FO

Following Blue Water

Jenny Sullivan

PONT BOOKS

For my husband Rob
with all the love in the world
and my thanks for 30 years of joy.

First Impression—1999

ISBN 1 85902 732 6

© Jenny Sullivan

Jenny Sullivan has asserted her right under the Copyright, Designs and
Patents Act, 1988, to be identified as Author of this Work.

This volume is published with the support of the
Arts Council of Wales.

Printed in Wales at
Gomer Press, Llandysul, Ceredigion

Madoc may never have existed.
He may not have discovered America
But then again, he might . . .

MADOG am I, the son of Owain Gwynedd,
  With stature large and comely grace adorned,
No lands at home, nor store of wealth me pleased
  My mind was whole to search the ocean seas.

Maredudd ap Rhys
Bard and Clergyman
mid-15th century

CHAPTER ONE

We were eyeball to eyeball.

'Back-packing around India! At your age?' I shrieked. 'For God's sake, Mum! The sixties was the time to do that. Not now!'

'In 1965, I was five years old, Angharad,' she shrieked back. 'I couldn't even have *lifted* a bloody back-pack, let alone *carried* one round bloody India.'

'So now, at thirty-five, you want to go off and discover yourself with a bunch of rackety friends. And you're going to dump me on my father and the Praying Mantis, so you can. That's really nice of you, Mum. Thanks a lot. Don't think about me, will you?'

Charlie, my mother's Insignificant Other, twitched. He hated it when we rowed, which in fairness wasn't often.

'Look, you guys,' he began.

'We're not guys,' we said in unison.

'And this is between us, so butt out, Charlie,' I hissed.

Charlie subsided. I slumped in the rocking chair, pushing roughly with my foot so the chair creaked, which I knew infuriated Mum.

'It isn't fair,' I complained. 'Other mothers are satisfied with little jobs in offices, or doing Open University courses. Some of them even go to proper college when they're old. But not *my* mother. Oh, no. My mother has to go traipsing through India. That means you'll be away when my A-level results come out, and I'll be stuck in north Wales in that god-awful place with Dad and that woman.' I could feel my bottom lip sticking out about five miles, but I didn't care. This was one guilt trip I had to make stick.

Mum ran her fingers through her hair, which didn't take long, because she'd had it cropped down almost to the scalp the day before. It showed off her lovely cheekbones and made her eyes look huge.

'Thirty-five isn't old, Angharad. I'm not ready for a rocking chair just yet.' Her voice took on a pleading note. 'Can't you understand? I'm still young. I got married when I was seventeen, because I was having you, and I haven't seen anything at all of life yet. Oh, please, Angharad, sweetheart, please don't make it difficult for me. I'll never have an opportunity like it again. And if Charlie doesn't mind me taking off for three months . . .'

Charlie didn't count, and we both knew it.

I humphed. 'But it means shoving me off, away from all my friends, for months. It isn't fair. Couldn't I just stay here? Look after the house?'

Mum gave me one of her Looks. The last time she'd left me, I'd sort of had a party, and there'd been a little bit of damage. Well, quite a lot, actually.

'Oh, all right. I said I was sorry, didn't I? And I paid for the breakages.' I changed tack. 'Can I stay with Ceri, then?'

'Ceri's mother would be fit for the funny farm if she had the two of you for more than a week. No, Angharad. It's your dad's turn to have you this summer anyway.'

'But not for three months, Mum! From the time I finish my A's in June, right up to the end of September before I go to university. It's not fair. What if I don't get the grades I need? What if I miss out on college altogether?'

'Your Dad will be there. And I know you don't like Myfanwy-the-Mantis, but your father said Ceri could go and stay for a while as well, and there will be other people there.' Her voice tailed off, pleadingly.

And that was another thing. My father and his new wife, Myfanwy (dubbed the Praying Mantis because of her habit of clasping her hands under her chin when she spoke. And because Mum and I hated her) had bought Tŷ Pendaran, a big old house near Rhos-on-Sea, and had started up a sort of hotel for writers and artists to go and stay at while they wrote and painted. They had professional writers and painters in residence, to lecture the arty types and show them how to do things. Dad's a writer, and Myfanwy paints (awful chocolate boxy portraits of people that make them look pretty, no matter how ugly they actually are). I had this horrible vision of me waiting hand, foot and finger on a dozen or so carbon copies of the Mantis, and didn't fancy the prospect one bit.

'He just wants me for cheap labour,' I grumbled, 'to do the washing up and make beds.'

'Well, he *does* need someone to help, but he's going to pay you the going wage. You'll get free board and lodging, and because there isn't anything much for you to spend your money on, you'll be able to save what you earn which will give you some extra money for college,' she finished, all in a rush. 'You're going to need it then, with all the grants and stuff disappearing.'

The truth was, I just didn't want to go. 'And how am I supposed to get there?' I whinged. 'If you think I'm going to bus it up through Wales – well, I saw that article in the *Western Mail* about that little trip – The

9

Upchuck Trail, that's what they called it, and you know I throw up even on short journeys. And if I went by train instead I'd probably have to go by way of London, Belfast and Outer Mongolia.'

Unfortunately, she'd already thought of that. 'Charlie will drive you.'

Charlie didn't look ecstatic at the prospect. Still, if I really had to go, it would be better to go up in Charlie's little red MG than have to do it by bus or train. And Charlie was OK, for a temporary, part-time, stop-gap Insignificant Other. There hadn't been many since she split from Dad seven years ago, when I was ten. Just Peter, who she'd dumped a bit sharpish when he clouted me, once; Adrian, who was a complete yuppie prat and lasted all of three weeks, and now Charlie, the first one threatening to actually move in, who was friendly, kind, generous, loved my Mum to distraction, but was a bit on the boring side, since he wanted Mum to settle down and get married, and it was fairly obvious that Mum was ready for anything but. He was 'letting' her go to India in the somewhat vague hope that she'd miss him like mad, come home after ten days and fling herself into his arms with faint cries of 'Marry me, Charlie, quick'. Yeah, Charlie. In a parallel universe maybe.

Part of me wanted to carry on moaning and thinking up reasons why Mum shouldn't go back-packing, and I shouldn't be banished to Tŷ Pendaran, but the rest of me was coming round to the idea. I loved the sea-shore, adored my Dad – even if he did go and marry Myfanwy the Mantis – and the up-side of getting away from it all for the summer was beginning to reveal itself despite. And besides, my conscience was saying, Mum's only

10

thirty-five. She hasn't had any life since she had me seventeen years ago, and she deserves this. Maybe, I told myself, maybe this will get the tickle out of her feet and then she'll settle down. Be a pinny-and-Victoria-sponge sort of Mum. Fat chance.

I heaved a great, big, martyred sigh. One thing about me, I always know when I'm beaten. 'All right. I'll do it. You can go. Mind you,' I scowled, 'no smuggling pot through customs or anything like that. I don't want to have to come and bail you out of Calcutta nick.' That was a joke. My Mum is so down on drugs that even getting an aspirin out of her is hard work.

Her smile broke through her scowl. I kept forgetting how pretty my Mum is. I suppose it's something you get used to, living with someone the whole time. She's tiny, with little bones, and huge eyes, and she's graceful. I take after Dad: even though I'm only five feet two, I galumph a lot. I think I was at the head of the queue when God handed out clumsy. And my hair is sort of brownish, and straight, and my eyes are sort of greeny-blue, and although my skin is nice, and my teeth – thanks to two years in a metal brace the size of the second Severn Crossing courtesy of the Dentist from Hell – are straight and white. The overall impression is sort of, I don't know, *ordinary*, I suppose. And I don't have boobs to speak of, which is a major downer. Mum keeps telling me I'll get them when I'm good and ready. Trust me, O-Goddess-of-Boobs, I'm good and ready *now*.

She gave me a hug. 'No Calcutta jails, I promise. I'll phone your father.'

11

The next months went quickly, as months tend to do before exams. I was taking English, History and Theatre Studies. I wanted to do anything around the theatre: scene painting, selling tickets, not just acting. I got horrendously stage struck at thirteen when a touring theatre company put on Groovy Bill's *The Tempest* in Raglan Castle. I'd never realised Shakespeare could be so amazing and wonderful. Since then I'd joined the Young People's Theatre, and we'd done all sorts of plays from Dylan Thomas to Orwell. In going to Rhos I'd miss not only my mates, but my chance to take part in the winter production, too, since it was always cast in September. Still, if the A-levels went well, I would be at university – Aberystwyth, hopefully – by January, when the play was performed, so that didn't really matter. I found it hard to believe that I was actually going to leave home and go to college. It seemed so final, somehow, so utterly *grown up* and *responsible* and *scary*. I'd cope, though. That's one thing Mum's taught me. How to cope in a crisis.

In the meantime, the history exam was *dire*. I'd apparently revised totally the wrong things, because I hardly recognised the questions as having anything to do with me at all. English wasn't too bad, and Theatre Arts was a doddle. I'd memorised huge chunks of Groovy Bill and Anouilh – we'd done *Becket* in the Youth Theatre, so I knew it inside out and wrote reams. I just hoped I'd scraped a reasonable pass in History, because I needed two Bs and a C to get into Aberystwyth, where I'd set my heart on going. I didn't want to go and live in a place like Preston, or Manchester, or Leeds, where it's cold, and damp, and in winter there's probably

12

permafrost. Aberystwyth is pretty cold in winter, I know, but it's got fresh, clean sea-winds blowing through it, and just about everyone can live in halls if they want. Which I did. I wanted my first time away from home on my own to be with loads of other young people, all in the same boat. I really wanted to go to Aber: I'd already started to learn Welsh, which is difficult in a border county like Monmouthshire, where an awful lot of people consider themselves more English than anything else.

Ceri and I officially left school on the day of our last exam, but we met up to take back our text books, say goodbye to our teachers (even the ones we didn't particularly like, we felt sad about leaving, which was a bit weird. We'd spent two years grousing about them, and now we were leaving them, suddenly they didn't seem so bad at all) and make arrangements for Ceri to come up to Rhos in August. I dropped in to see my year tutor, Mr Beaupré, to arrange to have my A-level results posted to me at Dad's, and it turned out he'd heard about Dad's place on some arty grapevine or other. Bit of a poser, our Mr Beaupré (which he pronounces 'Bow-pray': some of the kids wind him up by mis-pronouncing it whenever they can.) He always wears black roll-neck sweaters even in summer, and a jacket draped artily over his shoulders, and rumour has it he bleaches his hair. Still, he seemed impressed by Dad and the Mantis's venture. I'd have to stop calling her that, if I was going to live with them for three months. Not conducive to friendly relations, is it, name-calling? Mr Beaupré was still gushing.

'*Maaahrvellous* venture. Creative people *need* somewhere to go to find their *muse*,' he enthused. 'If

13

they ever decide to expand into theatre arts, please tell your father I'm his man.' He smiled, exposing his capped teeth, and fingered back his long, wavy hair. Which must have been painful, because it was gelled to the consistency of yellow corrugated cardboard.

'I'll mention it to Dad,' I said, knowing that I wouldn't. If Dad ever ventured in that direction, he'd go for someone famous. I mean, he had *Penry Pritchard* there for a whole month, lecturing on novel-writing. So he was *bound* to ask someone like old Bopers to help, wasn't he? Not.

Actually, I thought Penry Pritchard might be the one bright dot on the horizon. He's a brilliant writer, and I'd read so many of his books I felt as if I knew him. I'd never met him, but I bet having him there would almost make up for having to do housework. Me and housework don't get on particularly well. I don't see the point in shifting dust around when all it does is hang sneakily around in the air until your back is turned and then settle back down to where it was before you started. Still, I'd spoken to Dad and he promised me there was a dishwasher, so I needn't worry about having to do mountains of washing up, and I supposed I could manage a bit of bed-making once a week when the visitors came and went. It wouldn't be all bad.

There was also the sea, just across the road, and there were bound to be some nice people on the courses, by the law of averages. And Dad said he had a surprise for me, too. I thought a lot about this surprise – Keanu Reeves or Brad Pitt booked in for the whole summer? Nice thought, that. Well, I'd find out soon enough.

Meanwhile, our leaving day slipped through our

fingers. Ceri and I travelled home on the school bus for the last time. We were so miserable about leaving school (even though we'd looked forward to it since the year dot) that we couldn't even summon up the enthusiasm to bawl out the Year Seven kids who weren't sitting-down-and-facing-forward as per school rules.

We had only one more school function: the Leaver's Ball on the following Saturday night, and then that was it. I was off to Rhos on the Sunday (complete with hangover, probably) and Ceri was going to Spain with her parents until just before she came to Rhos to stay with me at the end of August.

We got off the bus and neither of us knew what to say. We held our blue sixth-form folders like barriers against our chests. This was it. Real life loomed.

'What if we fail everything?' Ceri said suddenly. 'What if we have to get jobs in Woolworths?'

'We won't. If we fail, we'll, we'll – I don't know what we'll do, but I'll think of something. We'll work our way round the world. Follow the sun. Pick grapes. Live on a kibbutz. Go vodka-testing in Russia. We'll do *something*.'

Ceri cheered up. 'Just you and me, kid?'

'Just you and me.' We hugged goodbye, even though we were meeting again that evening to decide once and for all what we would wear for the Ball. 'See you.'

She went down the hill towards her home, and I went down the other side towards mine, thinking about Dad's surprise. It wouldn't be a kitten. The Mantis was allergic to cats. I stopped suddenly, half way down the hill. *Driving lessons!* It had to be.

Things were looking up.

CHAPTER TWO

Mum woke me up at six on the Saturday I was due to go to Dad's. Since I hadn't gone to bed until around three o'clock (which felt like all of ten minutes ago), I had to be bullied awake and into the shower. And yes, I had a hangover. From two small glasses of wine and a whole lot of noise. My bags stood in the hall, ready, and, because we were renting out the house to an American family while we were all away, Mum was hurtling about with a duster in one hand and a vacuum cleaner in the other.

When it came time to say our goodbyes I got this most weird sensation. Half of me wanted to sulk and stamp and wail, and generally behave like a spoiled brat, because driving lessons and car or not (the surprise *had* to be that, didn't it?) I didn't want to go to Pendaran. The other half, the grown up half, wanted to smile sweetly, hug Mum, wish her a safe and happy trip, and go without making any waves whatsoever. Amazingly, the nice half won, which was a bit scary: almost as if I had got horribly responsible and adult overnight. Charlie was gobsmacked. He kept staring at me while he loaded my bags into the back seat of the MG. He also put the top down, because it was a sunny day.

I gave Mum a hug, and managed to smile and wave the whole time until we got away from the house and onto the Monmouth road. Then I let out a great wail and burst into tears, which made Charlie nearly drive into a lamp-post. He had the good sense not to say anything, though, just handed me a box of paper hankies and the directions on how to get to Pendaran to occupy my mind. He has this package on his computer which will work out a route between somewhere and anywhere, and he was very proud of it. He'd asked it for directions to Colwyn Bay, the nearest large-ish town, which it quite happily provided. We could follow signposts from there.

I quite enjoyed the journey up: even though bits of me felt sad that I wouldn't see Mum for three months, (OK, or Charlie, either. I suppose he had his good points) I would see Dad, and I'd be by the sea, and Ceri was coming to stay, and – and there was the surprise, wasn't there? It had to be driving lessons. Once I was legally mobile, watch out world!

We stopped at Ruthin for lunch, and Charlie took me into a pub and bought me a glass of wine with my steak and kidney pie and chips, which made me look at him quite kindly. I was relieved to see that he drank orange juice, though. He isn't always so responsible about drinking and driving, and if I had to go to Dad's, I wanted to arrive in more or less the same condition I started, with all my bits in approximately the right places. Maybe Mum had spoken severely to him: she's good at that.

Charlie is a bit younger than Mum, he's thirty-three, and I look quite a grown-up seventeen, so we didn't get any funny glances. If it hadn't been *Charlie*, who's a bit like furniture, I might have pretended I was on a date with a handsome millionaire, but Charlie's just Charlie. He's OK. If Mum decides to settle on him (assuming she doesn't run off with an Indian Rajah, if there are any left) I won't be too gutted.

By the time we reached Pendaran it was six o'clock. Charlie unloaded my bags into the hall and didn't hang about. I don't think he particularly wanted to run into Dad. Don't know why, though: Dad had gone off with the Mantis long before Charlie came on the scene. He wasn't likely to black his eye in whatchamacallit – *crime passionnel* – or something.

The house was big, much bigger than I'd expected (I suppose it had to be, to accommodate Dad and the Mantis, me, twelve guests and two lecturers at a time). The hallway smelled of lavender polish and old woodsmoke, and was cool and dark because of the oak panelling covering the walls. I wandered off in search of Dad, and finding the back door open, went through it.

I stood on a wide paved terrace overlooking a large garden, stretching uphill to woodland behind the house, and to the sea at the front, with an embankment on the other side of the beach road, to protect it from the sea. A high wall bordered the property all round. Near a wrought iron gate at the front of the garden a small blue dinghy lay upside-down on the grass. Lots of bushes and trees, the droopy sort that bend over and form leafy caves around their own trunks, made a sort of mini-wood on the right. I promised myself that I'd explore that bit, when I had a chance. I like private places. I've never quite grown out of the kidstuff thrill of having a den to hide in. I love being able to see, but not be seen, to hear but not be heard.

I heard the chug of a motor, and turned to see Dad coming round the side of the house on a little red sit-and-ride tractor mower. Seeing me, he steered towards me, and hopped off, enveloping me in a huge hug. When we'd finished hugging, and he'd given me a smacking kiss on the nose, which was his usual way of greeting me, he held me away from him.

'By the great town hall of Gotham City, Robin! Look at the size of you!'

I'd almost forgotten our Batman-and-Robin routine. I walked round behind him. 'Holy Toledo, Batman – no bald spot yet, but by the great town hall tower of Greater Gotham, there are a few grey hairs!' And there were, since I'd seen him last six – no, seven, months ago. He looked older than Mum, even though there was only a year between them, but then, he was married to Myfanwy the Mantis, wasn't he? Enough to give anyone grey hairs, that.

We grinned at each other like idiots. I suppose I was getting a bit old for kids' stuff, but families are like that, aren't they? Well, ours is.

'Where are all the arty types then, Dad?' I'd half expected to find people with long hair and quill pens, or stand-up easels and people in smocks and floppy velvet ties all over the place.

'Oh, they don't arrive until Monday in time for dinner. So we've got a whole day to settle you in – except that Penry's arriving tomorrow evening and Laetitia will be here Monday morning.'

'I've heard of Penry – the-famous-writer-you-were-once-in-school-with,' I said, before he had a chance to, because he was very proud of knowing a best-selling author, was Dad '– but Laetitia who?' We were walking, arms round each other, towards the house.

'Laetitia Barnard. Artist. Supposed to be very good. Friend of Muvvy's, from college.'

Ah yes. Myfanwy. Be polite, Angharad. 'How is Myfanwy, Dad?'

He beamed. 'She's – well, you'll see for yourself. She's gone into Colwyn Bay to get a bit of shopping.

She'll be back soon. Come on in and we'll have a cup of tea while we're waiting, shall we?'

Don't rush back for me, Muvvy, I thought. Stay away forever, if you like.

He led the way into the large, sunny kitchen, with a bright red Aga covered in drying tea-towels looming on one wall. A large dishwasher (thank goodness) occupied one corner, and three sinks and a run of tiled worktops hugged the sunshine-yellow walls. The biggest fridge I'd seen in my life hummed in the passageway behind me, and a half-open door revealed a laundry room and a huge freezer beyond the kitchen.

I leaned against a counter while Dad put the kettle on. Through the open window the garden sloped downhill, and trees rustled in the slight sea-breeze. Dad poured two mugs of tea and we took them through to the terraced patio at the back, overlooking the sea. From there I could see that a river ran just outside the walls, carving its way across the sand to the sea. I decided to explore the riverbank even before I picked myself out a den.

'What do you think of the house, Hari?' Dad always called me Hari (except when he was calling me Robin, that is), although to Mum I was always Angharad. She never shortened it. When I was 'little', I'd convinced myself that Dad only called me Hari because he'd really wanted a boy, and that was why he and Mum had split up. I was fairly miserable for a couple of months over that, but Mum kept at me until she'd got out of me what was wrong. The Spanish Inquisition has nothing on my Mum when it comes to finding out stuff.

Once she'd got me to tell her what I was miserable

20

about, she told me more about what had gone wrong between her and Dad. They'd married so young, straight from school in fact, they were still growing up. As the years passed, they sort of grew out of loving each other in *that* way. The funny thing was, they were still really good friends after splitting up. I understood a bit better then, I suppose, but I was still sorry they'd split up, and sorrier still when Dad had fallen for the Mantis. Still, I knew they both loved me, and always would, whatever happened.

'The house is amazing, Dad! It's *huge*. I knew it would have to be a bit on the large side to take all your visitors, but I hadn't realised you had so much land with it. I'm going to explore up the banks of the river, later.'

Dad hooted with laughter. 'Still the same old Hari.' Then he got serious. 'If you go on the beach, check the flags. If there are two red ones, it's dangerous to walk between them because of quicksands. The river was much bigger, once, and where the estuary has silted up, it can be dangerous. But if you're sensible, you should be OK.' He raised an eyebrow. 'Don't want to lose my darling daughter to a lot of slurping sands, do I? When you've finished your tea, I'll take you upstairs and show you your room. There's a spare bed in it for Ceri when she comes to stay. Is she still the same?'

'She's still an idiot, if that's what you mean.'

We finished our tea and, with Dad carrying my bags and leading the way, climbed the wide staircase to the top floor, three flights up. It was the type of staircase I often imagine myself Scarlett O'Hara-ing down in a long dress. Going up it, however, was a different matter: halfway up I had to stop and take a breather.

'Good grief, Dad, have you thought of getting a lift installed?'

'We'll get a chairlift put in, just for you, you poor old lady.' He pushed open a door. 'Old servants' quarters, this was. Right up in the attic, so you can see the sea.'

See the sea? I'll say! It stretched, a sheet of dark blue, towards the horizon, the bay curving round it protectively. It would be the first thing I'd see every morning, because there was no way I would ever close the curtains and hide that view. No one could look in at me in my knickers, I was much too high.

'Wow!' I breathed, crossing to the window. 'Gosh, Dad, whatever you paid for this place, it was worth it for the view.'

Dad chuckled. 'Glad you think so. Anyway, as far as paying for it is concerned, it's about one per cent ours and ninety-nine per cent the bank's at the moment.' A door slammed somewhere downstairs. 'That'll be Myfanwy home. Come on. We've got a surprise for you.'

Secretly hugging myself, I resolved to be suitably surprised when they presented me with the vouchers, the car keys, whatever, for my driving lessons. I hate it when people guess surprises, it totally spoils them. I'd done Drama: I could do surprised, *dim problem*. Myfanwy was in the kitchen, her back to us.

'Hello, honeybun. Look who's here,' Dad said. Myfanwy turned round, a welcoming smile on her face. I didn't have to act surprised, and I instantly forgot about driving lessons. Myfanwy was pregnant. Very.

'Here's your surprise!' Dad said, patting her bump gently, 'a new baby brother or sister. Mum didn't tell

22

you?' he asked anxiously, 'I asked her not to. I didn't want to spoil the surprise for you.'

I shook my head. I had to, I couldn't speak. I smiled, but my mouth felt stiff, as if I hadn't smiled for ages, and had forgotten how. 'Congratulations,' I finally managed to bumble out. My voice sounded weird even to me. 'Oh, great. Really great. When's it due?'

'Just over five weeks. It will be here before you go back to Raglan.' They were so wrapped up in each other, hugging and pecking little kisses on noses and stuff, I knew they didn't need me there. Not at all. Not ever.

'I'm going up to unpack, OK?' I said, and fled.

In my bedroom, I sat on one of the twin beds and shook. I couldn't think straight, my brain was numb. They didn't want me there. How could they? They had a new family on the way. But I was stuck there anyway, wasn't I? My mother was off to India tomorrow. I couldn't go home. I looked at my watch. Even if I phoned now, that instant, and begged her not to go, to stay home, to get me away from there, it would be too late. She couldn't call off her trip now.

I felt betrayed, as if I'd been shovelled out of the house so she could get away from me, and shovelled into Tŷ Pendaran because it was Dad's 'turn' to be lumbered with me. A fat, salty tear trickled down my nose and onto my upper lip. I licked it off. Nobody wanted me. Oh, yes, this was going to be a *great* summer.

I unpacked because I had to. There was nowhere else for me to go, nothing else for me to do. Forlornly I shoved T-shirts, jeans and shorts into drawers, hung up dresses and skirts and tossed shoes and sandals into the wardrobe bottom. I put my wash bag in the little

23

bathroom leading off the bedroom, and put my pyjamas and dressing gown on the bed. The sea view sparkled at me, mockingly, and sun glinted off the wardrobe mirror. I looked around me at the fluffy blue towels piled on the bed, the fresh flowers in the vase on the dressing table, the selection of books on the shelf, the little colour TV on a swivel arm at the end of the bed. It was just for show. It didn't mean anything at all. Dad didn't need me any more. He and Myfanwy were starting a new family. I was just his 'mistake', from when he was young.

I blew my nose, miserably, and stood up, catching sight of my red eyes and swollen nose in the mirror. What was I to do? I sighed. I had to make the best of it, that's what. 'Come on, Angharad,' I said to my reflection, 'you might as well get on with it. Keep busy, that's the answer. Then the days will go quicker, and before you know it Ceri will be here, and then it will be September and you can go home.'

There was a soft rapping at the door. 'Come in,' I squeaked, wiping my eyes. It was the Mantis.

'You shouldn't be climbing all those stairs!' I said brightly, 'not in your condition.'

She clasped her hands under her chin. I wondered when she'd started doing that. When she'd first met my Dad, she'd been thin as a twig, and the habit had made her look just like the insect in question. Dad introduced us all at a 'neutral ground' dinner at an hotel in Cardiff, when we'd all been horribly polite, like complete strangers.

After, when we were on our own, Mum said, 'I hope she doesn't start chomping your father's head off, like the real thing,' and we'd held our sides and giggled, and

24

rolled about, hooting with laughter. But now I realised that there must have been pain in it for her: she had been replaced and there had been no going back, even if they didn't love each other 'like that' any more. I understood, now, because I was feeling a bit replaced myself.

'Oh, I'm OK,' she said. 'Look, Hari –'

I winced. That was Dad's name for me.

'Hari, just because I'm having a baby doesn't mean your dad will love you any less, you know! Love expands to encompass all those you have around you to love. Love is infinite.'

Oh, yeah. I'd forgotten. She'd been a social worker once, hadn't she? Typical. Spouting that rubbish at me. How could she know what Dad felt? Or me for that matter.

I didn't say anything. I just looked at my hands.

'Your Dad thinks you're the best thing since sliced bread,' she went on. 'Ever since I've known him he's talked about you. Endlessly! Our baby won't make any difference to the way he feels about you, you know.'

'No? Well, you coming along certainly made a difference to the way he felt about my Mum, didn't it?' I knew I shouldn't have said it. I wished I could call the words back, but of course I couldn't. They were out, and she looked hurt.

'That isn't fair. You know it was over between your Mum and Dad long before I came along.'

I knew I should have apologised, but couldn't bring myself to do it. She came towards me as if she was going to hug me, and I backed away. I didn't want her touching me. 'Look, Myfanwy. I'm really, really pleased for you. I'll try not to be a nuisance while I'm here. But please don't expect me to be ecstatic about it, OK? It's your baby, and my Dad's. It's nothing to do with me.'

She bit her lip and tears welled up in her brown eyes. 'I said we should have told you earlier, but he wanted to surprise you.'

'Oh, he did that all right. But there are surprises and surprises, and so far as surprises go, I've had better, trust me.' I turned my back on her and went and stared doggedly out of the window. When I turned round, she'd gone.

CHAPTER THREE

Sunday passed in a sort of hollow haze of misery, as if I was seeing everything through the wrong end of a telescope. I helped Dad and the Mantis (the pregnant Mantis) make up beds, and worked with Marged the part-time cook in the kitchen helping prepare lasagne and salad ready for the arty types when they arrived on Monday, and I tried to smile, honest I did. I tried to make myself believe that the new baby wouldn't make any difference to Dad and me. But I knew it would, really.

It was a relief when Penry Pritchard arrived, sweeping up the drive in his four-wheel-drive and into the house like a whirlwind, clouting Dad on the back and kissing the Mantis, which made her giggle and blush, silly cow.

'And this,' Dad said, his arm across my stiffened shoulders, 'is Angharad, my daughter.'

'Angharad.' Penry took my hand in both of his, stroking the back of it with his thumb, and gazed into my eyes. His were very dark blue, almost lapis lazuli, and they glistened. His shoulder-length fair hair was tied back at the nape of his neck, and he wore jeans and an open-necked shirt, the sleeves rolled up over muscular arms. 'Angharad,' he said again, rolling the syllables around his tongue, and kissed my hand. 'Jack, old buddy. You didn't tell me you had such a beautiful daughter.'

The blush began somewhere round my toenails and slithered up to my face, and I wished someone would open a window. My bullshit detector was clanging bells. What a *creep*.

'No, I didn't,' Dad said, shortly, 'and you, my lad, can keep your paws off her. She's only seventeen. You're old enough to be her father.'

'Only barely, Jack. After all, you started rather before the rest of us in the fatherhood stakes, and,' he eyed Myfanwy, grinning, 'you're still at it, I see.' He still hadn't let go of my hand, and I tugged gently to get it back, because I was beginning to feel stupid, standing in the hallway having my hand held by old Teeth-and-Trousers. And I was getting angry. Especially with Dad watching. Penry gave my hand a final squeeze before relinquishing it, and honoured me with another blast of the lapis lazuli eyes.

'Come on,' Dad changed the subject. 'I'll show you your room.'

The blush began to subside, and eventually my face went back to its normal shade, but I made a mental decision to stay well away from him. I don't mind it when guys around my own age act flirtatious, but Penry was old enough to be my father, for heaven's sake. I can be daft, occasionally, but not even I'm daft enough to fall for *that*.

There were just the four of us for dinner: Dad and the Mantis, Penry and me. We ate at one end of the long, battered dining table, and Myfanwy put out the lights and put candles around the room so we wouldn't look like orphans picnicking in a baronial hall. It could have been quite romantic, actually. There's something about candlelight. Pity about the company. I put away the dress I'd been planning to wear, the new blue one with the low neck and the little petal sleeves, (the one that made me look twenty-two, honest), and the old silver Celtic pendant

28

which dangled into my barely there cleavage. Instead, I got out the old brown one with the high neck so that Penry wouldn't get any ideas. The last thing I wanted to do was encourage him. I was sorry not to wear the pendant, though. Mum had found it in an antique shop and bought it for me as a small reward when I got my GCSE results, which hadn't been nearly as bad as everyone had expected. Which is all I'm saying on the subject, OK?

Dad sort of looked me up and down and grunted, but I think the Mantis had had words with him about my reaction towards my new half-sibling, because he was treating me like some sort of distant relative. What did he expect? That I'd be over the moon or something? In your dreams, yeah, Dad. OK, if he could be off with me, I could be twice as off with him.

The Mantis had pulled out all the stops for the dinner: we began with smoked salmon (which I adore. If the devil popped up and offered a pound of smoked salmon for my soul, I'd think seriously before turning him down, and that's only because I couldn't hack the eternal flames and stuff. I'm a terrible coward). Then we had boeuf bourguignon, which was gorgeous, and then some creamy, lemony stuff, and two bottles of wine kind of disappeared during the meal, so that by the time we got to coffee and mints I felt it would be a really good idea to turn down the brandy. But Penry, smirking, poured some into my coffee anyway when Dad wasn't looking. I know from experience (not a lot, but some) that spirits and me don't mix too well. First of all I get giggly, then either I fall asleep or I get loud, and I certainly wasn't having that with Penry around, so I pointedly left the spiked coffee.

We sat round the table for ages, talking, and I joined in like a grown-up, and only once caught Dad glancing at his watch and looking at me as if he was about to tell me it was bed-time. I slipped my gaze away from him, and he obviously decided to let it go, so that I stayed up until almost two, when Penry broke up the party by yawning loudly.

'I'm knackered,' he announced. 'I had a long drive today. I'm going to bed. Wake me when the Blessed Laetitia gets here if I'm not already up. No breakfast. No early morning tea and toast. Just let me sleep, OK? Angharad can bring up some orange juice, later.'

Angharad bloody well won't, I thought.

The Mantis clasped her hands and nodded. I helped clear the table and stack the dishwasher, and then went upstairs. I could hear Penry moving about in his room as I reached his landing, and tried to slither past without making any noise. Nevertheless, he heard me.

'Goodnight, Angharad my sweet,' his voice said seductively from inside his bedroom.

I shot up the next flight of stairs to my room and shut and locked the door. It took me ages to get to sleep. What with being supplanted in Dad's affections by some noisy, smelly brat of a kid, and now Supercreep . . . I hadn't been looking forward to the summer, but had been prepared to make the best of it. Not any more. I just wanted it to be over.

Next day, Laetitia Barnard arrived. If I disliked Myfanwy the Mantis, I loathed Laetitia (dubbed 'The Locust' on sight). Not only was she dressed all in *grande dame* flowing green, but she had moist, slightly bulbous eyes, with long dark lashes, a long, thin body, and a way of poking her head forward when she spoke, just like a locust. To everyone else, that is. She didn't deign to address me directly, even though Myfanwy introduced us. She just bared her teeth, lowered her lashes and turned her back on me. Not being famous, I was obviously not worth her attention.

She put her head on one side and sniffed. Then she closed her eyes, pulled a face, and opened them again. 'I sense a cat, Muvvy,' she said sternly. 'I told you, no cats. Is there a cat?' She had a little-girly, breathy voice.

Muvvy shook her head, but the Locust gazed at her as if she were lying, for several seconds, while the Mantis squirmed, giving the impression that she had at least a dozen tomcats locked in a cupboard somewhere. I resolved to seek out the nearest moggy and tempt it indoors – with left-over smoked salmon if necessary. Thus getting at Mantis and Locust in one fell swoop.

Then at last, the Mantis was off the hook. 'My room, Muvvy,' Laetitia whispered, back of hand laid on fevered brow. 'I'm simply exhausted. I can't move another step until I rest and meditate. I need my *mantra* so *desperately*.'

Oh, this one's a right fruitcake, I thought. 'Would you like a cup of tea brought up?' I asked, being determined to make myself useful even if I was an unwanted child of a previous marriage.

She swivelled her head round on its stalk and stared at me as if I'd suggested a nice cup of arsenic laced with strychnine. '*Tea?*' she hissed, 'I never touch tea, or coffee, or any other artificial stimulant.' She turned petulantly to the Mantis. 'Muvvy, I *told* you. Nothing but Perrier. Tŷ Nant in dire emergency. But *never* ever *tea.* I hope there isn't a radio or television in my room?'

Myfanwy, hands clasped beseechingly under her chin, shook her head frantically, her lank brown hair flying. 'Of course not, 'Tisha! I made a note of what you said about radio waves and Jack took the TV out. And there's lots of Perrier, and lots of Tŷ Nant. The bottles are so pretty, aren't they? That lovely cobalt blue –' She tailed off helplessly at Laetitia's glare.

'And the vegetables for my meals? All organic I hope?'

Myfanwy nodded. I almost gasped. I'd taken them out of the Tesco bag about five minutes ago, to put in the fridge, and organic they certainly weren't. I began to respect the Mantis, even if I didn't like her. Sneaky wins points in my book.

'That's all right then. The girl can bring me some orange juice, later. Freshly squeezed. No pips, no peel. None of that supermarket rubbish. In about an hour, when I've finished drawing down my spirits and boosting my *Ka*. Now, show me to my room, please. Jack, you may carry my bags The bed is aligned east/west, isn't it? My Chinese holistic therapist insists on east/west. *Feng shui*, you know.' Her voice tailed off as she followed Myfanwy upstairs. Dad, after a comical grimace at me (which I ignored. He wasn't getting round me. I knew I was there under sufferance) picked up her mountain of luggage and followed.

Penry didn't surface until three, and recognising the bleary, semi-conscious, hung-over condition he was in (Charlie tied one on occasionally) I waited until he was slumped at the kitchen table and then put the vacuum cleaner, the dishwasher, the washing machine and the radio on, all at once, which made a wonderful din. It was quite satisfying. I enjoyed watching him writhe. After most of a pot of black coffee, however, he began to revive just as the visitors started to pitch up in cars and taxis. He was looking better, if bloodshot, but instead of staying to help greet them, he disappeared in the direction of the village almost immediately.

Everything was chaos for a time, with piles of cases in the hall and people wandering round the house and garden, exclaiming and exploring. My job was welcoming, making cups of tea and coffee, and passing round the shortbread that Marged had baked, while Dad ferried bags to rooms and Myfanwy and Marged washed salad and baked apple pies.

By dinner they had all turned up: there were only eight on this course, and they all seemed to be OK except for a Mrs Marchpoint, a small, dyed-red-haired, whiny lady from London. Mrs Marchpoint complained about the journey, the heat, the location of the house, the wind from the sea, the cost of the course, and the room she'd been allocated. It was too small. She was claustrophobic. So Dad asked one of the other guests to change with her, but that room didn't suit, either. So then Dad solemnly took her right round the house until she found a room she liked. But the only room she liked was occupied by someone who, perhaps recognising Mrs Marchpoint as a professional complainer, got stubborn and refused to change. They glared at each other for a while, and then Mrs Marchpoint sullenly and ungraciously accepted an empty one on the first floor, overlooking the sea, with a big bay window.

Penry, resplendent in an aquamarine shirt to echo his eyes and show off his tan, swept down the wide stairs, the focus of almost every female eye (but especially Laetitia's), when Dad hammered on the gong in the hallway, signalling dinner. Dad and the Mantis were at the head of the table and Penry and the Locust were at the foot, and although there were no candles tonight, the side lamps were lit rather than the overhead light, which lent an air of intimacy to the gathering. I was sandwiched between Mrs Marchpoint and a tiny, quiet lady with blonde, wispy hair, who squinched up into her chair with her elbows tucked in and her eyes lowered, and hardly spoke except to say 'please' and 'thank you'. I think she chewed every mouthful one hundred times, like a Victorian schoolgirl. It was rather an uncomfortable meal.

Miss Marchpoint complained about everything: the food, (although she ate it all), the lighting, the wine, until I wanted to up-end the left-over brussels sprouts on her head. I worked hard to ignore her and get the little lady on my other side to talk, but she just primmed her mouth, lowered her head and nibbled at her vegetarian lasagne, so in the end I gave up on her, too.

When everyone (except the Locust, of course) had been served coffee, Dad tapped his spoon on his glass for quiet and stood up.

'There aren't many house rules,' he began. 'Basically, we'd like you all to look on Tŷ Pendaran as home while you are here. My wife and I will help in any way we can. I shall be creative writing tutor, together with Penry Pritchard here –'

(Penry smiled his languid smile and a sort of Mexican

Wave of female primping went round the table. Even Mrs Marchpoint wasn't immune, it seemed). Dad went on, 'and my wife will be assisting with the watercolour painting course, although for obvious reasons she will confine herself to workshops in the garden and studio.' He grinned at the Mantis and she blushed. 'Laetitia Barnard –' he bowed towards her, and she tossed her hair, and bared her teeth, flashing her personality on like a lighthouse, then switching it off again, 'will be lead tutor for those wishing to venture further afield. All tutorials begin at nine-thirty sharp. Please help yourselves to breakfast: there is always cereal, toast, bacon, whatever you can find, but please leave the kitchen tidy after you. Lunch, once again, we ask you to help yourselves, and dinner will be cooked on a rota basis. Either my daughter Angharad or Marged will be on hand to help, but we would like you, please, to choose an evening and put your names on the list on the notice-board in the hall. It works out at two or three people preparing each evening meal, and if you've never cooked before, don't worry. It's great fun.'

I looked at Mrs Marchpoint's sour face and doubted that cooking with her would be fun. I made a mental note to check which night she put her name down for, and avoid it like the plague.

'There will be one more guest,' Dad continued, 'Rhidian Lloyd-Evans, but he's missed his train and will be arriving later. The circumstances of Rhidian's stay are a little different from the rest of you. He's a very talented young writer, and his English teacher, who's an old friend of mine, asked if he might come here on a work experience basis. He'll be here for the entire summer, and will be joining tutorials whenever possible. However, he will also be acting as a general dogsbody and handyman, so if you need anything in particular – say a light-bulb replaced or something like that, please see Rhidian about it. When he arrives, of course!'

Dad sat down and asked for questions. Except for Mrs Marchpoint, who complained about noisy seagulls, (what did she expect Dad to do about that? Shoot them?) there were none. Dad and Penry were going to read from their latest works during the evening, so the guests drifted into the library while I helped Marged clear up.

Marged had just left and I was on the point of slithering unobtrusively into the library for the reading when I heard an almighty crash outside the front door, which had been closed for the night. I peered through the bay window beside it, but couldn't see anything. Then I remembered Rhidian the late-comer, unlocked the front door and opened it.

I didn't see him at first: I expected him to be at eye-, not ankle-level. Not that he was short. When he stood up, he was about six feet tall, but right then he was lying flat on his back, his glasses askew on his nose, having fallen backwards over his suitcase, which he'd obviously put down while he bashed on the door. He scrambled awkwardly to his feet, shoving his glasses straight, and grinned at me. His hair stuck out like a cockscomb at the back of his head, and he had a crooked, shy grin. He was also blushing very redly, and I warmed to him instantly, not only because he looked to be about my age, but chronic blushers I know about. Besides, it was a nice smile.

'Hello, 's me,' he said, shuffling. 'Look, sorry I'm

late. Missed my train. Thought I had loads of time, but I got talking to this porter guy, and you know how it is. Really int'resting bloke, y'know?'

I nodded. I got the general picture. 'No problem. You're – 'I tried to remember, 'Rhidian Lloyd-Evans, right?'

'Rhid. Everyone calls me Rhid. Usually because it's what they want to do.' His glasses had slipped down his nose again.

I must have looked puzzled.

'Rhid. You know, get rid of me.'

'Oh. Yes.' I laughed, dutifully. His sense of humour needed some work. 'Come on in. Have you had anything to eat?'

He shook his head. 'But don't bother. I'll be OK, honest. I had a huge breakfast before I left.'

I started to grin. 'Breakfast? Do you know what time it is?'

He looked at his watch. 'Oh, wow. Nearly ten. Oh.'

'Look, put your case in the hall. Then I'll find you something to eat.'

I put the lights on in the kitchen. 'I can do you some lasagne, unless you're a vegetarian? The veggie stuff is all gone, I'm afraid.'

'God, no. Unrepentant carnivore. Omnivore, actually. Anything, honestly.' The glasses slithered again, and he tripped over a chair leg.

'Go on, sit down.' I slid a heaping helping of lasagne into the microwave and uncovered a cling-filmed dish of salad from the fridge. I could feel his eyes on me, so I chattered.

'I'm Angharad. My Dad is Jack Bowen. Myfanwy is my stepmother. You know, they run this place.'

'Your Dad's a brilliant bloke to let me come. I'm supposed to be sort of studying at the feet of the master, y'know?' The glasses were shoved upwards. 'Well, two masters, actually, 'cos Penry's pretty good, too. But your Dad's my main man.' He sighed, gustily. 'A whole summer, at Tŷ Pendaran, doing nothing but write and fix light bulbs and stuff. Wow.'

'Where are you from?'

'Cardiff. Ever been there?'

I grinned. 'Lived there for the first part of my life. Then me and Mum moved to Raglan, near Monmouth, when she and Dad split up. Only Mum's backpacking in India,' I pulled a face, 'so here I am. Summer with my Dad'. The microwave pinged, and I slid the steaming dish in front of him. I poured him a glass of wine and sat beside him while he ate, which he did with great concentration. I could almost hear the lasagne *boing* as it bottomed out in his empty stomach.

When he'd finished, I took him up to his room to dump his bags, and then we crept together into the library, earning a scowl from the Locust, who was sitting Very Close to a smirking Penry, and found chairs next to each other at the back of the room. Dad had just finished reading from his latest novel, and it was Penry's turn. I felt my ears go pink. Very fond of the four-letter Anglo-Saxon, our Penry. Even though I'd read his books, and I certainly knew the words, it felt different to hear a grown-up say them out loud in polite company. I noticed Dad's disapproving glance at me, as if he wished he could banish me and my tender ears. Honestly, if he could hear some of what goes on in the first-year yard at school, he'd faint dead away!

Rhidian and I sat up late that night, over cocoa in the kitchen, and in bed afterwards I decided that the summer might be bearable after all. Rhidian, being my own age, would at least be someone to talk to until Ceri arrived. And tomorrow I had an afternoon to myself, to explore.

CHAPTER FOUR

On my way to breakfast I checked the cooks' rota on the notice board. Mrs Marchpoint hadn't put her name down at all. Perhaps she thought it was beneath her. Neither Laetitia nor Penry appeared for breakfast, and since Mrs Marchpoint was already sitting at the breakfast table poking a spoon suspiciously into a pot of the Mantis's home-made strawberry jam, I took my breakfast out onto the patio so that I could look at the sea while I ate. I could do without Mrs Marchpoint at breakfast time.

Crunching crusts despite the hopeful squadron of gulls wheeling overhead, I didn't hear Dad until he flopped down on the bench beside me. I didn't look up. And I wasn't going to speak first. It wasn't me doing the abandoning, OK? He cleared his throat.

'Looks like a nice day for the race.'

I was supposed to say 'what race', and he would answer 'the human race', then we were both supposed to laugh. But I didn't feel like playing. He sighed.

'Look, sweetheart, please don't sulk –'

'I'm not sulking.'

'You are.'

''m not.'

'All right, you're not. But you aren't happy, are you?'

'I'm fine.'

'You aren't. You haven't said a word to me since we told you about the baby.'

'Yes I have. I just said several.'

'Only because I made you.'

'You didn't.'

'Oh, for heaven's sake.' He stood up, shoved his hands in his pocket and scowled at me. 'Look, Hari, just because Muv and I are having a baby doesn't mean I'll love you any less. Don't you know yet that love is infinite? That it expands to fit the number of people in your life that you have to love?'

'Oh yeah? Funny, that's exactly what Myfanwy said. So how come there wasn't room for Mum in it then?' That was a cheap and childish shot and I should have been ashamed of myself. I was, a bit. Dad looked hurt.

'That's not fair. I still love your Mum. I always will. Only not in *that* way.'

'Sex, you mean.'

He panicked at hearing the dread word from my mouth, started to pace, put his foot in my toast-plate, and shattered it. I picked up the pieces, and held them in my lap. I thought mournfully (and, yeah, a bit melodramatically, OK, I admit it) that my heart felt pretty much the same. Broken in two.

'Yes. And your Mum doesn't feel that way about me any more, either.'

'How do you know?'

'Because we discussed this *ad nauseam* before we decided to split, that's how. You're too young to under-'

'Oh, that's an easy get out, Dad. Too young to understand about sex,' I mimicked. 'Do me a favour, Dad. Do you think I'm a kid, or what? D'you know how many girls in my year at school are still virgins?'

That had the desired effect. It distracted him, even if it didn't shut him up. Thank goodness he didn't call me on it, and ask 'No, how many?', because trouble was, I didn't know either. I knew definitely that one girl

41

wasn't, because she'd left just after Christmas to have a baby, which is as good a proof as any. But as for the others – well, they talked up a storm, but who knows?

'Look, we're getting off the subject. All I want to say is that if the new baby turns out half as good as you, my darling daughter, I'll be a lucky man. And Myfanwy loves you, too.'

I'll bet, I thought. Myfanwy loves me like a turkey loves Christmas. But I was beginning to feel a bit better.

'All right?'

'All right.' But I wasn't backing down that easily. Trouble is, I love my Dad to bits, and making him suffer wasn't easy. 'Just try to understand how I'm feeling, will you, Dad? I mean, I know it's going to be my brother or sister, but I can't feel as excited about it as you do. When it gets here, I'll try. That's all I can promise right now.' I felt a bit mean for saying it, but I wasn't letting him off the hook entirely. Not yet.

'I'll settle for that. However. While we're on the subject of sex, I'm not one to run down my friends, and Penry has been a good mate since we were in school, but be careful of him. He has a reputation with women. I've warned him off, but –'

This was too much. 'Oh, for heaven's sake, Dad. Warned him off? I'm not a child any more.' I tossed my hair back. That always makes me look sophisticated. 'I know he's one of your best friends, Dad, but *honestly*. He's such a bullshit artist.'

Dad winced, but carried on regardless. 'You aren't quite as grown up as you think, Hari. At seventeen, you've still got a lot to learn about relationships between men and women. Trust me. Women fall for Penry quite easily, strange as it might seem. They drop like ripe plums.'

'Well, for a start, I'm a person, not a plum, and I happen to think he's a pretentious prat. OK?'

Dad grinned. 'OK. Nice bit of alliteration, there, Hari!' He glanced at his watch. 'Look, I've got to run, I'm doing a workshop this morning. What are you going to do?'

'I promised Marged I'd go with her into Colwyn Bay to do some food shopping, and then this afternoon I'm going for a walk up the river.'

'All right. But remember what I told you about the quicksands.'

'I'm not going on the beach. I just said, I'm going inland.'

After lunch, carefully avoiding Penry until he was safely holding forth to his workshop, I let myself out the front gate and after a few moments just enjoying the view and the sea air, I followed the boundary wall along the side of the house beside Afon Pendaran. The heat of the afternoon was tempered by the trees along the banks of the river, and sunlight tossed bright coins through the leaves onto the dried mud track, criss-crossed by gnarled roots and bordered with rabbit holes.

The higher reaches of the river had a strange oldness about them, as if they hadn't been disturbed for hundreds of years. I moved slowly along barely visible paths, enjoying the semi-gloom and secrecy of it all. Fallen trees lay uncleared, forming dens floored with damp leafmould, and I was aware of sudden sharp scuffles as small creatures moved away from my passing.

When I'd walked for a while, I came upon a sunlit clearing with a small stone bridge over a stream, and

43

leaned on the sun-warmed stones, chucking pebbles into the clear water. I'd brought a carton of orange juice with me, and after a few games of Poohsticks against myself, (some things a person never grows out of, OK?) I wandered down to the water's edge and dangled my feet in the river's shallows while I drank the juice, then paddled icily upstream for a while. I glanced at my watch and decided to start back: there was only just time to make it back, shower and change for dinner.

I didn't see the obstruction until I fell over it.

I sat on the damp bank, hissing pain through my teeth, clutching a barked shin and waiting until the agony went away and I could breathe again. What is it about raked shins that hurts more than anything else? When I could ungrit my teeth, and I'd mopped the blood up with a Kleenex, I looked for whatever had tripped me. I imagined it had been a loop of root, but when I looked, I discovered what looked like old, moss-covered stone-work. Not just stray stones, but large, business-like building stones set deeply into the ground. Purposeful, going someplace stones. The closer I looked, the further back they seemed to go into the scrub and bushes beside the river. I peered into the undergrowth – they seemed to stretch for two or three metres into the wood and in the other direction, too – I could see traces of it heading all the way back to the rear wall of Tŷ Pendaran. I couldn't imagine how I hadn't noticed it before. Interested now, I walked beside it, right up to the point at which it disappeared under Dad's garden wall. I squinted around me, getting my bearings. By my calculations, it should come out right where the mass of bushes and shrubs was in the garden, where I'd planned to make my den. Curiouser and curiouser.

Then I remembered how late I was, and making up my mind to ask Dad about it – it certainly wasn't just a wall, or the remains of a ruined house, it was far too big and important-looking for that – I sprinted (well, hobbled) the final yards to the house, and made it downstairs just as the dinner gong sounded.

Penry was there before me, and he patted the seat beside him for me to sit next to him. Fortunately, Rhidian also saw the gesture, and interpreted it as being intended for him. He slid into the seat, his face pink with mingled embarrassment and delight at being singled out by one of his heroes, promptly knocked over his wine glass, dropped his napkin, and by the time he had settled down I was sitting safely on the other side of him, well away from Penry – and Mrs Marchpoint too, thank goodness.

Dad was across the table, opposite me. 'What did you do with yourself this afternoon, sweetheart?'

'Oh, I went for an amble up the river.'

'Wandering about all on your own? That's not a good idea.' Penry's voice.

'Whyever not?' I asked, coldly.

'Well, anything could happen. Pretty little thing like you . . .'

Despite his smile, Dad's voice was icy. 'Nothing will happen to Angharad, Pen. I'm sure she's perfectly safe. At least while you are inside at a workshop.'

Ouch. Penry spluttered, suddenly finding his celery soup remarkably interesting. Laetitia was holding court at the top end of the table, rabbiting on about Impressionists, and Picasso's blue period, and Ceri Richards, and the success of her last exhibition, while

45

she daintily sipped her soup and picked at her salad. Between mouthfuls she batted her eyelashes and flashed her lighthouse smile in Penry's direction. I noted happily that she had lipstick on her teeth. Myfanwy ventured an opinion, but the Locust (wearing green yet again) squished her effortlessly, and ploughed onward to Gauguin, Toulouse-Lautrec and Van Gogh almost without pausing for breath.

'Boring old bat,' Rhidian muttered, and I read his lips and choked on my potato salad.

Dad came into the kitchen while I was helping Marged clear up. 'Can I have a word, Hari?'

I had a feeling I knew what was coming. 'Yeah. Why not?'

'Look, love. I know Pen's an attractive man, but don't let him turn your head.'

'Oh, for heaven's sake, Dad. Will you stop worrying! Turn my head? You make me sound like that girl in the Exorcist who sicked up pea soup. I'm not stupid. For the last time, I'm not interested, OK?' And just to allay his fears I spent the evening sitting next to Rhidian while the writers read their day's work and the painters showed theirs off. I couldn't work Dad out. Did he think I was going to throw myself at Penry because I was miffed about the new baby? Maybe he just couldn't cope with me growing up. Magazines sometimes have articles about father/daughter relationships, and apparently some Dads have problems with this. It's all to do with emergent sexuality, apparently. I certainly didn't intend to let mine emerge anywhere near Penry Pritchard.

Next day I made myself scarce after lunch and went to explore the place in the bushes where the stone structure should have emerged onto Dad's property. I hunted, but couldn't find a trace of it. Surely it couldn't just stop? Yesterday, I'd seen how the stones marched right up to, and then disappeared under the wall. It had to be here somewhere. I wandered across the garden to the shed where Dad kept his garden tools, and found a small trowel. Maybe if I dug around a bit. A little archaeology, why not? It would help to pass the time. I pushed my way between trees and under overhanging shrubs until I reached the side wall of the garden, and walked carefully along a ten metre stretch of it, where shade had prevented grass growing. Then, suddenly, I spotted a place where bare earth gave way to moss, and when I prodded it with the blade of the trowel, there was the unmistakeable chinking sound of metal on stone. Carefully, I scraped away the emerald fuzz, and uncovered a large stone just like the ones in the wood. At the stone's edge I slid the trowel down into the earth and uncovered still more, and inched my way along the buried wall until I'd reached the edge of the stone construction. It was, as near as I could estimate, five metres wide. I sat back on my heels. I couldn't work out what it could possibly be. As wide as this was, it had to be something substantial, like a castle, but it was wide even for castle walls. They'd have been massive. I stood up and scratched my head, wondering how deep the stones went into the earth. There was only one way to find out.

By the time I went in to shower ready for dinner I was three feet down the side of the stone wall, and hadn't reached the bottom yet. I plonked myself next to Dad at dinner, partly because I wanted to talk to him, partly because I didn't want to sit next to Penry. During the paté starter Dad was involved in chatting to Mrs Marchpoint – or rather listening to her complain about her bed, which was apparently too hard in some places and too soft in others, but when the main course arrived, I got his attention.

'Dad, I found this weird thingy in the garden – like a very wide wall. It starts way up-river, and it comes out under our side wall and goes along under the bushes on the river side.'

Dad frowned. 'Wall? I can't say I've ever noticed anything out of the ordinary, not that I've had much time to explore the garden that minutely yet. Trust you to find it! Where is it exactly?'

I explained, and he listened, then shrugged. 'Haven't got a clue. Maybe you can find something in the library. Or ask Marged. She's lived in the village since the year dot. She'll know if anyone does.'

I asked Marged later, while I helped in the kitchen. She brushed her greying hair back from her flushed, plump face as she listened. 'Old stones by the wall? Oh, yes now. That would be *yr hen gei*.'

'*Hen gei*?'

'You know, the old whatchamacallit. Jetty. The quay.' She tore off a sheet of cling-film and covered the left-over paté with it. 'Once, long ago, the river was wider, and not so silted up. They say quite big ships used to sail out of Pendaran, times gone.'

'When? Victorian times?'

Marged turned from the fridge. 'Victorian? Oh, no, *cariad*. Much, much longer ago than that. Right, right back. When there were proper Welsh Princes, that far

48

back.' She shook out a pot-holder and hung it on the side of the Aga. 'All this, where this house, Tŷ Pendaran, is, used to be quayside, they say. Only the river changed its course, and the bit by the estuary silted up, and the jetty sort of ended up inland. You should be able to find something in the library, if you look.'

'What, this library, here in the house? Or is there one in the village?'

'One in the village? Some hopes! Mobile's what we get, once a fortnight. There's a library in town, of course. But the book you want's in the library here, I think. I'll look it out for you, tomorrow.'

But by tomorrow I knew a lot more than Marged could tell me.

CHAPTER FIVE

There was no doubt about it: Penry was not a morning person, which was fine by me because it meant I could at least eat breakfast in peace. Well, not in peace exactly: having breakfast with Rhidian was anything but. Rhidian's room was across the hall from mine, and I began to suspect that he was listening for me to leave my room, because he appeared in his doorway the instant my bedroom door opened. That was OK. That morning, feeling generous, I made him some toast and buttered it while he waded through a vast bowl of muesli.

'What are you going to do today?' I asked.

He pulled a face. 'Well, Mrs Marchpoint has decided she's got a mouse in her room. The obvious thing would be to borrow a cat, but of course Laetitia won't have one in the house. So I've got to spend the morning buying mouse-zapper and putting it down in her bedroom.' His glasses had slithered down his nose, and he pushed them up with the hand that held his toast, getting smears of butter in his hair. 'To be honest, I'd rather get rid of Mrs M. and keep the mouse. Mice are OK. At least they don't complain. Unlike Mrs Marchpoint. What about you?'

'Archaeology,' I mumbled through marmite toast, 'when I've finished helping Marged peel potatoes for dinner. Organic ones, of course.'

He grinned. I'd shared the Mantis's subterfuge with him. 'Digging up the past, eh? Where? A local dig?'

'Not yet. I'm just about to start one.'

He raised his eyebrows. No one could have accused him of being handsome, but he had a nice, big-brotherly sort of face, with freckles, and a wide, white, friendly grin. 'You are? Where?'

'I've found this weird wall in the garden. Well, actually, not only in the garden. It goes quite a way up the river bank as well. Marged says it's the remains of a medieval jetty, and I want to see how far down it goes.'

'D'you mean how far down beneath the soil, or how far down towards the sea.'

'Well, both, really. I think if I can uncover a fair bit of it, Dad may want to make a feature of it in next year's course brochure. If I can find out who built it, and when, and why. Stuff like that. It could be a summer project. Help to pass the time.'

'Mmm. Where is it? Perhaps when I've finished mouse-trapping, I can come and help. If you don't mind me butting in. I've got plenty of muscle, even if I am a bear of very little brain.'

I beamed. I never could resist a Pooh fan. Besides, he was a bear of quite impressive brain, judging by the discussion he was having with Dad last night about writers I'd never even heard of. 'That'd be great. I'm not very good at digging. I get blisters.'

He wiped toast crumbs off his mouth with the back of his hand. 'If you wear an old pair of gloves, they'll help. But don't do too much. Let me do the donkey work. You can be foreperson.'

I waited for him on the patio after lunch, but he didn't turn up. I wandered into the kitchen, where Marged was discussing the evening's menu with the cooks for the day. By some awful mischance Mrs Marchpoint and the man who had refused to change rooms with her had ended up on the same team, which should make for a lively cooking session. I resolved to be back in time so that I could eavesdrop.

'Sorry to interrupt, but have you seen Rhidian?' I asked.

Mrs Marchpoint glared. 'That boy's useless. He spent the entire morning crawling about under my bed and in the wardrobe and the wretched rodent is still scuttling around. I've sent him to buy some proper traps. Spring-loaded, old-fashioned wooden ones. And I've told him he's to bait them with chocolate. Never fails, chocolate. Those old traps will break their backs just like that.' She snapped a piece of celery, and I shuddered.

'But he's supposed to be off duty this afternoon,' I protested. 'He was going to help me to –'

'That's *your* misfortune,' Mrs Marchpoint interrupted. 'His first priority is to keep the guests happy, remember? Not mess around with you.'

She said 'mess around' as if it had some dark hidden meaning. 'Some hopes of keeping you happy,' I muttered darkly under my breath, and turned away. She wouldn't be contented in paradise, that one. Mrs Marchpoint went back to her cooking. 'Look,' she was saying to her unfortunate partner as I closed the door behind me, 'you don't hold a vegetable peeler like that, you silly man. Hold it this way!'

I rummaged in Dad's shed until I found a ratty old pair of gardening gloves and a spade with a sort of heart-shaped blade as well as a trowel for fine work and a padded plastic kneeler to protect my jeans from mud and my knees from wear and tear. Then I headed for the shrubbery. Before disappearing into the bushes, sensing eyes on me, I glanced up towards the house. In the bay

52

window overlooking the garden Penry stood, watching me, and then someone demanded his attention and he turned away, letting me slip into the bushes unseen. I was glad he was stuck in his tutorial for a couple of hours. I didn't fancy being followed into undergrowth by Penry Pritchard! Laetitia, the Mantis and six arty types were clustered on the patio with easels, their backs to the house, painting a long-distance sea-view, some pink hydrangea and a few trees in the foreground. So no one saw me slip into the shrubbery near the wall.

The smell of leaf-mould strong in my nostrils, I found the patch of wall I'd uncovered the previous day, and began to pace it out, prodding with the point of the spade until it didn't clank any more, which meant I'd reached what had probably been the sea-end of the old jetty. I went to the side of it, and began digging the spade in and waggling it along the length of the wall, marking it out clearly so that Rhidian and I could uncover it. Well, some of it. We'd need an earth-mover to shift it all. But if we could uncover the top foot or so all along the length of the jetty, I'd have something to show Dad, and maybe he'd get someone in to help open up the whole thing. Someone with a big spade, a broad back, and lots and lots of stamina, I thought, as I dug into the soil at the end of the wall.

At least the earth was soft here, where the overhanging bushes and trees had kept it shady and sheltered and stopped sea wind and sun drying it out. After about an hour, I stopped for a rest and surveyed my work, which didn't look like much, because I kept running into tree-roots and having to move on and start again a little further on. But a definite curve was being revealed, the recognisable, rounded end of the arm of stonework which had stretched out to sea. I'd brought a can of Coke with me, and unzipped it, pouring most of it down my throat in one long, thirsty gurgle, while I flexed my aching back.

I went to the edge of the bushes to see if there was any sign of Rhidian, but apart from the painters on the patio, the garden was empty. Turning, I walked back into the bushes, towards my dig.

I didn't see what I tripped over: probably a stray root or something, there were plenty of those, but I remember falling, plunging forward, the half-empty Coke can airborne. Then a crack, and all the lights went out.

I came round to the sound of voices, speaking, unmistakably, in Welsh. Now, being in North Wales, which does tend to have the odd Welsh speaker hanging about, Welsh voices aren't that unusual. But (a) I didn't recognise any of the voices, and (b) I understood every single word. Which, since I speak only schoolgirl Welsh, and not very good schoolgirl Welsh at that, is pretty amazing. I can get by in shops buying stuff, and I can say please, and thank you, and what a nice day, stuff like that. But this was proper Welsh conversation between two Welshmen, and I was having no trouble at all in understanding it.

I began to open my eyes, but the light hurt. And that was strange, because when I'd tripped, the light had been dim and greenish, an under-the-bushes sort of light, and now it was bright, glaring sunshine. Perhaps they – whoever they were – had dragged me out onto the lawn to bring me round.

My head ached. I covered my eyes with my hands, shading them from the sun, and peered out, cautiously.

'Ah, look, she's coming round,' an unfamiliar voice said. 'There, sweeting, don't sit up. Looks like you had one of your turns, and hit your head when you fell. We've sent for your father.'

'I don't have turns. I tripped.' I sat up, despite the hampering hands, and stared at the two men kneeling beside me. They were strangers, and to say the least, they were dressed weirdly, in rough wool jerkins and baggy trousers made of what looked like coarse sacking. One had leather boots, and the other wore a rough piece of cloth wrapped round each foot, tied with leather thongs. The one on my left was young, about twenty, I suppose, with a friendly but not terribly bright expression that wasn't helped by the tooth missing in front and the rough mane of straggly, matted hair falling into his eyes, one of which was aimed directly at his nose. The one on my right was older, his eyes slitted against the sun, greying hair cropped almost to the skull.

'What is this?' I rubbed my head gingerly. I had a huge lump on my forehead. 'The Sealed Knot or something?' I looked around me, baffled.

I was sitting on the curved wall of a large jetty thrusting out towards a blue, calm sea. Beside me, tied up to the grey stone wall, was a boat the like of which I'd never seen before; strange, wide-based, with a large square sail, and a jaunty, cork-like look about it, all curved wood and overlapping planks. Painted on the bows in letters of gold were the words *Gwennan Gorn,* and at the seaward end of the boat a ferocious dragon's head of carved and painted wood gazed out to sea. The ship's deck was covered with men cleaning, coiling ropes, stacking casks and packages, barrels and wooden

55

boxes into the tiny, dark hold. More than anything, it resembled a a Viking longship, and seemed well out of place for a Sealed Knot event.

'Sealed Knot?' The older man looked puzzled. He was still talking Welsh, and I was still understanding it. 'I never heard tell of any Sealed Knot. What would that be, now?'

'Oh, you know.' I rubbed my elbow where I'd bashed it, falling over. 'The Sealed Knot. They go around old castles reconstructing battles, that sort of thing. English Civil War. All in costume, with cannons and stuff.'

'English War?' The man spat, with great feeling. 'Bloody English and their wars. The English King goes to war, and Welshmen suffer.'

My head was aching. English king? Last I looked, old Liz was occupying the throne, with the terminally blighted Charlie next in the queue. I looked behind me, where a cluster of cottages huddled at the base of a small hill, beside which the wide river ran to the sea. It looked vaguely familiar, but as if something was missing from it, the way a city street looks when an old building has been demolished, and soon no one remembers what it looked like before the demolition.

'Where am I? Where's Tŷ Pendaran?'

'Don't you worry, Angharad. We've sent for your father. You just lie still and rest. You and your funny turns. Still, you wouldn't be our Angharad without them, would you?'

. 'I've never had a funny turn in my whole life,' I said, shortly, shaking off his patting hands. 'There's nothing wrong with me except I bashed my head when I tripped. And I'm not your Angharad.'

The younger man, now kneeling beside me, slapped his thighs with both hands and roared with laughter, his mouth wide open showing that more than one tooth was missing. His mouth was a disaster area, and would have kept my dentist happily humming old Beatles songs and whirring his drill for weeks on end.

'Never had a funny turn in her life, she says!' he roared. 'Never 'ad a funny turn. 'At's a good one, in't it, Iolo? 'At's a good one! There's me supposed to be Tom Twp, but she's the *twp* one now, in't she, Iolo, eh? In't she?'

Iolo shook his head, smiling. 'Perhaps Angharad doesn't think that they are funny turns, Tomos.' His eyes were kind. 'But without your turns, Angharad, you wouldn't be our wise one, would you?'

Eh? 'You what?' I said, now totally mystified. I was beginning to wonder if insanity was a prerequisite for being allowed to join the Sealed Knot. This lot were totally nuts, that was for sure.

'Ah. Here's your father now.'

Oh, Dad, great. Thank goodness for that. I turned my head, wincing at the pain. I seemed to have cricked my neck when I tripped, too. An elderly man, leaning heavily on a stout wooden stick, was making his way up the jetty towards us, but there was no sign of Dad. My companion – the slightly more intelligent one, though neither of them seemed likely to get on *University Challenge* – raised an arm in welcome.

'She is here, my Lord, and safe, praise be.'

I still couldn't spot my Dad coming. The man drew level, and stood beside me, gazing down. He was old and bent, but his eyes, although set beneath bushy white

57

eyebrows, were a clear and sparkling green, and unlike the eyes of any old man I've ever seen.

'Angharad, girl. Are you all right? Your forehead is bleeding. Iolo, may I borrow two of the men to carry her back to the house? Tomos, you will do for one.' He called to one of the sailors on the bobbing deck. 'And you, Siôn One-Eye. Leave what you are doing, and fetch a litter. I will speak to your master later.'

'If you think,' I said firmly, 'that I'm going off with you somewhere when I've never met you before in my entire life, then you'll *have* to carry me, chum, make no mistake. Put one finger on me and I'll scream blue murder.'

The old man looked worried. 'Blue murder? Ah. You've had one of your visions. When we've got you safe home, and seen to that head, then we'll try to interpret it. But until then, child, rest easy. There's nothing to be afraid of. Look, here is Tomos with the litter.'

I looked wildly around for something to hang on to. 'I'm not going, I'm not go –'

But I was dumped bodily onto the stretcher like a sack of potatoes, and, Siôn in front, the half-witted Tomos chortling gap-toothed down at me, the old man hobbling along beside, I was carried off down the jetty towards the beginning of the dark wood's edge. I wasn't going in *there* without a fight.

Just as we reached the end of the jetty, a voice bellowed from behind us. 'Siôn? Tomos? Where the hell do you think you're going?'

'Ah, my boy! It's you.' The old man turned. 'Angharad has taken a fall, and they are carrying her home for me.'

58

He was tall, broadshouldered, his skin tanned dark brown, his pale eyes vivid against sun-bleached hair tied behind his head. He moved like a great, golden lion, although he walked with a slight limp. 'They have other duties, father, but for Angharad –' he grinned at me, exposing straight white teeth, 'for Angharad I will allow them a rest.'

The litter had come to a halt, and seizing my opportunity, I legged it. I legged it so fast I forgot to check first that I was steady on my feet. I wasn't. I fell over and the lights went out yet again.

CHAPTER SIX

'Angharad, you OK?' I squinted one eye open. I was in the gloom of the bushes again, and Rhidian's face peered anxiously down at me.

'Ow. I hit my head.'

'I can see that. You're bleeding. Here – and here. How did you manage to crack your head in two places?'

'Must have bounced, I suppose. Here, help me up.' Rhidian put his arm around my back and heaved. My head whirled, and my legs sagged. I almost sat down again, hard.

'Thank goodness I decided to come and find you when I got rid of Mrs Marchpoint.' He clutched me anxiously, holding me upright. 'You might have been out here for ages if I hadn't come looking. Can you walk OK?'

'Of course I can.' I tried your basic one-step, and nearly fell over. 'Whoops. Not properly. If you help me, I'll be OK to get into the kitchen, I think.' My head ached.

We must have looked quite a sight, tottering across the lawn, arms around each other like Romeo and Juliet. My head was pounding as if lots of little men with hammers were inside it, but I wasn't feeling so bad I didn't notice Penry's expression. He was staring out of the window as we approached the patio, and it wasn't until we got closer that he noticed my bloodstained face.

Flinging open the window, he yelled, 'What's happened? Are you all right?' Then over his shoulder, 'Jack, Angharad's hurt herself. Rhidian's bringing her in now.'

If I'd been worried about the way my Dad felt about me, it would have been banished by the look on his face. Of course, I reminded myself bitterly, this is now. When the baby comes, it will all be different. He loves me now, now there's just me. But what about then? So I was fairly short with him when he shot out of the kitchen door, the Marchpoint hard on his heels, and grabbed me.

'Get off, Dad, stop fussing. I'm all right. I just had a fall and hit my head, that's all. It's nothing, honest.'

'She was unconscious, Mr Bowen,' Rhidian chipped in. 'Must have taken a hell of a whack.'

Dad peered into my eyes, and Mrs Marchpoint shoved her hand in front of my face. 'How many fingers have I got up? How many fingers?'

I withered her with a look. 'I said I'm all right. I'm not concussed. I've just bashed my head and given myself a bit of a headache. Please, Mrs Marchpoint, don't fuss.'

Mrs Marchpoint folded her arms. 'If you'll take my advice, Jack Bowen, you'll take this child to casualty. Can't take chances with head injuries. Could be in a coma by tonight. You mark my words.'

Thanks a bunch, I thought.

Dad gently wiped the blood from my forehead. 'It's only a graze. Well, both sides. How you managed to hit yourself twice, I can't understand, but I think Mrs Marchpoint's probably right. Come on, Rhidian, help me get her into the car.'

Protesting loudly, I was stuffed in the front seat of the car and driven to hospital, Rhidian leaning over the back seat anxiously, occasionally patting my shoulder, as if I were a carthorse. Dad glanced at him in the rear view mirror and grinned. 'She'll be all right, Rhidian. But it's as well to check it out. Her brain wasn't much cop before. We don't want it any worse.'

'She scared me witless, Mr Bowen, lying there.' Rhidian shuddered. 'All cold and still like a corpse.'

I rolled my eyes in disgust. Honestly, men! And they say women fuss.

They wouldn't let me out of the hospital that night, they kept me in for observation after they'd X-rayed my skull. Observation apparently meant waking me up about every five minutes throughout the night to peer into my eyeballs with a little torch, and take my pulse and blood pressure, which meant the amount of sleep I got was zilch, and about three in the morning I quit altogether when an ancient crone in the next bed with no teeth or hair began to snore loud enough to wake the dead and talk to herself into the bargain. And hospitals are supposed to help you get well.

I lay there, starched sheets crackling each time I twitched, totally fed up, listening to the nurses giggling at the ward desk, the old lady snoring and rabbiting, the sound of the traffic outside, the odd ambulance blatting into the casualty department, and tried to make sense of what had happened to me.

It had to have been a dream, right? I'd been unconscious, hadn't I? It had been mightily strange, though. Where, for instance, had the people my dream had conjured up come from? The 'Pendaran' bit was obvious. But what about the men? What were their names? Oh yes. Iolo and Tom Twp. I didn't know anyone with names like that, and I didn't think they'd been in any book I'd read recently either. But what puzzled me most of all was that the place I'd dreamed up seemed so strange-and-familiar, which is a bit of a contradiction in terms, I suppose. Obviously, the jetty was the one I'd found beside the river and in the garden, and my subconscious had gone and imagined it as it once had been, but the surroundings, the river, the hill, the lie of the land, everything except the wide sea estuary had seemed so familiar, somehow. And so real. There'd been hard, knobbly, sun-warmed stone under my back, the brightness of the sun in my eyes, and, now I came to think of it, I'd smelled seaweed, salt, raw fish, and quite a lot else that hadn't been as pleasant or as easy to identify.

By the time Dad came to fetch me home next afternoon, I'd persuaded myself that I'd imagined the whole thing. The immediacy of it began to pale, the way a dream gradually fades throughout the day, until eventually one can only remember fleeting images of it. Of course it had been a dream.

I was excused helping out at Tŷ Pendaran that day, and the next, but felt so tired that I stayed in bed and slept for most of the time. Marged brought me meals on a tray and made a fuss of me, but I wasn't particularly hungry, and after two days of watching lousy daytime TV, I decided I'd be better off downstairs. The visitors had been given the day off to either carry on with writing or painting, or wander off and explore the hills with Dad and Rhidian in the minibus, so apart from the Mantis, who was resting, and Marged, preparing vegetables in the kitchen, I had the house to myself. I decided to join Marged in the kitchen, and began stringing beans companionably beside her at the kitchen table. I'd already decided Marged was Good People: she was comfortable and friendly.

'Feeling better, lovely?'

'Mmm.' I zipped the knife from one end of a bean to the other, and began slicing the bean into neat diamond shapes. Very satisfying, seeing the emerald pile grow in the bright yellow china bowl. 'Marged, what do you know about that old jetty? Are there any – well, I don't know – local stories or anything? Like legends, you know.'

Marged paused in mid-bean. 'Stories. Let me think.' She began stringing again, thoughtfully. 'Now you ask, the people that had this place before your Dada and Mam –'

'Stepmother,' I said sharply.

Marged gave me a long, assessing look. 'Stepmother. Right. Anyway. The Llewelyns had it for years and years until the old man died, and the old lady decided it was too much for her to handle, no children to help out, see, so they sold it and she's in an old folks' home down on the sea-front in Rhos. I used to help out here, when they had dinner parties and like that, and I remember her talking one night, while I washed up. Sitting right where you are, now I think of it. Drinking cocoa, she was, and –'

'What did she say?' I demanded, impatiently.

'She was on about that bit of shrubbery, where that bit of stone jetty is, being haunted. Said she'd heard voices, and nobody'd been there when she'd gone to look.'

'Late at night?'

'No. Any time, really. I said, well, probably someone on the other side of the garden wall, something like that, but she said no. Convinced she'd heard a ghost, she was.'

64

'She never *saw* one though?' I persisted.

Marged shook her head and stood up to put the bean-strings in the compost bin outside the back door. Her voice echoed back into the kitchen.

'Not to my knowledge. But anything old, like that, though, there's bound to be something about it, isn't there? All that time, and it still being there, hidden under the ground.'

'If there's nothing else I can do to help, Marged, I think I'll have a look for that book you mentioned.'

The library was cool from the trees outside the window, and the sun made leaf-patterns on the walls. It took me a while to find the book, *The History of Tŷ Pendaran*, but at last I discovered it on the top shelf. I had to stand on a stool to reach it, and blow dust off the top.

It was a thick, heavy book, the pages freckled brown with age. On the fly-leaf it read

The History of Tŷ Pendaran
by
Elianor Llewelyn

Llewelyn. Perhaps the author was the old lady that had owned the house before Dad. I flopped into one of the over-stuffed arm-chairs, the book propped open on my tucked-under knees, and began to leaf through it. Most of it was dry, giving details of the architecture, work done on repairs and renovations, the removal of an old stone cottage from the garden, the extensions and modifications that were done over the years. I yawned. There didn't seem to be anything relevant in it. It all seemed to be about the house itself. I skim-read the last chapters, looking for any reference to the jetty, but all I found was a sketch map of the river's probable old course in relation to the house, and the jetty marked in dotted lines on it. Underneath, in brownish, faded ink, were the words

> *There was sufficient river-depth in mediaeval times to permit the negotiation of the channel by quite large, sea-going vessels. It has been suggested that Madoc ap Owain Gwynedd may have sailed from this point.*

All very helpful. I'd never heard of any Madoc ap Owain Gwynedd. Then something clicked in my head. Oh yes – there was a Portmadoc lower down the coast, on the opposite side of the arm of Wales. I seemed to remember reading somewhere that the place had been built by someone called Madoc, or Maddocks, something like that, a couple of hundred years ago, although I couldn't remember exactly when. That must be him. So that was that. I closed the book, pulling a face at the puff of dust from the pages, and slipped it back into the gap on the top shelf. Then I heard voices downstairs, and recognised Rhidian's among them. I banished ancient history from my mind and went downstairs.

Dad was looking worried. 'Myfanwy isn't feeling too good,' he said. 'She doesn't feel up to joining us for dinner. Now the baby is so close, she gets tired very easily.'

'She should be resting most of the day at this stage, with her feet elevated.' Mrs Marchpoint, of course, had an opinion. 'The final months of a pregnancy are the major growth months. She's doing far too much. Pregnancy is something I know about. I had four children, and it's a wonder I survived any of my labours. I shall take her some tea and advise her.'

'*Tea!*'

I hid a smile. Laetitia the Locust had just come through the front door.

'You want to give a pregnant woman *tea*? You might as well give her poison.'

'Rubbish. Nothing wrong with tea.'

'It's a *stimulant*. Crammed with caffeine – not to mention tannic acid. It will dangerously over-stimulate both mother and child.'

Rhidian and I exchanged glances and crept off to the kitchen, leaving the battling women to it. Dad opted out, too, and followed us, still looking worried.

'Look, Dad, I'm sure she'll be OK,' I reassured him.

'But she's never had a baby before,' he rubbed his scalp, hard, making tufts of hair stick up.

'No, but you have. It can't be too bad, can it? Don't take any notice of Mrs Marchpoint. I expect Mum managed it without any fuss,' I said, meanly, then wished I hadn't.

He sighed. 'I suppose so. Oh, I'm sure you're right. But she looks so tired and white.'

I hadn't noticed. I tried to care, but could only manage a sort of luke-warm, slight concern. Myfanwy-and-brat I didn't care about. Dad, I did.

'Look, Dad, don't worry. I'll help out as much as I can. I'll take her up a tray tonight, and make sure she's OK before dinner. I can't do the painting workshops for her, but I can do some of the rest of the stuff if she tells me what to do, can't I?'

Dad grinned with relief. 'That would be such a help, Hari. Maybe you could manage the big shop, tomorrow? Marged can drive you in, and Rhidian can go with you to help carry it.' Then he remembered I'd only just come out of hospital. 'Only if you feel up to it, of course.'

I laid up a tray once the dinner was cooked, and, for Dad's sake only, you understand, put a pretty tray cloth on it, and a flower in a little vase. The steak pie steamed, and the runner beans and creamed potatoes smelled good. Myfanwy was sitting up in bed when I pushed the door of the room open. Two cups of liquid, one a murky green, the other tea-coloured, stood untouched on the bed-side table.

'Oh, thanks so much, Hari,' she said, pushing herself up and plumping pillows. She did look exhausted. I supposed carrying some great lump of a baby around inside you would make a person tired. 'Are you sure you can manage without me this evening?'

'Of course. It's a general reading session tonight – this lot of guests' last night.'

The Mantis frowned. 'And there's all the turn-round to do on the bedding, tomorrow. Oh, I'll never be able to cope. We'll have to take someone on from the village, and –'

'Nonsense,' I said, more confident than I actually felt. 'Rhidian and I can manage, and Dad and Marged will help us, I'm sure. Don't worry. Just rest.' I pinned on an artificial smile. 'Mustn't get over-tired, not with the baby coming.'

As if I cared.

CHAPTER SEVEN

The bad news was, Mrs Marchpoint decided to stay on, having completed the painting course, and give the writing a try. And unfortunately we had a room free, and she knew it.

'I've always,' she said, grandly, 'felt I could be a writer,' which made Dad grimace and me hide a grin. Dad's usual, rather testy, answer to anyone making that particular claim was 'Well, why aren't you, then?', but Mrs Marchpoint was a paying guest, so he couldn't. He says there's nothing more infuriating than having someone say that, as if it was something one could just 'do', just because one felt like it.

'You wouldn't expect to throw a perfect pot, or paint an Old Master, first time you tried, would you?' he fumed, later, 'so why do people seem to think writing's so easy? Arrogant, self-opinionated old bat.'

'Chill out, Dad. She'll soon find out it isn't as easy as it looks, and she is paying you! Give her some of your really mind-blowing writing exercises to do. That'll fix her.'

He grinned, evilly. 'I know exactly the one I shall start her off with. It's been known to make strong men cry. By the way, Hari, speaking of blowing minds, I think you'd better stay away from that old wall thing you've found. I don't want you ending up in hospital again.'

'Oh, come on, Dad!' I protested. 'That was just a one-off. I'm not going to fall on my face and knock myself out every time I go near the bushes!'

'You might. You always were clumsy. No, Hari, I think it's best if you stay right away from it.'

'That's not fair. I'll be OK. And it would be such a selling point for Tŷ Pendaran if it is that old quay, Dad. Oh, please let me carry on digging!' I got crafty. 'Suppose I only dig when Rhidian can help me? How would that be?'

He thought about it. 'Well, I suppose so. But only when Rhidian's there, all right? I'm worried enough about Muvvie, without having to worry about you, as well.'

Oh, knickers to Muvvie, I thought as I drifted into the kitchen to help the day's cooks and Marged serve the dinner. 'Did you find the book?' she asked, draining a steaming pan over the sink.

I shook my head, piling fluffy mash into deep dishes. 'Yes. Nothing significant in it.'

'You could try the library in Colwyn Bay. They'd have something, I expect.'

I shrugged. 'I'm not that worried. If I can just dig out the stonework as far as I can and find out what it looks like, that'll satisfy me. I mean, it's just an old stone jetty. There was a map of the area in the book, showing where the jetty was, in relation to the old course of the river. That's all I needed to know, actually. I'll carry on with the digging, but Dad says I mustn't unless Rhidian's with me.'

'What?' Rhidian came into the kitchen and picked up a tureen of soup.

'You. Help me dig the jetty out.'

'Oh. Sure. No problem. Am I allowed to eat first?'

I pulled a face, and followed him into the dining room with a basket of warm rolls. I forgot amateur archaeology. I was hungry.

Changeover weekend was horrendous. Every bed had to be stripped, re-made, and the linen laundered, every bathroom scrubbed, every hall and bedroom cleaned, and provisions bought in Colwyn Bay to feed the hordes due to arrive on Monday. Penry, wearing shorts, disappeared in the general direction of the beach (he always seemed to vanish when there was work to be done), and Laetitia the Locust betook herself in pursuit of him. She was allergic to dust, of course, and so couldn't possibly help out. All that bedding being shaken about would certainly trigger off her asthma.

'Hope you get sucked into the quicksand,' I muttered at her retreating back, 'slurp, slurp, gulp and no more Laetitia'. I resolved to scour Tesco for the most irradiated, hormone-stuffed non-organic vegetables I could possibly find, especially for her.

When we'd done the vast shop – three trolleys full, by the time we'd got everything – and Marged had headed off to have her hair done, Rhidian and I went into the library and took out temporary visitors' cards. Then I immersed myself in the history section, while Rhidian hit the horror. I found one about the Princes of Wales, and another called *North Wales – People and History*, which looked as if it might be useful. Rhidian joined me at the check-out desk with an armful of gory covers. I pulled a face.

'Oh, Rhidian! That's such junk!'

'I *like* junk. It helps me to sleep. Especially a good horror story. What have you got?'

I showed him.

'It's weird,' Rhidian pushed his glasses up his nose. 'D'you realise that just about every bit of history we've ever been taught has been English history?'

'No, it hasn't. We did the Rebecca Riots and the Chartists for GCSE. That's not English history.'

'All right. So that's Welsh. But what do you actually know about Owain Glyndŵr?'

'I can summon spirits from the vasty deep, I quoted. *'That great magician, damned Glendower.* And soon I shall know loads more.' I waggled my library books at him.

'And that was Shakespeare rewriting Welsh history to flatter his Tudor masters!' Rhidian said triumphantly. 'Welsh history as it affects England, that's what we're taught!'

I noticed the librarian waiting none too patiently for our books, and handed mine over.

'Is that your hobby-horse, Rhid?'

He grinned, sheepishly. 'Yes, I suppose. I'll shut up, shall I?'

I grinned back. 'Come on. I'll buy you a coke and a doughnut before we head back. Marged will be a while, yet.'

We found an empty table in a crowded cafe and grabbed it. There were tourists everywhere, all wandering about in that aimless, 'I'm on holiday but it's not nice enough for the beach,' expression on their faces, their peeling arms scarlet. There seemed to be an awful lot of Liverpool accents about.

When we'd ordered, I idly flicked through the North Wales book. 'I'd really like to carry on with digging up the jetty,' I said absent-mindedly. 'I still think it's a worth-while project.'

The coke and doughnuts arrived. 'Me too,' Rhidian said jammily. 'If we can uncover a fair bit, maybe we'll find something: masons' marks, old pottery. Who knows. Only don't go bashing your head again, OK?' He wiped a smear of jam from the corner of his mouth. 'My heart nearly stopped when I saw you lying there, out cold. And then when you started talking to yourself with your eyes shut, well!'

'I *talked* to myself?' I was mystified. 'What did I say?'

Rhidian shrugged. 'Oh, I don't know. Strange thing was, you seemed to be talking in Welsh. But I must have misheard. You only said a few words.'

I put my doughnut down, slowly, the jam squishing out of the middle. 'What did I say?'

'Oh, come on, now, Angharad! I don't speak Welsh. It *just sounded* Welsh, is all. It could have been complete gibberish. Or Martian, even. After all, you don't speak fluent Welsh either, do you? So it couldn't have been, could it?'

He was right, it couldn't. But nonetheless, it gave me the shivers. But by the time Marged, curled until her greying hair looked like corrugated iron, met us in the car park, I'd almost forgotten.

Back at Tŷ Pendaran the house was in turmoil while the shopping was put away and everything finally prepared for the new batch of visitors.

Fortunately there was no one in the new lot to rival Mrs Marchpoint. In fact, they seemed like a pretty nice bunch. There was one totally prattish female who took one look at Penry and fell like a ton of bricks. Honestly, you could almost hear the thud. Tara-Louise, her name was, and she was blonde, and wore low-cut tops to show off her large boobs. They were like large white blancmanges. I hope I never get boobs like that. Boobs, yes, but not wobbly mountains. Once Penry clapped eyes on her he immediately forgot about me, which was great so far as I was concerned, but I got the impression Laetitia's nose was a little out of joint. At dinner Penry gazed into Tara-Louise's eyes stroking her bare arm so that she got goosebumps and all the little dark hairs on her arm stood up. She wasn't a natural blonde, then. She'd already asked Dad if he would be an 'absolute daaahling', and let her switch courses from painting to writing.

'Certainly,' Dad said, 'no problem. You can be in my group.'

He winked at me from the end of the table, and I grinned back. I think he'd stopped worrying about Penry making a play for me.

The Mantis wasn't with us. The Doctor had called during the day, and suggested she keep to her bed for a few days and rest. Her blood pressure was up, and her ankles were swollen, which apparently isn't a good thing in late pregnancy. Fine by me. She was out of my hair. I didn't have to look at her.

Laetitia didn't appreciate having to do all the workshops by herself, though. It meant that instead of having two groups of three a day, she had two groups of six, (or, actually, one of five, since Tara-Big-Boobs had deserted her) which she felt was altogether too much.

Dad told her she should try working in an inner city comp, like he had, with classes of nearly forty, and see how she liked that, which didn't go down too well. However, as Dad said when she'd stomped irritably away, she needed the money he was paying her, so it was

74

hard luck, really. But she sulked a lot. I had a sneaky idea that most of what she was sulking about was that Penry hadn't made any sort of pass at her: first he was oiling up to me, then he was at it with Tara-Louise, and she obviously felt quite put out. I wouldn't have thought Penry was her type, but who knows? Maybe she wanted him to try it on so she could turn him down.

It was Tuesday, out in the minibus day, before I got a chance to visit my jetty again. Unfortunately, Rhidian had gone off with Dad and the visitors, because they were going down to Portmeirion, and he'd never been there. I shouldn't really have disobeyed Dad and gone into the shrubbery alone, but I still felt he was over-reacting. Lightning doesn't strike twice in the same place, does it?

Glancing over my shoulder to make sure no one could see me – although Marged was busy upstairs with her vacuum cleaner and Myfanwy and Dad's room was at the front of the house and no one was likely to spot me – I slithered into the dark green-ness.

The stones of the jetty were as I'd left them, trowel and spade forgotten, a bloodstained, damp tissue that Rhidian had used to dab at the blood on my forehead crumpled on the ground. I was only going to look, honest, but it was almost as if the stones drew me. Mesmerised, I picked up the trowel and knelt beside the projecting mossy stones. I began to scrape, digging down deeper and deeper, clearing packed earth away, digging down and down.

That was too slow: I picked up the pointed, heart-shaped spade, its wooden handle damp from being left out of doors for the few nights since my accident, the blade already showing signs of orange rust, and thrust it deep into the soft earth. It was cool under the trees, but I soon warmed up and stripped off my sweater. I dug and dug, and by the time I heard the minibus crunching on the gravel of the drive, I had cleared the earth away from several feet of jetty to a depth of about eighteen inches. I was hot and sweaty, but I'd made progress. I left the spade and trowel under the bushes. If I was caught putting them back in the shed I'd catch it from Dad for not having Rhidian with me. Come to that, Rhidian wouldn't be too pleased when he found out. Perhaps it would be better if he didn't.

I peered cautiously out of the bushes to make sure there was no one about before hurtling across the lawn and into the kitchen. I remembered to kick off my earth-clogged trainers in the outhouse first – muddy shoes would have been a dead giveaway, and nobody asked where I'd been or what I'd been doing all afternoon.

I took Myfanwy's tray up to her that evening and almost felt sorry for her. Her face was puffy, and she was even paler than usual. She looked like – oh, I don't know – a sort of skinny white whale, with that great grotesque bump and her stick insect arms poking out of her pink frilly nightie. She struggled to a sitting position and I put the tray so that its wooden legs straddled her swollen stomach.

'That looks good, Hari.' She brushed lank hair from her face, and picked up a fork.

'How are you feeling?' I enquired, with a sympathy I didn't really feel.

She grimaced. 'Awful. I feel so tired all the time, and Pudden,' she patted her bump affectionately, 'little

76

Pudden is kicking me to bits. I can't believe there are almost four weeks still to go. I feel so huge and heavy.'

Pudden! Yuk. I crossed to the door. I'd done the polite bit. Now I wanted my dinner. 'Well, four weeks isn't so long. It'll be over before you know it.'

Her eyes rested on me. 'Hari, I wouldn't tell your Dad this – but I'm so afraid something will go wrong.'

'Don't be silly,' I said briskly. 'This is the twentieth century. What can possibly go wrong?' Then I felt a bit guilty. 'Come on, Myfanwy. Cheer up. Just think, soon you'll have your baby to cuddle.'

CHAPTER EIGHT

Next day, as soon as I was able, I tried to sneak out the back way. Just my luck. My hand was actually on the door-handle when Rhidian came in.

'Where are you off?' he enquired.

'Who, me?' I knew I looked guilty.

'You. Oh, I get it. You're sneaking off to do some more digging, all by yourself, aren't you?'

'More digging?' I tried to look innocent.

'Yes. I went and had a look at your bit of wall last night and I saw you'd been hard at it. You were supposed to have me there with you, remember?'

'Oh, all right,' I said ungraciously. 'I'm going to do a bit more, now. Want to come?'

'Course I do. I'll fetch a spade.'

I went ahead down to the shrubbery, and pushed my way into the bushes, scratching my face on a twig. I picked up my spade, and leaned on it, trying to decide whether to carry on where I'd left off, or move down a bit. The day was windy, and a stray gust rattled the leaves, piercing the gloom. Sunlight spackled the ground, making it look as if the earth was moving. One stray gleam picked up the edge of something slightly shiny at the bottom of yesterday's trench. I bent down, and gently scraped away the dirt with the corner of the trowel until I worked it free. Whatever it was was clogged with dirt, and I rubbed it between my fingers until the earth flaked away, leaving me holding a small, round, flat disc of silvery metal, a hole pierced through it close to the edge. A design was chased into it, and I moved it this way and that, trying to catch one of the elusive sunbeams, to make out what it was. No good. I moved into the light, and gasped.

A dragon chased its arrow tail around the disc, mighty jaws belching fire, ridged spine sharp, talons curved and wicked. Rhidian arrived, tripping over his spade.

I started to say, 'Look what I found in the trench, Rhid,' but stopped myself just in time. I wasn't sure why. I slipped the disc surreptitiously into my shorts pocket. 'Come on, Rhid, let's get digging.'

'Slave-driver!' he said amiably, but went obediently to work.

The day was hotter than yesterday despite the breeze. Perspiration poured off us, and when we'd been digging for an hour Rhidian straightened his back and wiped his forehead. 'Look, I think we ought to take a break, or we'll both drop dead from heat exhaustion. I'll go and get us a drink from the kitchen. You have a rest.'

I embedded the spade into the turf, and surveyed the trench we'd already dug. More and more of the wall was revealed, and we'd almost uncovered the entire curve of the end of the jetty wall. It was quite exciting, seeing bits of history come above ground for the first time in goodness knows how long. I sat down on the exposed wall and took the disc out of my pocket to have another look.

The world went blank. I couldn't see, couldn't hear, couldn't think, for a second. It was as if a mighty bolt of lightning had struck me dead centre. Then sounds came back, and I could see again.

Thinking, though, that was difficult. I couldn't for the life of me grasp where I was. Then I knew. I was still sitting on the curved end wall of the jetty, my legs dangling over the edge into space where seconds earlier they'd touched solid earth, and before me was the open sea, slightly choppy, reflecting the clear blue of the sky. I heard voices behind me, the creak of wood against wood, and the slap of waves against stone. Slowly, stiffly, I got to my feet, turned. The disc fell from my numb fingers. Before me was the hustle and bustle of the same strange quayside that I'd dreamed – hallucinated? – before, and the same broad-beamed, curved-sided longship drifted beside the jetty wall, tied by thick hawsers to iron rings, its dragon head prow snarling above me. I bent, and picked up the disc. As my fingertips touched it I was back in the gloom of the shrubbery, and Rhidian, a glass of orange juice in each hand, stood before me, his glasses slithering down his nose.

'Here,' he said, holding one out to me, shoving his glasses up, and taking a long swig of his juice.

I tried to speak, but couldn't. Slowly I reached out and took the glass of juice, slipping the disc into my pocket. Maybe that bash on the head had scrambled my brains. Maybe I was getting sick. Sunstroke, maybe. Maybe it was something worse. A brain tumour! Maybe I was just going quietly doo-lally. Or was I? Only one way to find out.

'Rhidian,' I began, and then cleared my throat. 'Rhidian, hold my glass for a minute, please, and watch what happens.'

Mystified, he took the glass. I walked to the centre of the wall and reached into my pocket, wrapping the disc firmly in my fingers. It happened again. Bright light, deaf-and-blind – and then I was back on the sea wall, a little lower down this time, the boat closer now. I let go the disc for a second, dropping it loose into my pocket, then held it tightly again. I was back in the shrubbery.

'What?' he said, sipping orange.

'Did anything happen?'

'Yeah. You sort of twitched and pulled a face. Like this.' He pulled an expression like a panic-stricken bull-frog. 'Why?'

'Nothing else?'

He shook his head. 'Like what?'

'Oh, nothing.' I walked to the very end of the wall, where the boundary wall of the house covered it, and clutched the disc again. This time I was close to the land end of the jetty, about the place I'd been when I'd leapt off the stretcher last time. I released the disc in my pocket, and took time to look around me. To my left, above the shoreline, a small group of mud and wood shacks huddled, smoke trickling from holes in the untidy thatched roofs. On the right, the land sloped up to dark woods, and a river disappeared into the trees. And suddenly, I knew where I was. On my right, some time in the future, Tŷ Pendaran would be built.

Ridiculous, impossible as it seemed, somehow I appeared to have slipped into the past. I turned, and saw the boat, the gilded name *Gwennan Gorn* gleaming in the sun. On the deck a tall man, fair hair tied at the nape of his neck, bent over a coil of rope. His back was bare, and muscles rippled under a tanned skin. I seized the disc again and was back with Rhidian.

'Are you all right?' he said, crossly. 'I've been talking to you for the last ten minutes, and you haven't said a word.'

'Ten minutes?' Surely I hadn't been away that long?

81

'Well, five. OK, so I exaggerate occasionally.'

That made me feel better. Not much. 'Look, Rhidian. D'you mind if we pack in digging for today? I think the heat is getting to me.'

He looked relieved. 'Fine by me.' He swigged the last of the orange juice and tossed the glass nonchalantly from hand to hand. Well, almost. I caught it before it shattered on the stones.

'Oops!' he said, grinning sheepishly. Honestly, he gave a whole new meaning to clumsy.

We carried the spades back into the shed, bashing them on the ground to shake off the loose earth.

'Fancy an ice-cream on the front?' Rhidian asked.

I shook my head. 'No thanks. I'm shattered. I think I'll go and have a rest before dinner. If you don't mind,' I added, seeing his face fall.

I felt guilty, going upstairs to my room and leaving him to wander off to the ice-cream kiosk by himself, especially after all his hard work digging, but I needed time to think.

Once in my room I took the disc out of my pocket, rinsed it in the washbasin, polishing it dry on my towel. Holding it between my hands, I felt nothing; nothing happened, not even a tingle. Not the disc, then. Maybe it had to be a combination of disc and wall.

I shook myself. I spoke to myself severely, out loud. 'Oh, come on, Angharad. Time travel? This isn't Doctor Who! This is real life!' I put the disc on the duvet, lay on my stomach, and considered it. Yet something had happened. The disc gleamed smugly at me, the dragon's incised eyes catching the light. I came to a decision. I'd sneak away, somehow lose Rhidian, and find out if it really worked, whether I could really slip back into the past whenever I felt like it. Time-travel. I had a peculiar feeling, deep inside me. Almost like sitting in the dentist's waiting room.

I looked at my watch. Quarter to five: no time to do anything today, I was needed in the kitchen to help with dinner. I had a quick shower, and went downstairs, joining Marged in the kitchen.

Dad came in quarter of an hour later, and went up to see the Mantis. Downstairs again, he worriedly chewed his thumbnail.

'I think I'll get the doctor out again tomorrow if she's no better,' he muttered. 'She looks so tired and pale. She's lost all her bounce, somehow.'

'Dandelion leaf tea,' Laetitia said, coming into the kitchen to check the preparation of her 'organic' vegetables. Marged just managed to whisk the Tesco spinach bag into the bin before she spotted it.

'Pardon?' Dad said, mystified.

'Dandelion leaf tea. Excellent diuretic. Cure the puffiness. I swear by it.'

'Can't do any harm, I suppose,' Dad said.

'Might poison her,' I muttered hopefully, under my breath. Fortunately, he didn't hear me.

'What have you been doing all day, Hari?'

'Who, me?' (Popping back in time a bit, you know how it is, I thought.) 'Nothing, really. Rhidian and I did some digging on the jetty. We've uncovered quite a bit of it now.'

'Find anything interesting?'

I shook my head. I didn't want to show him the disc. Not yet. Not until I'd had a chance to see if it really worked, or if I was just imagining things. 'Just a lot of old stones.'

It was quite nauseating, watching Tara-Louise snuggle up to Penry over the parsnips, and even more sick-making watching him enjoy peering down her Jersey cow front. Almost, but not quite, put me off Marged's sticky toffee pudding. Laetitia, however, looked like she'd bitten unexpectedly on a lemon.

After dinner, I joined the groups in the library, where the guest reader was just beginning her talk. She'd written a biography of Charlotte Bronte, and since *Jane Eyre* is one of my all-time favourite books, I wanted to hear her. But somehow she managed to make even Charlotte seem boring, waffling on about the politics of feminism and stuff like that, which was all very well in its place, but I wanted to know what old Charlotte had been like as a person. Penry fell asleep, and I switched off half-way through one of the complicated speeches that comprised Laetitia's questions, and thought about the disc nestling in my jewel case upstairs between my locket with Mum and Dad's pictures in, and the little gold cross and chain my Godmother had sent me for my confirmation. I didn't like leaving it there: I was afraid someone might see it, or it might miraculously disappear. I felt I needed to keep it close.

When I went up to bed I locked the door behind me and quickly took it out of the box. I had an idea. In the bottom bit of the case, where I kept my junk stuff, I had a smallish pewter CND pendant I'd picked up in a junk shop hanging on a leather thong. I tied it around my neck. The pendant hung on top of the disc, obscuring it completely, the twin discs nestling in the hollow of my throat. I turned my head this way and that in front of the mirror. Nothing showed. Great.

'Are you going to be digging this afternoon?' Rhidian asked at breakfast next morning. He swallowed his mouthful of toast and took another bite.

I shrugged. 'Don't think so. I might go into town with Marged. I want to pick up a couple of things for myself. Want to come with me? I need a new dress,' I added, craftily, knowing instinctively that Rhidian, being male, would loathe trailing round the shops after me. Especially me trying on dresses. I was right.

He shuddered. 'No thanks. I'm – I'll – I've got things to do, OK?'

'Fine!' I said, happily. That was me free and clear. Of course, I had no intention of going into town with Marged or anyone else.

No. I was going upriver.

CHAPTER NINE

I helped Marged stack the lunch dishes in the machine, and then went upstairs to get my sweater, because the day was grey, with a chill breeze blowing in from the sea. I checked that there was no one about and slipped through the gate, following the garden wall round to where the jetty's stones reappeared on the far side of the wall. I didn't walk on it. I wanted to go deeper into the woods, where no one could see me, before I tested the dragon disc again. I mean, it was impossible, wasn't it? It had to be some sort of throwback to the bump on the head. After all, I had been in hospital overnight, so the Accident and Emergency staff had taken it seriously, even if I hadn't, particularly. Maybe hallucinations were a symptom of delayed concussion or something.

There had been rain overnight, not much, but enough to settle the dust and make the track beside the wall sticky underfoot. I walked until the trees closed behind me, and when I was certain that no one was about, I fished the pendant from the neck of my T-shirt, separated dragon from CND sign, and clutching the dragon disc in my hand, took a deep breath, closed my eyes, and stepped onto the wall. As soon as my second foot joined the first on the mossy stones, there it was – instant white-out.

Cautiously, I opened my eyes. I was still in the wood, beside the river, but before me in the distance was a small building that certainly hadn't been there the last time I'd walked upriver – in my time, that is. Keeping under cover of the trees, I crept closer. When I was only a few yards away I hid behind a handy trunk to inspect the house more closely. It was square-shaped, but unlike the others nearer the sea, because it was built of roughly dressed stone rather than mud and wood. The roof was neatly thatched, and it nestled in a clearing in the trees like a witch's cottage in a fairy tale, smoke drifting upwards from a hole in the thatch. I watched for a while, but apart from the smoke, there was no sign of life.

Chopped logs were stacked neatly against the wall under an overhang of roof, and an axe leaned against them. A leather bucket stood outside the rough wooden door, but there were no windows to speak of, just narrow slits in the walls covered with what looked like animal hides.

I edged closer, listening for sounds, wondering how fast I could get back to the jetty if anyone suddenly came through the wooden door and caught me. When I was close enough to touch the pile of logs, I cautiously slithered round to the nearest wall-slit, and listened beside it. Silence. I poked my nose and one eye up against the slit, but couldn't see past the leathery hide stretched across it. But the hut seemed to be empty: it was completely silent, and it had an unmistakable 'nobody's home' feel about it. What harm could there be in just looking?

Promising myself that if there was any trace of warty old ladies in pointy hats, small children in cages or bowls of porridge in threesomes, I would run like a bat out of hell back to my time, I pushed open the door, wincing at the loud creak – it sounded like Count Dracula's front door. It took a while to get used to the gloom. Smoke sucked up from the firepit by the opening door billowed in acrid clouds, filling the room and stinging my eyes. Eventually I stopped coughing and could see through my streaming eyes.

Despite the minute size of the place, a platform had been built on stilts to make a rudimentary second floor, with a ladder leading upwards. Below the platform the earthen floor of the hut had been covered with rough planks, on which stood a long, light-wood chest and on the chest, something wrapped in leather. Over the firepit was an iron fire-dog, with a blackened pot hanging from it, steaming gently. Curious, I went further into the hut, over to the bubbling cauldron, lifted out the ladle resting on the rim, and sniffed. Some sort of meat stew, from the smell of it. I went back to the door and peered out to make sure that no one was coming, and then cautiously climbed the rickety ladder to the platform and peeked over the edge. Coarse sacking covered a pile of hay, and sheepskins were folded neatly beside it. A russet woollen gown hung on a wooden peg from the roof-beam, and floppy, shapeless leather shoes stood beneath it. On the other side of the roof-space hung a second gown, longer, bigger, obviously a man's. Another chest, this time of dark wood, and with a curved lid, stood on the platform near my right hand, and curiously I opened it, and found it full of small pottery jars and little wooden boxes. I opened one: it contained some sort of pinky-grey gritty paste, which smelled faintly of roses and mint. I guessed at some sort of ointment.

Just as I was beginning to feel vaguely guilty about snooping, and was about to climb backwards down the ladder and leave, I heard the door to the hut open. I shot frantically upwards as if I'd been poked with a cattle prod. Inside, I groaned. Hadn't I learned anything from Goldilocks?

I flattened myself on the platform, waiting to be discovered. I fished for the disc on its thong, but when I found it, clutched it and squeezed my eyes shut, nothing happened. Away from the jetty, apparently, I was trapped. Slowly, carefully, I poked my nose over the edge. Just below me was the silvery hair of an old man: the one who had organised the stretcher-carriers on the jetty. He bent over the cauldron, stirring with a long wooden spoon. He turned suddenly, and I pulled my head back so that I was out of sight, trying to make myself even flatter against the floor. My heart beat so loudly that I could feel it thudding against the rough planks of the floor.

And then the worst happened. I breathed in dust, and felt a sneeze coming up from my toes. Now, my sneezes are legendary. They can be heard (according to my mother, anyway) across at least six counties on a clear day. Ladylike, they ain't. Frantically, I groped for my jeans pocket to find a tissue in the vain hope of muffling it: perhaps the old man was deaf, perhaps he wouldn't hear me. But I couldn't find either pocket or tissue. My jeans were gone, and in their place was a rough woollen skirt. Flabbergasted, I rolled onto my side and looked down at myself. The gown was green and caught at the waist by a rope girdle, and was like nothing I'd ever seen before. The sneeze broke before I could stop it, and a mild voice spoke from down below.

'Angharad, my child. Are you feeling better?'

Reluctantly, feeling horribly trapped, I looked over the edge, and met those startling green eyes again.

'Ah, good. You look rested. Better. You have colour in your cheeks at last. Come down and have some broth.'

Well, what could I do? I could hardly stay up there, could I? Not once I'd been discovered. What would happen, though, when I got downstairs, he got a close look and he didn't recognise me? I'd probably end up locked in a dungeon somewhere. Shakily, I edged backwards down the ladder until I stood on the wooden platform. The old man glanced in my direction and beckoned.

'Here. Come and sit down.'

He didn't turn a hair! Obediently, my mind working overtime, wondering if I could make a dash for the door and leg it for the jetty and sanity, I sidled towards the wooden stool he'd hooked forward to the fireside with his foot, and perched gingerly on it. He ladled some steaming soup into a bowl and handed it to me, a wooden spoon propped against the rim.

'Eat,' he commanded, and I obeyed, not knowing what else to do. It tasted good, but it might as well have been ashes for all I cared. What on earth was I going to do? The old man busied himself about the hut, folding clothes which he'd brought in from outside in a wicker basket (I wondered fairly hysterically where the washing line was – I hadn't spotted one) and stacking wooden bowls. He didn't seem to notice that I was a different Angharad from the one he was expecting!

'There is good news,' he said at last, breaking the silence that was just about the most uncomfortable I'd ever known. 'Your foster brother is back.'

My who? 'Oh, great.' I said, warily.

The old man turned, and looked at me strangely. 'Great? What an odd choice of words, Angharad. What do you mean?'

I gulped. I was going to have to watch the twentieth century slang if I was going to hang around whatever time this was for much longer! Not that I intended to. As soon as I could, trust me, I was out of there. 'Um. It means I'm glad. Pleased. Happy.'

The old man sighed. 'You young people. You have a language all your own.' Which was the point at which I realised that, once again, he – and I – were speaking Welsh. I didn't want to ask where my 'foster brother' had been, or even who he was: obviously I was supposed to know that. Considering I wouldn't know my foster brother from Adam even if he came and bit me (which I hoped he wouldn't) I decided the best thing to do was to keep quiet and speak only when I had to. I slurped some more soup, but it was beginning to make me feel sick. I put the bowl down. The old man looked at the half-full bowl and sighed.

'You must eat more, Angharad. You are too thin and these strange, swooning spells of yours tire you. Three you've had now, in as many days, when before you had them only once a month when your time was upon you.'

Now that was interesting. Perhaps his Angharad – whoever she was – was having the same trouble as me! 'I'm all right.' I ventured. 'I'm just not hungry.'

'Perhaps an apple?'

I shook my head. The old man cocked his head on one side, listening. 'I hear someone coming.'

I couldn't. His face broke into a smile. 'I'm right. It's him.'

The door opened, and a tall man – the man who had been on the jetty – came in. He stooped to avoid bashing his head on the lintel, then straightened, smiling. He seemed to fill the hut as he swept the old man up in his arms, hugging him, whirling him in a circle until the old man bellowed to be put down.

'Stop it, you oaf! Madoc, stop this at once! Have you no respect for age and infirmity? Put me down this instant.'

My, he was handsome! Drop-dead gorgeous, in fact. Pity he was supposed to be my brother. His hair had started out mousy brown, I guessed, but sun and sea had bleached it into gold and amber streaks, and the blueness of his eyes was vivid against his tan, and crinkled at the corners when he set the old man carefully on his feet and glanced at me.

'Angharad! You've changed so much!' he said, starting towards me.

You're telling me! I thought. *You'll never know how much.* I managed a weak grin. What had the old man called him? Madoc. 'Hi, Madoc.' Damnation, slang again. 'I mean, hello.' Oh, crumbs, did they even say hello?

Apparently, they did, or he didn't notice my slip. He bent and gave me a smacking kiss on the cheek. He smelled of woodsmoke, salt and fresh sweat and his bristly chin rasped my cheek. 'You're growing so fast we'll have to find you a husband before long.'

'Over my dead body,' I retorted, before I could stop myself. Madoc roared with laughter, slapping me on the back so hard I almost fell off the stool.

'She doesn't change, Pendaran. Still the old Angharad.'

That, I thought, *is what you think, chum!* Then I realised what he'd called the old man. Pendaran. Dad's house: Tŷ Pendaran. Another clue. So this was Madoc. The one responsible for building Portmadoc? Somehow, I didn't think so. So who was he? More to the point, who was I?

Pendaran ladled more soup into a bowl and Madoc began eating with great enjoyment, but not much in the way of table-manners. The old man watched him with a wry smile.

'You still make the finest broth in Wales, Pendaran.'

'And you still eat as if there will be no more food on this earth, Madoc,' Pendaran replied. 'Tell me what has been happening to you, my boy. It has been so long since you were home.'

No it hasn't! I thought. *You were here just a few days ago!* Unless, of course, I was popping in and out of time all over the place, and not in any particular order. Curiouser and curiouser.

Madoc sat on the floor to eat his broth, one long leg bent, the other stretched out, his booted foot almost touching mine. He scraped his bowl, and held it out for a refill. 'I've been in Ireland with Rhirid,' he began.

'Ah. How is your brother?'

Madoc shrugged. 'As always. Glad to be away from our father. Owain Gwynedd casts a long shadow, but even he can't reach Ireland in a hurry. Rhirid wanted me to stay there, make my life with him and his family, but the land isn't for me. Those who own land own trouble, and I've had too much trouble already in my life.'

Pendaran smiled. 'That's true, my boy. But why are you back?'

93

Madoc set his empty bowl down beside him. 'I've been thinking, Pendaran. There must be lands beyond those we know. The sea is so vast, so much of it uncharted, that there must be more. There must, don't you see? More lands. More people. Perhaps wonderful lands and amazing people. Maybe lands as good as Gwynedd. Empty lands, perhaps, with no one shedding blood for them. The *Gwennan Gorn* is seaworthy, strong, and I have a mind to see how far I can sail her. I shall take her and sail into the sunset until I find something. There's nothing for me here but bitterness and bloodshed.'

Pendaran sighed. 'It will be hard to lose you, Madoc. But you must do as you will.'

Madoc fidgeted. 'Before I go, Pendaran, I need your help. I must see my mother before I leave. Please don't argue. It may be for the last time. A sailor at Rhirid's court told tales of sea-monsters beyond the blue waters. I need to see her.' He pulled a comical face. 'In case I'm eaten up entirely.'

Pendaran picked up our bowls and held them, stacked one on the other, on his bony knees.

'And how do you propose to do that? Your father does not know you are alive. Do you plan to march up to his castle gate and demand to see Brenda? You will be turned away by Owain's men. Or dangled kicking from a hempen rope.'

'Oh, come, Pendaran. You are still Owain's bard. Couldn't you smuggle me in as your apprentice?'

Pendaran looked at his foster son steadily for a few seconds, and then his face twitched, his shoulders heaved, and he began to laugh until tears ran down his cheeks.

94

'Madoc, you are tall and comely, but you have the voice of a tone-deaf rook!' he spluttered at last. 'You could never be my apprentice in a million years!'

'I don't need to sing, Pendaran. All you need to do is tell them I am your apprentice. Then, while you entertain, I can slip away and see my mother. Please?'

They were both so wrapped up in Madoc's plan that they were ignoring me. Nonchalantly I got up, stretched, wandered innocently towards the door, and through it. Then I legged it for the jetty and grabbed the disc hanging around my neck.

And I was back in the woods, and in my own time.

CHAPTER TEN

I was wearing jeans and sweatshirt and my feet were snug in trainers. I turned round: there was no sign of the little house with the stacked logs sheltering under its eaves, just a quiet woodland glade with an unwilling, watery sun struggling through.

I was glad to reach the rear wall of Tŷ Pendaran, and see the comforting sight of the house. I didn't feel like going back and talking to people, so I headed for the sea front instead. The beach was empty except for a few hardy souls wearing anoraks and cowering behind windbreaks: it was a bleak place when the sun wasn't trying very hard. Jumping from the sea wall onto the sands I walked towards the blue-green, distant coast of Rhos-on-Sea, trying to work it all out.

The disc alone didn't do it: it had to be the disc *and* the jetty stones, apparently. So how come I'd time-slipped the first time, before I had the disc? Maybe the bash on the head had done it. I'd read about stuff like that, people bashing their heads and losing their memories or discovering psychic powers and things. After all, I'd never done anything remotely like this before, and there were certainly plenty of old places around Raglan where I could have slipped if I'd been able to, the Castle for one. That was right at the end of my road, and I spent loads of time there. But I'd always stayed boringly plugged into the twentieth century, and yet now, apparently, I was able to travel backwards to – well, when?

The trouble was, I didn't have a clue where – or

rather, perhaps, when – to start looking. The book in Tŷ Pendaran library hadn't been much use at all, except for Elianor Llewelyn's brief reference to Madoc. The Madoc who'd built the town, according to Dad when I'd asked him, had been (or so he thought, anyway) some 18th century bod. And if not 18th, then 17th at the earliest. And where – or rather *whenever* – I had landed up, it was long before that. Perhaps there was some other Madoc I hadn't run to earth yet.

I remembered the book I'd got out of the library, *North Wales – People and History*. It was still sitting on the dressing table in my room, untouched. Maybe there would be a clue in that.

The house was almost empty when I got back, except for Marged in the kitchen, and a small group of writers glued to the word processors in the writing room. I slithered past the door and up the stairs to my room, picked up the book and turned to the index of people and places at the back of it. I ran my forefinger down the Ms. There seemed to be rather a lot of Madocs. I sighed, and began methodically to look up each one. I was almost at the end before I found the one I thought I wanted.

> *Madoc ap Owain Gwynedd: Subject of a legend which gained some unlikely popularity during the nineteenth century when the artist George Catlin produced a series of paintings of what he described as Welsh-speaking white Indians, thus lending some credence to the ancient tale of Madoc discovering a pre-Columbian America in 1170.*

And that was it. No further information at all. Frustrating, or what?

Could I really have travelled back to 1170? My common sense said 'get a life, Angharad'. But deep down inside, I wondered. It had all felt so real, so everyday clear, not dreamlike at all. And Madoc – whoever he was, had said that he was going to sail beyond the horizon to find new lands. Across seas where there were sea-monsters, beyond the blue water. But America? I thought of the size of the *Gwennan Gorn*. Nah. Impossible. That little shiplet would have been tossed around like a cork if it hadn't sunk in Caernarfon Bay on day one!.

But then, corks float. And besides, weren't the Vikings supposed to have made it to America? And then there was that little raft, the *Kon-Tiki* – that had made it across the Pacific, or nearly. It was something to do with the Gulf Stream Drift. And hadn't I read somewhere that two men rowed across the Atlantic once? If a raft and a rowboat could make such epic journeys, why not a sturdy little ship like the *Gwennan Gorn*? Maybe it was possible.

I shook myself. Oh, come on, Angharad. There is no way that Madoc, whoever he was, could have reached America before Columbus *and nobody have noticed?* Three hundred and thirty-two years before Columbus, and no one bothered to write it down? Unless of course he hadn't made it back, so no one knew for certain.

It was no good. I'd never know. I fingered the dragon disc. I didn't think I'd risk trying the time-slip again. It was too scary. I mean, suppose I slipped back and caught the Black Death, or leprosy, or one of the other killer bugs that were rife around then? Good grief, even tonsillitis might be fatal without antibiotics to zap it with, and let's face it, I've always been a martyr to tonsillitis. No, it was too risky. I wouldn't do it again. Suppose I got stuck there, in whenever-it-was, and couldn't get back?

And while *I* was *there*, where was the real Angharad? There had to *be* a real Angharad, because they thought I was her. They had recognised me, so I must look exactly like her. And whoever she was, and wherever she got parked while I was literally in her shoes, she had funny turns, too, so where did *she* go? I sighed. My head was aching. I snapped the book shut and went downstairs to help Marged. But I'd decided: no more time-slipping. I'd hand the disc into the museum next time I went in to Colwyn Bay, tell them where I had found it, and forget about Madoc. While I still had it, the temptation to slip would be too great.

Well, that was what I intended to do. Honest. I went into town, the disc in my purse, and went into the museum. I was heading for the curator's office, when my eye happened to fall on a glass case. Inside was a curious contraption, a wooden bowl, filled with (pretend) water – it was probably perspex – and a crude needle floating on a splinter of wood on top. Beside it was a dusty, insignificant lump of metal, a rough 'N' carved into one end of it, and beneath the whole thing was a sign which read:

A LODESTONE:
THE EARLIEST KNOWN COMPASS

But what really caught my eye was the inscription beneath that again:

Prince Madoc ap Owain Gwynedd, the 'Sailor Prince' would probably have navigated by the stars and by means of just such a crude compass as this, in his vessel Gwennan Gorn. *Madoc is believed by some historians to have discovered America in the year 1170.*

For an instant, I couldn't breathe or move: it was like a sign, and I knew I had to find out more, Black Death and rampant tonsillitis be damned. I was going back. Then, I took the disc out of my purse, slipped it onto the leather thong around my neck, and left without speaking to the curator. I was going back.

I didn't get a chance to slip away for almost a week, but in the meantime Rhidian and I dug away at the jetty wall in our spare time, uncovering it, digging deeper, finding the remains of shellfish embedded in the earth, traces of sand, broken clay pipes, bits of crockery. We didn't reach the bottom of the wall: it had to be tremendously wide and deep to withstand the force of high sea tides and the constant wash of the river, but we got down to about two feet, and carried on digging until we had revealed almost half the length of the wall buried within the garden boundaries. And all the time I was conscious of the small weight of the disc swinging free around my neck. I was careful not to touch it when my hands were in contact with the wall. I didn't want to slip unprepared.

Meanwhile, the Mantis wasn't getting any better, and the doctor insisted she stayed in bed. I took up her supper one evening and found her crying. For the first time I felt a bit sympathetic. Not a lot, but a bit. I hate to see people upset, it makes my insides go panicky. I plonked the tray down and sat on the edge of the bed, careful not to get too close in case she grabbed me and wanted to cry on my shoulder. I didn't want to get that involved. Not hugging involved.

'What's the matter, Myfanwy?' I asked, quite kindly for me.

'What do you think?' she said, unreasonably, still turned away from me.

'I don't know. That's why I asked.' I could hear an edge of exasperation creeping into my voice, and tried to stifle it. 'Why don't you tell me? I might be able to help, you never know.'

She rolled over, dabbing at her red eyes with a soggy Kleenex. I passed her the box, and she struggled into a sitting position, fished one out and blew, hard.

'I'm just so useless,' she wailed. 'Having a baby is such a simple thing to do, but I'm even making a mess of that.'

I hate self-pity. 'Don't be silly,' I said, shortly. 'You aren't making a mess of anything. You aren't well, that's all. I expect that's what's making you depressed. Cheer up, it won't be long now, will it? The baby's almost here.' (Oh, goody-goody-goody, my innermost nasty side said).

'But I look so ugly. I've never been fat before, and I sometimes feel that I'm going to be fat and awkward for ever.'

'You won't be. You're just feeling sorry for yourself. Come on, Myfanwy. Sit up and have some soup. Dad will worry if you don't eat.'

'And that's another thing. He can't concentrate on his workshops because he's worrying about me all the time, I know he is. And I can't help Laetitia with the art workshops, or Marged with the cooking, or anything. Oh, I feel so useless.'

I sighed. 'You aren't useless, Muvvie. Everyone understands, so just stop worrying, OK?' God, I hate self-pity. 'I'm here to help, so's Rhidian, and Laetitia can manage perfectly well, she just likes playing the martyr, that's all. Just try to stay calm. Getting all weepy won't help the baby, now, will it?'

Saved by the gong. Its loud clanging echoed up the stairs. 'Look, Myfanwy, I've got to go down and help with dinner now. I'll get Dad to pop up afterwards, before the talk starts in the library, OK?'

She nodded, picked up her spoon, and dunked it half-heartedly in the celery and stilton soup. It was my favourite, and I wanted to get downstairs before it all disappeared. Especially since Rhidian was rather partial to it, too. I glanced back at the doorway. She was listlessly sloshing her spoon around, not eating at all.

I caught up with Dad just as he was going in to dinner. 'Dad, Myfanwy's feeling very down again. I told her you'd pop up after dinner, before the talk begins.'

He raked his fingers through his hair. 'I just don't know what to do, Hari. Half of me wishes we'd never started this baby –' (you and me both, I thought) '– and the other half wishes she was in hospital, and the other half wants to keep her close so I can be with her.'

'That's one too many halves, Dad,' I joked.

'Oh, you know what I mean.' And he looked so worried that I relented.

'Yeah. Oh, look, Dad. I'm sure she'll be fine. And my new baby brother or sister,' I added, pinning on a false smile.

'You are looking forward to it a bit, aren't you, Hari?' he pleaded.

'Of course I am, Dad,' I lied. 'Can't wait.' Then I reached for the soup. Rhidian was tonsil deep in it already.

While we were waiting for the guest reader (some art gallery owner from London) to begin his talk, Rhidian whispered, 'I can't do any digging tomorrow. I promised your Dad I'd go with him to Colwyn Bay and take the guests on a guided tour.' He grinned, smugly. 'He's letting me drive the second bus.'

I groaned. 'Heaven help the rest of the world. Clear the roads, Rhidian's driving.'

He scowled. 'I passed my test first go, thank you very much.'

'But Rhid, you're so clumsy!'

'Look who's talking! It wasn't me who fell flat on her face and bashed her head. And ended up in hospital.'

'That was an accident. Could have happened to anyone.' I was suddenly seized with an overwhelming desire to tell Rhidian about the disc, and opened my mouth to blurt it out. Then, fortunately, the gallery chap got up and started waffling, and I didn't. I was glad, after, that I hadn't told him. I wanted to go back to the cottage in the wood again – only once more, I promised myself, just one last time – before I handed over the disc to the museum. If everyone was heading for Colwyn Bay tomorrow, maybe I'd have my chance then.

Before my next trip back in time, though, I decided to make some preparations. Although my watch had disappeared as soon as I had stepped on the wall, and my modern jeans and sweater had mysteriously been

103

exchanged for a scratchy green dress, I wondered if there was anything I could take back with me which might help, just in case of problems. Obviously, anything modern would disappear, but it was possible that if I took a modern version of something that had already been invented, perhaps it would be exchanged for the twelfth century equivalent.

For instance, I hadn't been left starkers when I crossed, had I? No, my clothes had gone, but I'd been given others in exchange (thank goodness). So what would happen if I took, say, a knife with me next time? Something to protect myself with. I mean, way back then, there were wolves and wild boars, if I remembered my history correctly. Briefly I wondered how much good a little knife would be against a big, hairy, muscular wild boar with dripping fangs and gory tusks – and then pushed it firmly out of my mind. I decided to stay well away from large pigs with Attitude and stray wolves. But I thought I might try the experiment anyway, if only in the interests of science.

Dad wanted me to go with him to Colwyn Bay, but I pleaded tiredness. 'Anyway, Dad,' I added, my fingers firmly crossed behind my back to cancel out the lie, 'someone ought to stay around here because of Myfanwy. We can't all go, and Marged is going into town to see her mother this afternoon, isn't she?'

Dad nodded. 'Yes, I'd forgotten. It would be better if you could stay behind. She's asleep now, but maybe you could play Scrabble with her when she wakes up? She loves Scrabble. It might take her out of herself a bit.'

Yech! I'd rather scrub the Channel Tunnel with a toothbrush, I thought, Scrabble being my least but one

104

favourite board game ever. Least of all was a tie between Monopoly and a terrible, juvenile game called "Sorry!" which had once caused me to hurl the game-board across the living room, but that's another story. I smiled instead, and nodded. 'You go, Dad. Don't worry, I'll keep an eye on her.'

I almost did. I crept upstairs and poked my nose round the door before I left the house. She was huddled in a large round ball, curled round the lump that was the baby, fast asleep and snoring. Good. I crept back downstairs and into the kitchen, opening drawers, looking for a suitable knife. I discarded the foot-long cooking knives and settled for a sturdy, six-inch blade that Marged used to peel vegetables. I started to tuck it into my jeans belt, but then stopped. It might drop out as soon as I time-slipped. There was a hole in the wooden handle at the top, so I found some string and threaded it through, and then tied the whole lot round my waist, under my jeans. I could feel it prickling my skin. I then imagined tripping while wearing it, shuddered at the thought, and slid the knife round to the back where it dug into my bottom.

That taken care of, I headed for the garden gate and the river path into the trees.

CHAPTER ELEVEN

Slipping unseen out of the gates of Tŷ Pendaran, I was ever so slightly nervous, but mostly I was excited. I had to slow down – I was breaking into a run, eager to get away from the house before anyone spotted me, and I was afraid I would fall flat on my face and break my leg. I might die of starvation, lost in the wood, before I ever had a chance to time-slip again.

When I reached the place where the cottage would be (or had been?) I clutched the dragon disc and stepped onto the wall. The strange, white-out sensation hit me, and when I dizzily opened my eyes again, I was standing right beside the cottage. Pendaran, hoe in hand, stood a few feet away, gazing at me, a concerned expression on his wrinkled face. He reached out a hand to steady me, as if I was about to fall over.

'These wretched spells are coming more often, Angharad.' He led me inside, his arm round my shoulders, hooking a bench towards him with his foot. I sat down.

'The last few haven't lasted so long – only moments – but this one was a deep one,' he said, his voice troubled.

'Deep?' I looked at him blankly.

'You have been standing still, not seeing, not hearing, for several minutes, as if you had been turned to stone. Do you feel ill?'

I shook my head. 'Nah. It's OK.'

His bushy white brows slid together. 'Oh Cei? Who is Cei?'

I mentally kicked myself. I was going to have to watch my language, weed out twentieth century slang! Trouble was, the way I talk is the way I talk, right?

'I mean I'm fine. I'm all right. I don't feel ill. Just a bit shaky, that's all.' I smiled reassuringly.

He was still watching me closely. 'Angharad, when you have these turns, where do you go?'

'Go?' Inside, I panicked. 'I –'

'Are you conscious? Do you see and hear?'

I thought, quickly. As close to the truth as I could get it would be a good idea. 'It's really strange. There's a sort of light, and a rushing sensation, like standing in a high wind. There's a sort of white noi—.' I stopped myself. White noise wasn't a twelfth-century concept at all! 'A sort of hissing sound,' I amended. 'I can't hear much at all.' If the other Angharad was travelling forward while I was travelling back, she'd be able to see into the future. Goodness knows what she thought of the twentieth century. If, of course, she got that far. Maybe she got stuck in the near future, instead of the distant. Maybe she was in some sort of limbo. Well, I couldn't worry about that now. It would have been useful if the other Angharad could have left crib notes around somewhere – assuming she could read and write, which she most likely couldn't.

Pendaran sighed. 'You are so like your mother. She suffered these spells until she died. She, also, knew strange things.'

Died? A goose walked on my grave in hob-nailed boots. I took myself in hand. Don't be daft, Angharad. Your Mum's alive and well and back-packing round India, and your Dad's not Pendaran, either. You've only borrowed this world for a bit.

Pendaran went on, 'It's a pity you didn't foresee the trouble with Madoc. A timely vision might have saved me from a most unpleasant night in Owain Gwynedd's dungeon.'

'Trouble?' I asked, tentatively.

'Don't tell me you've forgotten!' Pendaran stared at me.

I put my hand to my brow in best stage heroine style. 'My mind is blurred,' I said, vaguely. 'When I have my turns I forget things.' Then I remembered that Madoc had talked Pendaran into smuggling him inside Owain Gwynedd's castle to say goodbye to his mother. 'Oh, yes. Remind me, please – did Madoc see his mother?'

Pendaran threw up his hands, exasperated. 'Oh, by all the great geomancers,' he groaned, 'what a mistake that was! I should never have let him talk me into it.'

'It was bad?' I asked, uncertainly. 'How?'

Pendaran sighed. 'I managed to get him inside the castle, and then I entertained Owain while Madoc went in search of Brenda. Well into the banquet, we were, me singing old Owain's praises like a lark, and then on to the love-songs, my voice sounding better than it has for months, the court attentive, the ladies dabbing tears and sniffling. And then a servant slithered up to Owain and whispered in his ear. Leapt from his seat like a scalded cat, he did, and shot out of the great hall as if the devil was after him.' Pendaran put his head in his hands and waggled it, mournfully.

'Owain caught Brenda in Madoc's arms, and Madoc had to fight his way out, past his father and past Owain's steward. Not to mention the castle guard.'

'Why?' If Brenda was Madoc's mother, and Owain his father, what was the problem?

Pendaran lowered his hands and peered at me. 'Why? My child, when Owain last saw Madoc he was a newborn, knot-footed, crippled baby, which he ordered to be slaughtered. You know the law: a physically flawed man may not inherit. Owain took it a step further. A crippled child born to his wife? An insult. Dispose of the brat immediately.'

I couldn't believe my ears. '*His own father?*' I gasped. 'You mean his own father tried to have him killed? Madoc?'

Pendaran nodded. 'Brenda lied; told him the child was dead, and had him smuggled secretly to me to foster. Oh, come, now, Angharad,' he said, testily, 'you've known this tale since birth. Your foster-brother has told you, I have told you.'

I shrugged. 'Yes, but –' I thought fast on my feet, 'but these strange turns I have seem to affect my memory.' Pendaran looked doubtful. 'It comes back after a while, no problem,' I reassured him.

Pendaran's face cleared. 'Ah.'

'So what happened?'

'Owain, summoned by that weasel of a servant, found Brenda in another man's arms, and assumed that Madoc was her lover. Even though Brenda is old, and grey, and –'

'– and will not live past this next sunrise,' I said, absently. Then stopped, as if I'd stubbed my toe. Why had I said that? And yet I knew it was true.

Pendaran, too, was taken aback. 'How do you know this?' he whispered. 'Has Owain harmed her?'

Scared, I shook my head. 'No. I just know that she is going to die soon. Don't ask me how I know, but I do.'

'And then? What will Owain do?'

I shook my head. 'Don't know.'

Pendaran shook his head. 'Poor Brenda. Worn out by child-bearing, replaced by his women – poor lady.'

'But what about Madoc?'

'Madoc has taken the *Gwennan Gorn,* and set sail for Ireland to his brother Rhirid who gave him sanctuary once before. He will remain there until these ill winds blow over.'

'So he hasn't headed for Amer— um, for his new world, then, just yet?'

Pendaran lifted a small cauldron of water onto the hooked iron firedog, spilled droplets hissing and steaming on the ashy logs. The room smelled of burning brambles.

'Let me brew you a nourishing drink, Angharad,' he muttered, bending over the crudely-made wooden cupboard on the far side of the cottage. 'Perhaps something to clear your mind. Maybe then you will remember what will befall poor Brenda.' Then he suddenly straightened, listening. 'There's someone coming.'

I listened, but at first I couldn't hear anything. Then I could. Hoofbeats – many hoofbeats – thudded on firm earth, and the slap of leather on leather echoed round the cottage. My throat tightened: I was suddenly very, very scared. My head thumped, hard.

Seconds later, the cottage door was hurled open with a mighty crash of wood against stone, and the small room rapidly filled with large men in leather helmets and body armour, holding swords menacingly in gauntletted hands, their eyes bleak and cruel, emphasised by the vertical leather strips of their helmet nose-guards.

'Edwall.' Pendaran drew himself up to his full height and met the leader eye to eye. 'Why do you violate my home with drawn swords? Remember, my boy, that I am a Druid and your father's Chief Bard. My home is protected. I must be respected. You may not enter in this way.'

Edwall, prowling round the cottage, whirled suddenly on the balls of his feet, wordlessly thrusting his sword upward between the boards of the sleeping platform. I gulped. This was getting altogether too medieval for my liking. Someone could get hurt. Me, for instance.

'Where have you hidden him, Pendaran?' he snarled, his blade now at the old man's throat.

'Him?'

'Him. He that Owain Gwynedd discovered making free with his wife.'

'Owain Gwynedd has no quarrel with him.'

'He saw him with his own eyes, Bard! It is treason, to toy with your Lord's wife!'

'Edwall, Edwall,' Pendaran began, mildly. 'The boy is Owain's son. Brenda is his mother. He is your own younger brother.'

Edwall shook his head, pityingly. 'So Brenda would have us believe,' he jeered. 'Owain's sons, my brothers, are all accounted for. Some dead, some exiled, some behind bars, but all, all are accounted for.'

'Remember, Edwall, the crippled child? The one Brenda bore Owain eighteen years ago? The baby boy with the foot turned and twisted, knotted like old tree-roots?'

Edwall stared. 'That child died. He was marked, blemished. Owain does not suffer imperfections.'

I spoke, suddenly, not knowing where the words were coming from. 'The Druid Pendaran took the boy at

Brenda's request. He healed him with ointments and bandages, and long and painful hours of massage. Madoc is perfect, a son for any man to have pride in. But Brenda's end is near, and it was right that Madoc should see her for the last time in this life. Owain Gwynedd will have Crisiant, now.'

All eyes turned to me. My head thudded sickly, my stomach lurched, and I felt redness rising in a great wave up my neck to flood my hot face.

'This is the Wyrd-Girl? She who knows the unknowable?'

Pendaran spat, accurately, into the fire. 'It is. When she speaks, Edwall, wise men listen. In England, they would call her a witch.'

'In England, Pendaran, the Sais would burn her.'

Pardon me? I didn't like the way this conversation was heading.

'In Wales, Edwall, we are more civilised. We listen to our wise ones. We do not destroy them.'

Edwall slashed upwards at a cross-beam, leaving a notch in the wood. He was like a violent caged animal in that small house. He strode across the room to stand directly in front of me, staring into my eyes. I wanted to look away, but knew, somehow, that it would be dangerous to do so. His dark eyes glittered each side of the leather nose-guard, and this close to him I could smell his sour, rank sweat. I held my breath for more than one reason!

Suddenly, his eyes narrowed, his hand shot out, grasping the dragon disc hanging in the hollow of my throat, ripping it from my neck.

'This is the boy's token. He bears a dragon figurehead on his ship. I shall have this.'

'That isn't Madoc's!' I yelled, reaching for it, 'That's mine! Give it back!'

He held it above his head, out of reach. Pendaran grabbed my wrist. 'Let him have it, Angharad. Madoc will give you another.'

Edwall swung round. 'You expect him back, then?'

Pendaran shrugged. 'Who knows? Perhaps tonight. Perhaps next month. Perhaps next year. Perhaps never. But for now, Edwall, he is long gone. To Rhirid, his brother, exiled in Ireland with Brenda's kin.'

Edwall tossed the pendant in his gauntleted fist. 'Until he returns, then, I shall keep this.' He grinned, exposing disastrous teeth. 'It shall lie with him in his traitor's grave. Unless we throw his body to the dogs.'

'No!' I yelled, knowing I couldn't get back to my own time without it. 'No, please, Edwall, it is mine. I must have it back.'

Edwall turned at the door and grinned. 'Must? Strange words, Wyrd Girl, to your better. Perhaps in time. Perhaps not. Mine is the power here. Perhaps you can witch it back. You could try. See if your power is equal to mine.' He flexed his muscles. 'My power is in my sword. This power I believe in. And my sword can slit your throat like butter, for all your far-seeing.'

He strode out of the hut, bending his head to pass beneath the doorpost. Pity. I'd have liked to see it knocked from his shoulders.

Desperately, I rushed to the door behind the departing men and watched them mount their horses and ride away

113

through the trees. My dragon disc, my only means of escape, going with them in Edwall's leather belt-pouch.

Now I was in trouble. I burst into tears. 'I must have it back, Pendaran. I need it.'

'Oh, come, Angharad!' Pendaran patted my shoulder. 'It was only a trinket. In Edwall's present mood, we were lucky to escape with our necks intact and you worry about a necklace! Madoc will fetch you another. I will send word to him in Ireland. Don't let it distress you so much.'

'You don't understand!' I wailed. 'Without it, I'm stuck. I can't do anything.'

'What do you mean?'

'I can't go back to my own time, I—'

I realised that Pendaran was staring at me.

'What do you mean, your own time? This is your time. What other time do we have but that which the Great Power allows us on this earth?'

'I mean,' I stammered, thinking fast, 'I mean without Madoc's dragon pendant my powers will fade. I won't have any turns. I can't see the future.'

Pendaran wiped tears from my face with a grimy thumb. 'Oh, don't upset yourself, Angharad! This is nonsense! You've had your powers from the day you were born. Madoc's gift to you is but a year old. He gave it to you last Mayday on your fourteenth birthday.'

'I'm *seventeen!*' I wailed, 'and I want to go home!' The headache was almost unbearable.

That was when, as well as the pain in my head, I felt the tugging. The pushing. *She* wanted to go home, too. The other Angharad was making her presence felt.

114

CHAPTER TWELVE

It was a weird sensation: a dizzy, tugging, strangeness. The closest thing to it I'd ever experienced was standing up too quickly after lying on the floor reading a newspaper: almost a blackout, the world turning dark and a whirling inside my head. I cried out, clutching Pendaran for support. I felt as if I were being roughly pushed out of my own mind.

'What is it?' he asked, alarmed.

'I don't know. A strange feeling: sort of dizzy.'

'One of your turns?'

'Yes. No.' I saw a way out. 'Yes, I think so.'

'What did you see, this time?'

'Nothing. At least, nothing I can put into words.'

But I had *felt* something. I'd felt the presence of a stranger inside my head. She was afraid, pushing hard against my mind, trying to get back into her own body. The other Angharad. And without the dragon disc, I was stuck in her time, while she was stuck – where? Inside me? I shuddered. It was like having an alien on board, inside my brain, and I didn't like it.

'Pendaran,' I grasped the old man's sleeve. 'Pendaran, you must help me get the dragon disc back. It is very important and precious to me. Without it, my powers are not as strong. I can feel, but I don't know what the – the – the spirits are trying to tell me. Somehow you must make Edwall give it back to me.'

Pendaran stroked his chin, his rough hands rasping on white stubble, and his green eyes stared thoughtfully into mine. 'You have never mentioned spirits before, Angharad. Is the dragon trinket so vital?' he asked.

'Yes,' I said, clasping my hands beseechingly, feeling a bit like Myfanwy. If it worked, so what?

Pendaran considered, then came to a decision. 'Then tomorrow I will go to Edwall, try to persuade him.'

'Tomorrow!' I yelped, 'but that means I have to spend the night here!'

Pendaran looked at me strangely. 'And why not? You've slept here every night since you were born!'

'But –' I stopped. How could I begin to explain? I was going to have to resign myself to staying in the Middle Ages overnight. After all, what else could I do? Only Dad was going to go ballistic when I got back. If I got back. If Edwall didn't kill me first.

Supper was cold meat and a sour, beer-like drink, and bed came as soon as the sun went down. Pendaran soon slept, snoring on the far side of the up-the-ladder bit, but I lay awake on the other Angharad's scratchy straw mattress and worried about getting the disc back, returning to my own time, explaining to my father exactly where I'd been overnight – and that was going to take some doing – and wishing I'd thought to bring my toothbrush with me. Not that I could have: the knife I'd borrowed from Marged's kitchen hadn't travelled through. They probably hadn't invented Sheffield steel yet, I supposed. It was the only weapon I'd had. Now I had nothing, not the knife, not the disc, and my teeth felt coated and horrible. I *always* brush my teeth before bed. Miserably, I scratched a lump on my thigh, then another that had appeared on my arm. Oh, God, not fleas, too? That started me off thinking: flea-bites = plague rats = Black Death for sure. I spent most of the night waiting for buboes to pop up in my armpits, but somewhere along the line between bubo and plague pit I

116

must have dropped off, because the sun slanting in through gaps in the thatch woke me.

I lay for a second or two with my eyes shut, trying to work out why my bed was so hard, and why I could smell woodsmoke instead of bacon. Then I remembered, and opened my eyes. A spider, a large one, lurked about an inch away from the end of my nose. I shot vertically off the mattress, shrieking blue murder.

'Aaaagh! A spider! It's a spider, kill it someone, quick!'

Pendaran, below, laughed. 'One day, Angharad, you'll get over your fear of small creatures. They are more afraid of you than you are of them.'

'Wanna bet?' I muttered. I climbed down the ladder, feeling sticky, my mouth feeling like the bottom of a budgie's bedroom. I yawned, and the other Angharad pushed again. I fought her back down. I opened my mouth, intending to ask if I could have a wash, but what came out wasn't what I intended.

'Owain's wife, Brenda,' I said absently. 'She died last night.'

Pendaran turned, slowly, his face pale. 'What did you say?'

I stared back at him, just as bemused. 'I said –'

'I heard. This could mean trouble.'

'Why?'

'Because yesterday Edwall heard you foretell this death.'

'But –' I began, but Pendaran interrupted me.

'Quickly, get washed.' He shoved me towards the cottage door, and I saw that there was a wooden bucket of water and an old piece of sacking outside, waiting.

'Get dressed. Put on your good dress. We must get to the castle quickly, pay our respects.' He stopped, and took my face in his hands. 'Are you certain, Angharad?'

Strangely, I was. The other Angharad, whoever, and wherever she was, was in no doubt, and she let me know it.

Within the hour we were on the road, my face washed and my teeth rubbed with a piece of dry sacking. No wonder people ponged. We reached the square, no-nonsense stone keep surrounded by a big wooden stockade before the sun was high overhead. We approached the sentry at the gate, and Pendaran demanded admittance.

'What business do you have with Owain Gwynedd?' The sentry standing just inside the little door in the stockade was scruffy, bearded, his leather jerkin rubbed shiny where his sword rested, and grease-spots down his front testifying to his lack of table manners. He didn't smell too good, either, so I tried to block out most of it with a hand across my nose.

Pendaran stood up straight, and managed to look considerably taller than he actually was. 'That is not your affair, Dafydd ap Gwyn,' he said sternly. 'I am Druid and Bard to Owain Gwynedd, and not answerable to the likes of you, my boy. As you know well, and will know to your cost if I am kept waiting an instant longer. Admit me at once.'

That seemed to do the trick.

The sentry looked vaguely embarrassed. 'Sorry, my Lord Druid. Wasn't thinkin' straight for a minute, there.' He yawned, stepping back to allow us through the wicket gate. 'Up most of the night, what with all the comin' and goin' about the Lady Brenda.' He widened his eyes conspiratorially. 'You'll not 'ave 'eard that the Lady died, all of a sudden in the night, Lord Druid?'

Pendaran humphed. 'Heard? Dafydd ap Gwyn, my daughter *foretold* the Lady Brenda's death. *Yesterday.*'

The sentry's jaw dropped, and we were through the little door like rats up a drainpipe. His eyes widened when he saw me lurking behind Pendaran, and he hurriedly found something very interesting stuck to his bootsole when I stared him down. I tried very hard to look like a convincing seeress, and it seemed to work.

It was much larger inside the keep than it looked from outside: thick stone soared upwards, and flights of stairs disappeared into arched doorways. A huge, if rather grubby, tapestry decorated one wall behind a raised wooden platform furnished with a long table, benches, and two high backed chairs. I recognised Edwall sitting on the edge of the platform, and nudged Pendaran.

'There he is,' I hissed. 'Go on, Pendaran. Get my dragon pendant back, please.'

'Be quiet, Angharad. I must be careful how I go about this.' Pendaran squared his shoulders and, me scuttling behind him, strode to where Edwall sat. He didn't look up, being moodily engaged in a curious game which involved chucking a knife into the earthen floor between his booted feet. It looked like the sort of game that led to Casualty, stitches and anti-tetanus injections to me.

'Edwall,' Pendaran began, and the man glanced up, suddenly aware of us. To my amazement, he scrambled to his feet and shot backwards, stumbling over the edge of the platform, until he had put the wooden table safely between us and him.

'What do you want, Pendaran?' he stammered, but his eyes were on me. I suddenly realised that he was afraid, but couldn't work out what of. Surely not me?

'I want you to return the trinket you stole,' Pendaran said, sternly. 'It belongs to Angharad, my daughter. You must give it back to her immediately.'

Edwall fumbled in the pouch dangling from his belt. 'Here, take it,' he muttered. 'I didn't believe the girl had such powers, but now –'

I cottoned on, suddenly. 'But now that Brenda is dead,' I said, sternly, 'you believe me.' And then, suddenly, the other Angharad was speaking, in my voice. *Now that Brenda has confessed on her deathbed that she disobeyed Owain Gwynedd; that she sent Madoc to Pendaran for his protection and uprearing, now you believe. Believe this, too, Edwall. Owain Gwynedd will take Crisiant to wife, and all Christendom will roar with outrage.*

Couldn't believe I'd said it, whatever it was supposed to mean. Edwall held out the dragon disc, still dangling from its chain, in a trembling hand, and I took it, clasping it round my neck, feeling an uprush of joy as the cool metal slithered into the hollow of my throat. And as it touched my skin, I felt the other Angharad recede, pushed back by the presence of the pendant.

'Quick,' I muttered out of the side of my mouth, 'let's get out of here, Pendaran. Before Edwall decides to change his mind.' That comment about barbecuing witches was still lurking around in the back of my brain. I didn't want to put the (I felt, anyway) very reasonable Welsh reluctance to burn witches to the test!

Pendaran looked shocked. 'I must sing Brenda to her

tomb. Praise her goodness, her virtue, her beauty, her, her . . . That is my solemn duty as Bard to Owain Gwynedd. You know that, Angharad! We cannot leave yet. What are you thinking of?'

Thinking of? Getting back to the twentieth century, quick, is what I was thinking of, that's what! But I couldn't. I had to stay for interminably long and extremely scary hours and hours, seated on a hard wooden stool, while Pendaran sang doleful songs to a long, person-shaped bundle wrapped in white cloth. I could have made believe that it wasn't a dead person inside, except that the late Brenda's fat, grubby feet, yellowish and peppered with corns, were sticking out the end, which was nerve-wracking and a bit sick-making, both.

After the first few dirges, I tuned out, and listened to the gossip of the court ladies clustered around me. Around me, but none too close: I guessed my reputation had preceded me. My ears pricked up when they caught a familiar name.

'He will take Crisiant, next, according to the Wyrd-Girl,' a fat, fair-haired woman whispered behind her hand, 'and Holy Sainted Brenda not cold or even in her tomb yet, poor thing.'

'He will feel it is his right,' replied her companion. 'Brenda disobeyed him. She gave the Druid the crippled child she gave birth to.' They tutted, and shook their heads.

'But Crisiant . . .' her hook-nosed companion whispered, 'surely Crisiant . . .'

'. . . is his cousin. And when Canterbury hears of the marriage –' The fat one rolled her eyes, meaningfully – 'well!'

Canterbury? What on earth were they talking about?

'Becket, for all his carousing with the King in his young days, is an Archbishop to be reckoned with these days, they say.'

I tuned out, trying to work out when – and who. Becket? As in Thomas à, and *Murder in the Cathedral*, that Becket? I fumbled around in my memory for Kings-and-Queens. Drat modular history courses! If it wasn't for Theatre Arts I'd probably never have even heard of Becket. I tried to remember the play. Yes – when Becket was around, Henry II was on the throne of England. Good grief! I tuned back in again.

'– and Crisiant is Owain's cousin. His first cousin. He may not marry her. The Church will not allow it. The Archbishop –'

My eavesdropping was interrupted by the door of the chamber crashing open. A great shambling, untidy bear of a man, more like a Viking than anything else, swayed unsteadily in the doorway. The assembled ladies and courtiers leapt to their feet, bowing and curtseying, up and down like yo-yos. The man in the doorway took no notice, but strode across to the bed, hurling himself to his knees, weeping noisily (and rather theatrically, I thought). The unmistakable smell of second-hand wine fumes rose from him, and his clothes looked as if, somewhere along the line, he had been rather sick.

'Brenda, Brenda,' he howled, clutching the bare, yellow feet at the bottom of the bundle. 'I forgive you, Brenda. You spoke truly, my beloved wife. The boy is whole and perfect. It would have been a mortal sin to kill him. The Lord guided your heart. He will be my son, in your good memory. When he comes back –' He blew his nose and belched. 'If he comes back, he shall be made welcome for your dear sake. Oh, Brenda, Brenda, Brenda, Brenda.' He threw his head back and howled, mournfully.

Crumbs, don't overdo it, chum! I thought. *A little dignified grief, yes, but this doesn't quite ring true.* I was right. I saw a small, piggy eye slide sideways until it reached the face of a young woman sitting at the head of the bier, and remain fixed on her, while Owain Gwynedd wept noisily, if not particularly wetly. I remembered one of my favourite Groovy Bill quotations, '– full of sound and fury, signifying nothing'. That just about said it all.

'Brenda,' he wailed, 'I shall keep my oath to you.'

Oath?

'Oath, my Lord?' Pendaran was helping the big man to his feet, sympathetically offering him a white cloth to wipe his apparently perfectly dry eyes.

Owain Gwynedd hiccupped. 'I promised Brenda – on her deathbed, no less –' he added earnestly, blinking blearily at the Bard, 'that I'd take poor Crisiant as my wife, Pendaran!' He straightened up, glaring round the room, as if daring anyone to disagree.

Crisiant didn't look up, but from her expression I got the distinct impression that if Owain Gwynedd vanished from the face of the earth, Crisiant wouldn't be too upset.

There was a hiss of 'I told you so's' from the assembled ladies, and several self-satisfied nods.

'Shall I sing some more, my Lord?' Pendaran asked with a sympathy I didn't really think he meant.

'No more dirges,' Owain muttered, flapping his hands irritably. 'Lay my late Lady to rest. She would not have me mourn over-long.'

123

Overlong? She hadn't popped her clogs more than a couple of hours ago! The court of Owain Gwynedd drifted away, and a priest and a pair of monks came in. Pendaran and I took the opportunity to make ourselves scarce, lagging politely behind the court ladies, until freedom beckoned in the shape of the open door.

'Quick!' I hissed, hurtling out into the sunshine, and heading for the wicket gate, Pendaran hard on my heels. I clutched the dragon disc as I ran: I wanted to make sure it was safe.

CHAPTER THIRTEEN

While I ran, I debated whether to keep going until I got to the jetty wall and then hurl myself through into my time. That seemed like a really good idea, but just as I reached Pendaran's hut, he caught my trailing dress and jerked me to a standstill. He was dead fast on his feet, for a wrinkly!

His face was very red, and he wheezed like an ancient carthorse. 'Wait, Angharad!' he puffed, clutching his chest, 'no one is chasing us. You ran as if seven devils from hell were after you.'

Not quite, old buddy, I thought. *But nearly!* Unwillingly, I turned round. He let go my dress.

'What will happen next, Angharad?' he asked, looking at me curiously. 'Did you see more? You knew that Brenda would die, and that Owain would have Crisiant. Is there more?'

I shook my head. 'No, Pendaran. Nothing comes to mind, yet.' I still hadn't shaken off the barbecued witches idea. Maybe it would be wise to hold off with the predictions for a while.

He sighed, his colour returning slowly to normal. 'I must get word to Madoc that his mother is dead. His meeting with her was nigh-on disastrous, but that is in the past. Praise the Power that he saw her one last time.' His eyes became more brilliant suddenly, filled with glistening tears. 'She was a good woman, Brenda. She left Erin barely out of childhood, a thin, quiet scrap of a girl, to be Owain's bride, and none ever heard her complain or say a word against him. He is a hard man,

125

Owain Gwynedd, to have to live with, and although she came to him without the gift of love, she bore his rough ways without a word against him.'

'Pity,' I said. I hadn't exactly taken to Owain. 'If she'd given him an earful occasionally, maybe he would have been a better husband.'

Pendaran looked puzzled. 'He was as good a husband to her as most Lords are to their wives. He beat her but rarely, and his mistresses, though many, were always ladies of the highest rank.'

I shook my head, disbelievingly, opened my mouth to argue, and then changed my mind. It was going to be a while yet before any sort of women's lib came along. 'Pendaran, you go home. I need to be by myself for a bit. I'll be back later, OK?'

'Oh, Cei,' Pendaran repeated. 'I do not know this "Cei". And why do you constantly call his name? Are you – erm – fond of him?' His bushy white eyebrows slanted together in a frown.

I hid a grin. I really must take more care how I spoke. 'It's just a way of saying "all right", Pendaran. All is well. I'll be back.'

Before he could reply, I turned away, and walked swiftly into the wood towards the end of the jetty. I wouldn't be back. This time, I'd learned my lesson. The other Angharad could have her body to herself, and as far as I was concerned, she could keep it. I had no intention of coming back. Not ever. Having almost got stuck permanently in the 12th century, I wasn't going to risk that again.

Holding the disc cupped in my hand, I stepped onto the wall, staggered as the light and white noise hit me,

126

and found myself back in my own time, wearing jeans and sweater, the knife still digging uncomfortably into my backside. Fat lot of good that idea had been! I debated dropping the disc into the trench and covering it, but I would still know it was there, and Rhidian might even uncover it. No, the only way to make sure I wasn't tempted to go back again was, this time, to turn it over to the Museum to put in a glass case. I couldn't get it back, then, even if I wanted it. Which I didn't.

I looked at my watch. It said five to five, and from the height of the sun, that was about right. I'd been away overnight, and I racked my brains for something to tell Dad, who was going to be, probably in equal proportions, frantic and furious. I knew from experience, however, that once he knew I was safe, furious would take over entirely. I debated telling him the truth, and then decided against it. Then I toyed with the idea of saying I'd been abducted by aliens. Then, I decided on a simple lie. He'd believe that. I'd say I'd had a funny turn in the woods, and passed out. It would probably mean more time in hospital, having a lot of useless tests and wasting NHS money, but he certainly wasn't likely to believe the truth, was he? And it was, sort of, a funny turn. They don't come much funnier, that's for certain.

I toed off my shoes, without untying the laces, outside the back door and padded into the kitchen. Marged was there, with two of the guests, preparing the meal. She glanced up, and I waited for the shrieks of relief – or possibly fury.

'Hello, Angharad, love,' she said, 'had a nice afternoon?'

127

I stared at her. Was that any way to greet someone who'd been away overnight, missing, perhaps mugged and left for dead somewhere, her lifeblood draining into the leaf-mould? 'Um, yes, thanks,' I said, feeling fairly bemused. 'Where's Dad?'

'Oh, your Dad is still out with his bus party.' She glanced at the kitchen clock. 'He should be back any minute, I expect. And that Rhidian will be starving, as usual. Hollow legs, that boy.'

I couldn't understand it. I'd been missing for at least twenty-four hours, and she hadn't even noticed.

I went into my room and shut the door. I decided to play it by ear rather than ask anyone what day it was. But if I hadn't been away overnight, no one would know I'd been missing, would they? Maybe my time-travelling was in a different time-span to the everyday one. I went back downstairs and picked up a newspaper from the hall table: according to the date, it was still yesterday. Or today. Unless that was yesterday's paper. Oh, rats.

Dad and Rhidian arrived home in convoy from Colwyn Bay in the mini-buses, and neither of them said anything like 'Where the hell have you been?' or 'My darling daughter, I've been so worried!'. So I guessed, then, that it was today's paper, and somehow time was different between then and now. It was something to think about. If I could pop back and forward without anyone noticing I'd been away, then, maybe I could . . .

I pinched myself, and went to set the table for dinner. I *wasn't going back*, and that was the end of it. The disc was going to the Museum, and I was staying firmly put in the twentieth century. Much safer. When the table was ready, I nipped up to see Myfanwy, feeling guilty that

I'd abandoned her all afternoon when I'd promised Dad I'd be with her. She was lying on her back, still snoring, so I sneaked away again. With any luck, she'd been asleep all afternoon and hadn't noticed I'd not been in to play Scrabble with her.

Next day, though, I went with Rhidian to the library, and couldn't resist doing some research. Knowing about Owain Gwynedd gave me so much more to work on, and meeting him had tickled my curiosity. I discovered that old Owain popped up all over the place, in all sorts of history books, usually disagreeing violently with other people, either his neighbouring Welsh Lords, or the English king. Most of the books, however, ignored Madoc completely. One of them said that Owain might have had as many as twenty-seven children by various wives and girlfriends! I shuddered. Horrible old beast. I wondered how many more of them he'd had slaughtered because they'd had something wrong with them, like a squint, or a birthmark, or a club foot, like Madoc had had.

And then I hit, as they say in American movies, pay-dirt. I found a whole book all about Madoc. Even though it had a sort of disclaimer in the front, saying that Madoc 'may not have existed', it also said that there was strong evidence that he had. After Owain Gwynedd's death (and yes, Archbishop Thomas à Becket had excommunicated him for marrying Crisiant), the land of Gwynedd was sort of up for grabs, and all of the males in the pack of twenty-seven children started right in fighting over the spoils. They slit each others throats, put out each others' eyes, locked each other in dungeons, chopped off various bits (imperfect or disfigured may not inherit, remember?) and generally made everybody's lives miserable, hoping to reduce the competition a bit, I suppose. Nowadays they'd have been labelled a 'dysfunctional family', and the social workers would have had a field day. To put it mildly, the sons of Owain Gwynedd didn't get on at all well, and they'd obviously never heard of family solidarity.

Madoc, being one of the youngest, would have been way down the list for inherited goodies anyway, and he (and this book said, his brother Rhirid, from Ireland) sailed away in their boat and discovered America.

'*A plaque,*' it said, '*has been raised to commemorate Madoc's discovery of America, sponsored by the Daughters of the American Revolution, on the shores of Mobile Bay, Alabama, where Madoc is believed to have landed and begun his journey up the banks of the Alabama River.*'

They even knew where he'd landed, in the Bay of Mexico. Short hairs rose and prickled at the nape of my neck, and goose-bumps appeared on my arms.

He'd made it! No matter what the historians said, I now knew he'd existed and also that he'd made it to America. I was still grinning like an idiot when I tried to check the book out of the library to take home with me. Unfortunately, it was in the reference section, and the librarian wouldn't let me. Never mind, I'd be back, just as soon as I could find time, read to the end and find out what happened to him.

The inane grin lasted all evening, right through the reading-of-the-writers' work and the showing-of-the-painters'-paintings, because it was the guests' (including Mrs Marchpoint's, hooray, hooray!) last night.

Afterwards, Rhidian followed me into the kitchen where I was stacking coffee cups and wine glasses in the dishwasher and zapping milk in the microwave ready for bedtime cocoa.

He sat at the kitchen table, studying me. Then at last, he said, 'If you don't tell me what you are looking so smug about, I'm going to get really ratty. I may shove you in the dish-washer and turn it on.'

I stared at him. 'Smug? Me? I don't know what you're on about.'

'You've been grinning like a Cheshire cat all evening. What's going on, Angharad?'

I shrugged. 'Nothing, really. I just went to the library today, and found out a bit about Madoc – you know, the one who's supposed to have sailed from our jetty.'

'And?'

'And it looks as if he made it all the way to America!'

Rhidian stared at me. 'So?'

'So, it's really amazing that he managed it. Nearly four hundred years before Columbus a Welshman makes it to America.' I was so pleased with what I'd found out that I didn't realise I was babbling as I stirred chocolate powder into hot milk. 'I'm just so pleased for him, that's all.'

Rhidian picked up a mug and sipped, staring at me thoughtfully over the steaming rim. 'Angharad, do you know you're talking as if you actually know him?'

'Well, I –' I stopped myself, just in time. I'd been about to say 'I do'.

Rhidian raised an eyebrow, quizzically, which had the effect of making his glasses slide down his nose. 'Why do I keep getting the feeling that there's something I don't know? Something's going on, isn't it? Something to do with that jetty wall?'

I looked at him, about to lie, to say no, there was nothing, he was imagining it all. But a little devil prodded me, honest. I slid into the seat opposite him, and looked him straight in the eye. 'If I tell you, you won't believe me.'

'Try me.'

'OK. But don't forget, I warned you.' I grinned at him. 'You'll think I'm daft, or winding you up.'

He scowled. 'Get on with it, woman.'

'OK, you asked for it. The other day, I found a round sort of medallion thingy, where we were digging. And if I stand on the jetty holding it, I sort of trip out of now and into then.'

Rhidian gazed at me disbelievingly for a bit, and then began humming the X-Files theme. 'Pull the other one, Angharad. It's got bells on. Or have you been smoking Penry's wacky baccy?'

'Wacky baccy?' I said, my interest caught. 'Penry smokes funny fags?'

'Never mind Penry,' Rhidian said crossly. 'You must think I'm daft, telling me that. So what's the big secret, Angharad?'

'Told you you wouldn't believe me!' I said, triumphantly, picked up my cocoa and went to bed.

Despite my milky drink, though, I couldn't sleep. My mind kept slipping back to Madoc, and what it must have been like, taking that tiny boat across the Atlantic. If there had been rough weather – and there must have been – the waves must have been like trying to sail up Snowdon. And no stabilisers. I can get sick on a

132

lilypond, and I shuddered to imagine what the *Gwennan Gorn* would have been like on such an amazing journey. I wondered how long the journey had taken. A month? Two? I couldn't even guess what it might have been like.

A soft rapping came at my bedroom door, and I slid out of bed and put my dressing gown on. I put my ear to the door, but couldn't hear anything.

'Who is it?'

'It's me.'

'Who's me?' I had no intention to opening the door to Penry.

'Me, you dingbat. Rhidian.'

I opened the door. He was frowning.

'I've been thinking about what you said. And the way you said it,' he whispered. 'You meant it, didn't you? You weren't joking.'

It was my turn to raise an eyebrow quizzically. 'Who, me?'

'Look, can I come in?'

The house was quiet. Not that anyone was likely to catch him leaving my room in the early hours and jump to the wrong conclusions anyway. I chuckled inside. As if I'd get off with Rhidian. Ha! Rhid was my friend. He was like Winnie the Pooh. Clumsy and comfortable and rather sweet.

'Oh, all right.'

He edged inside and I closed the door behind him.

'Right,' I said. 'You can sit there,' I indicated the window-seat, 'and I'm getting back into bed. My feet are cold.'

He sat where instructed, and stared at me. 'You weren't joking, were you?' he repeated.

133

'Joking?' I hedged. 'When?'

'You know perfectly well. When you said you'd done a wossname. A time-slip.'

Me and my big mouth. What was I going to do? I could lie, or I could tell him. Our eyes met. It was no good. I was going to have to tell.

Quickly, I outlined what had happened to me, and he stared, disbelievingly. 'You actually sort of swapped minds with this other girl?' he asked when I'd finished.

I nodded. 'Well, either I swapped, or she budged up a bit and we shared,' I said.

'And you met Owain Gwynedd? And the old Druid guy? And Madoc?'

I nodded. 'Yes, yes, and yes.'

'Wow!' His glassed slithered again, and he took them off, slipping them into his shirt pocket. 'Wow!' He leaned forward, urgently, his eyes strange without his glasses. 'When are you going back?'

'I'm not.'

'What?' He sort of shouted it in a whisper.

'I said I'm not going back. Last time I almost got stuck there. I don't want to spend the rest of my life in medieval Wales, ta very much, Rhid. It's smelly, for a start, and people tend to wave nasty sharp things around. And they fight a lot. And there's no antibiotics and stuff. People die.'

'But the experience, Angharad! You've got to go back!'

I was about to say 'If you're so keen, then you go back,' when I paused. Deep down inside, I really did want to go back. I wanted to go back and tell Madoc that he'd actually find America, although of course he

134

wouldn't know it as that. I wondered what he'd call it. New Gwynedd, perhaps. Or New Wales. He'd believe me. I was the Wyrd Girl, wasn't I? The girl who knew the unknowable.

Rhidian had got up off his window-seat and was sitting on the edge of the bed, his face inches away from me. 'You've got to go back, Angharad! I would, in your shoes, honestly. Think of the historical novel I could write, after!'

I stared at him. I'd had an idea. 'Next time, Rhid, why don't you come with me?'

His mouth fell open, and then he shut it again. A great, lollopy grin spread across his face. 'D'you think I could? Really?'

'I don't know. But you could try, couldn't you?'

He couldn't sit still. 'We'll go tomorrow. Both of us. As soon as all the guests have gone, when we have our hours off, we can go. Oh, this is so *wild*!' he crowed.

He whirled past me, hugging himself, then he stopped, turned, hugged me, instead. Then he kissed me. On the lips, no less.

He didn't kiss like Winnie-the-Pooh.

CHAPTER FOURTEEN

He did it again, and I quite enjoyed it. Then I slung him out. I wanted to think about this. Both thises. Rhidian and me, and Rhidian and going back.

I turned both ideas round in my head for a while, and then found I was hugging myself. I could also feel a silly grin stretching practically from one ear to the other. This was ridiculous. It was still ridiculous two hours later, when I finally fell asleep.

A gull landing on my dormer window woke me. They always sound as if they've got hobnails on, seagulls on the roof. I was late for breakfast, and it was see-off-the-guests-day. I shot into the shower and out again, threw on some clothes and scuttled downstairs. Rhidian's door was still closed, but I grinned at it as I passed. Old Rhid! Who'd have thought it?

Tara-Louise with the boobs was sitting disconsolately at the kitchen table with a cup of black coffee. She and Penry had stayed up after everyone else last night, and I think there might have been a lot of red wine involved, because she had that look about her which said 'hung over'. I clattered the toaster, loudly, which, OK, was a bit mean. But.

Penry didn't put in an appearance before she left, and she was obviously fairly miffed about that. She hung around and hung around, looking at her watch, until the last possible minute before she went out to the minibus which would take her to the station. Before getting on she scribbled a note and put it in an envelope, sealing the flap. She looked a bit pink around the eyes.

'Look, Angharad, will you give this to Penry, please? I can't wait any longer. He promised he'd come down and say goodbye before I left –'

Hah! I thought. I smiled sweetly. 'Of course, Tara-Louise. Just as soon as he comes down.'

Penry must have been watching from an upstairs window, because as the bus disappeared through the gate, he came into the kitchen.

'All alone, little one?' he enquired.

I looked exaggeratedly around, then under the table. 'Looks like it.'

He chucked me under the chin. I hate being chucked, but especially by him.

'But now I'm here, so you aren't alone any more.'

'Pity you didn't come down earlier. Tara-Louise wanted to say goodbye. She left you a note.' I nodded towards the forlorn envelope on the breakfast-table.

Penry ripped open the envelope, glanced at the note, then tore it in two, chucking the pieces in the waste-bin.

Creep.

'You're very quiet this morning.'

'Mmm?' I didn't want to encourage him. I wanted to eat breakfast, help with the clearing up operation, and get back to Madoc. I'd already decided that I should finish reading the book before going back again, just so that I knew exactly what was going to happen to Madoc. And anyone else I happened to meet. I already knew what had happened to Thomas à Becket, who had excommunicated Owain for marrying his cousin Crisiant. Becket, of course, had been bloodily murdered. I shivered. Now *that* was creepy!

I jumped as a hand slid across my back. 'Cold?'

I shot up as if someone had stuck a pin in me. 'No! Stop it.' Flustered, I picked up my half-finished toast and threw it into the waste bin.

'That was the wrong bin. The food waste goes in that one. Am I disturbing you?'

'Yes.' I said, shortly.

'But Rhidian didn't disturb you, did he? When he sneaked into your room last night? Very late, as I recall. And he was there quite a time, wasn't he?' Penry was grinning from ear to ear.

I stared at him. 'You what? Are you trying to suggest something, Penry? What business is it of yours what I do?'

'Ah, so you were doing something, were you?'

'No, I was not. And neither was he!'

'But he was there, wasn't he? I went to bed late last night, remember? And my room is just below yours. I heard the two of you, talking.'

'And that's all we were doing, Penry. Talking.'

He smirked. 'Pull the other one, Hari, my love. What, you, sweet seventeen and never been –'

I went red. 'Why don't you keep your filthy mind to yourself, Penry Pritchard? For the last time, we weren't doing anything.'

'I believe you. Thousands wouldn't. All the same, I don't expect Jack would be too happy though, would he? Rhidian lurking in your room until the early hours.'

I glared at him, at a loss for words, then went out, slamming the door. I bumped into Rhidian on the stairs.

'Don't go in the kitchen,' I warned. 'Penry's in there, and he heard you in my room last night.'

'So?'

'So he's sort of threatening to tell Dad.'

Rhidian looked horrified. 'About what? Nothing happened!'

I didn't like that. He'd kissed me, hadn't he? That wasn't nothing. At least, I didn't think so. He caught my hand as, feeling ever so slightly mortally offended, I pushed past him.

'We're going back this afternoon, OK? As soon as we've helped clear up and had lunch?'

I scowled at him. 'Nothing, eh? Well for your information, Rhidian, it wasn't nothing to me. So there. And no, we're not going back. I'm going to the library to read up on Madoc first. If I go, I want to be properly prepared for anything that might happen.'

His early morning brain clicked into gear. 'Um. What wasn't nothing?' he asked ungrammatically, furrowing his brow so that his glasses slid.

'You kissed me.'

'Oh, that.'

'Oh, *that?*' That was the last straw. Torn between slugging him extremely hard and bursting into tears, I fled upstairs.

When I'd made my bed and flung my clothes into the laundry basket I felt a bit better, if only for the energy expended. I sat on my bed, idly brushing my hair, unsure what to do. The commonsensical part of me told me to go back to the library today, but the other, less prudent part wanted, most definitely, to go back and see if Madoc was there, tell him what had happened – or would happen. But then, he might still be in Ireland, with Rhirid – or on his way to America already.

I managed to avoid Rhidian most of the morning, because he was helping Dad mow the lawn. He thoroughly enjoyed playing with the little sit-and-ride lawn mower, and would mow the lawn as soon as a daisy poked its head up, which was a pity, because I like daisies. Penry, of course, had made himself scarce. Well, there was work to be done, wasn't there?

When the chores were finished I took the Mantis's lunch up, because Dad was away in Colwyn Bay seeing the bank manager. It was a best suit occasion, and he looked as if he was off to his own execution. Afterwards. if he survived, he was going on to speak to a writers' group somewhere, and wouldn't be back until around midnight, so Marged and I were going to be looking after the Mantis.

That meant I couldn't really sneak off to the library for the afternoon: Marged would be away by five-thirty, when she'd finished baking a load of fruit pies for the freezer. I debated staying and helping her, and then decided that I'd do a bit more digging instead. I didn't need to time-slip. I could just dig, see what more I could uncover.

And then Rhidian shot into the kitchen, just as I finished unloading the dishwasher and putting the crockery away.

'Can't stop!' he muttered, 'I've just heard that Gwilym ap Emrys is in John Menzies this afternoon, in Colwyn Bay, signing his new book. You know, he's the one who thinks he's a reincarnation of the son Arthur and Guinevere never had. The nutcase. Your Dad is giving me a lift in, and I'll bus it back. I've wanted to meet him for ages. He's completely off his head, he's so cool. Do you want to come with me?'

I shook my head.

'I thought you were going to the library today. Finish finding out about –' he glanced at Marged, '– you know who,' he whispered.

'No. I'm going to stick around here.'

'OK. See you tonight.' And he shot out again. A second later, he was back, grinning at me. 'Sorry,' he said. 'It wasn't nothing for me, either.' And he was gone.

I felt the inane grin coming back, and switched it off. That decided me. I wasn't going to time-slip without him.

I wasn't. I didn't intend to. Honest.

I left the kitchen door open, because it was a hot day, and the heat from the Aga cooking the pies made the kitchen oppressive. Collecting my trowel from the outhouse, I meandered across the lawn, slipping into the trees when I was certain no one was watching. Actually, the only person I was worried about following me was Penry, and he was well away from Tŷ Pendaran, probably holding forth to a crowd of admirers in the pub.

It was cool under the trees, and a slight breeze stirred the leaves overhead, making a peaceful, whispering sound. I sat beside the length of wall that we'd already uncovered, poking desultorily at the earth. It was hot work, and soon I stripped off my T-shirt and worked in my bikini top. I planned a swim, afterwards, to cool off. On the other side of Tŷ Pendaran was a small, secluded cove that was perfectly safe for swimming, according to Marged.

I uncovered the next bit, and moved along, shuffling backwards on my bottom. Which may be why I overbalanced, falling against the wall and grazing my arm. Without thinking, I scooted myself up onto the top

141

of the jetty, and examined my arm. The sudden flare of light and white noise were instantaneous and unexpected. And I hadn't even touched the dragon disc.

I was sitting on the edge of the jetty on the seaward side, watching a small, battered, square-sailed boat slip into the shelter of the harbour wall, dripping oars flashing diamond sparkles in the sunlight. The crimson paint of the dragon figurehead was cracked and dull, the gilt lettering of the name had worn partly away, and one of the masts had snapped off, almost at deck level, where it jutted like a broken tooth. Beside the wrecked mast, amidst a maelstrom of busy figures preparing to tie up at the quayside, stood the tall, tanned figure of Madoc ap Owain Gwynedd. He was waving to me.

Happiness spread inside me like a warm wave, and my welcoming smile broke like sunshine across my face. I raised my own arm in response. A cool breeze fluttered the rough fabric of my sleeveless, sea-green dress, and my feet, grimy and toughened by shoeless summer days, dangled over deep, sunlit sea-water.

Madoc looked older: from the corners of his eyes white laughter-lines radiated in his tanned face, and his hair was stiff with salt. He wore it differently, too, in two braids, instead of one short tail of hair, and with a shiver of disbelief I realised that feathers dangled from the leather thongs binding each plait. About his neck was another, beaded thong, carrying the unmistakable roundel of a small Dreamcatcher.

I knew about Dreamcatchers: cobwebs of thin silver or fine thread interlaced with feathers and beads. They had passed into hippie shops and market stalls, in my time, but Native American Indian legend was that they protected a

142

sleeper from bad dreams, allowing only the good dreams to flow through the web into the sleeping mind.

And Madoc, twelfth century Prince of Gwynedd, was wearing one about his strong, brown neck.

Madoc had reached America. And returned. He was safe.

It was more than two hours before Madoc had finished supervising the laying up of the *Gwennan Gorn*, and all the time I sat on the quay wall watching, my eyes feasting on his tall figure, watching the play of muscles under the shadowy skin. And I had this weird feeling. At first, I couldn't make it out, recognise it for what it was. Part of me felt, for Madoc, the way I'd felt when Rhidian kissed me. And yet I wasn't in love with Madoc, I couldn't be. I hardly knew him. As far as I was concerned, he didn't exist – whatever had happened to him, he'd died hundreds of years before I'd been born.

And then I understood. The other Angharad was in love with him, not me, and I was picking up her feelings the way a radio antenna picks up radio waves. I tried to look at him critically, through my eyes, not hers, fight down the feelings that were hers, not mine.

The limp was still there, despite Pendaran's minstrations, but his bare back was muscular as he bent and stretched, coiled ropes and called orders, his strength in his manner as well as his body. And all the time the inescapable proof of the success of his odyssey swayed at his neck.

At last, he swung hand over hand up the rope ladder to stand beside me, put his arms around me as I stood up, shyly, to greet him, and lifted me off my feet. He swung me dizzily round and set me down again, planting

143

a smacking (but brotherly) kiss on my lips. Then he held me at arms' length, and regarded me critically.

'You have grown up, Angharad. Have you taken a husband yet?'

I opened and shut my mouth, rather like a goldfish. What sort of question is that to ask a girl? The trouble was, I didn't know. Fairly obviously, time had passed there since the last time I'd 'slipped': maybe in the meantime Pendaran had married me off, but the way I – or rather the other Angharad – was feeling, I hoped not. Holy Toledo, Batman! I hoped not! Time-slipping was all very well, but a husband would be a horrendous complication. I resolved to keep my running feet on, ready for a quick sprint back to the wall if it turned out I was a married woman, especially a reluctant one, which BOTH Angharads definitely were. I certainly didn't want to get caught here at bed-time if I had a husband to contend with.

I decided the best tactic was to pretend I hadn't heard.

'You look well, Madoc.' Then I remembered he'd probably been away for a year at least, and I hadn't seen him for ages. For all I knew, way back then, the other Angharad might have expected him to have been eaten by a sea-monster. 'Did you find your new country? Your free and beautiful land?' smiling up at him, teasing him, knowing all the time, of course, that he had, hugging the knowledge to myself.

His arm casually about my shoulders, we began to walk in the general direction of Pendaran's cottage. 'Oh, Angharad, I have such tales to tell! Sea-creatures, whales big as mountains, spouting great plumes of water while their great tails splash mightily down on the sea!

Once, a great whale almost sank the *Gwennan Gorn*! We flew like birds in the crashing of its tail on the waves, but landed safely, praise be. You will not believe the things I have seen.'

'Oh, I think I would,' I said. 'You crossed wild seas, Madoc, and braved great danger. And you discovered your new land. And that's a fact.'

'Oh, Angharad. Such a new land. It is –. But no. Wait until I have seen Pendaran, and have eaten. Afterwards I will tell you everything. There is so much to tell!'

And quite a lot of it, I could tell you, I thought. *Things you will never even dream of.*

Pendaran was inside the cottage, bent over a chest in the far corner of the room. I peered into the murk. There didn't seem to be any stray husbands hanging around. But maybe I didn't live there any more.

It wasn't until Madoc called his name that the Bard realised that we were there. He turned, and his old face lit with joy at the sight of Madoc. He opened his arms wide, and Madoc went into them, stooping to clasp his foster father. There were tears in the old man's eyes as the two men pulled apart. Pendaran was visibly older, more stooped, the hair whiter and thinner than before. The amazing eyes, though, were bright and green as ever. He beamed at us.

'Angharad knew that you were coming home,' he said, triumphantly. 'She sensed it a week ago, and today she has been waiting at the water's edge from the instant the tide turned.'

Madoc gave me a strange look. 'Pendaran, is she a married woman yet? I asked the question, but she managed to avoid giving me an answer.'

145

Pendaran tipped his head forward, and his shoulders shook. At first I thought he was crying, but then realised that the strange, muffled, snorting noise was his laughter. 'Married, Madoc? Angharad? No. Although,' he went on, 'your brother Edwall has been pursuing her for months now, since the day she first terrified him almost out of what little wits he has. He stole the trinket you gave her – the one bearing the likeness of the *Gwennan Gorn*'s figurehead. She recovered it, but his small brain obviously decided that it was better to marry her than have her running around loose, working against him. For two years now, since you left, he has pestered her to marry him. She has refused him time and time again, but still he asks her.'

'I'd rather marry Attila the Hun,' I said, shortly, remembering the smelly, stocky figure, and the unpleasant, glittering eyes behind the leather nose-piece. Pursuing me for two years, eh. Dream on, Edwall. I don't know how the other Angharad felt about him, but he could go jump in the lake for all I cared.

Madoc frowned. 'Attila the Hun? So, there is someone,' he said, plaintively. 'Is this Attila of good family, Pendaran?'

Pendaran stared at me. 'Angharad, you have never mentioned this person. If he wishes to marry you, it is only right that he should ask me for my blessing. I am your father. He should show respect to me. I am also,' he drew himself up to his full height, and his eyes flashed, 'Druid and Bard to the Great Owain Gwynedd. And family,' he added. 'How long have you known this Attila?'

Oh, crumbs, me and my big mouth. 'Attila the Hun,' I

said, trying frantically to think how I could explain. Then, I remembered I was the Wyrd Girl round this neck of the woods. 'Oh, he's no one for you to worry about, Pendaran. He is an ancient king who appeared to me during one of my visions. Not a nice person at all. And centuries in the future.' I frowned. 'Or possibly the past, I can't remember.' I grinned.

Both faces cleared. So that was all right then.

Pendaran lost interest in me – and Attila the Hun – and gazed once more at Madoc. 'You are thinner, Madoc. Come, we shall eat.'

CHAPTER FIFTEEN

Madoc hadn't lost his appetite. He demolished everything Pendaran set before him, and ended up by eating what looked like half a treeful of apples.

'Fresh fruit, Pendaran! We left home with great barrels of it, but being at sea for nigh on three months, the fruit was eaten quickly, before it rotted in the casks.' He burped, covering his mouth politely with his hand. The smoky tallow rushlight flickered on his face, illuminating the hollows beneath his cheek-bones. I hadn't noticed his eyelashes before: although his hair was bleached almost white, now, by salt and sun, his lashes were long and dark, and cast shadows on the flat, strong planes of his face.

We left the rough table and benches and, while Pendaran seated himself on an upright wooden chair, Madoc lay, face up, his head resting on his crossed arms, and I sat beside him, my knees drawn up beneath my skirt, my chin resting on my knees. We talked softly in the firelight while the evening slipped away.

'We saw such storms, Pendaran,' Madoc began. 'Many, many times we thought *Gwennan Gorn* would not survive the tossing she endured.' He grinned, revealing white, even teeth. 'But she is built from finest Gwynedd oak, and her planks are fastened with nails fashioned from the horns of stags that roamed the Gwynedd hills, so how could she not survive? But sadly, all of us did not finish the journey: we lost ap Rhys and Llewelyn One-eye, from fever. Sion ap Geraint also. He died even as we sighted the new land, from a broken leg.'

148

'He died, from a broken leg?' I said, amazed. Then I remembered that I wasn't in the twentieth century any more.

'Aye. He fell in heavy seas, and the bone thrust through the flesh, and festered. He died, all right. He had no chance but our prayers, and they were not enough.' Madoc closed his eyes, remembering. 'He died hard, in great pain.'

I shuddered, and wished there was some way of bringing antibiotics with me into the past. This time, I hadn't even tried to bring the knife. Marged had been using it to peel apples when I left. Not that I'd been expecting to take this particular trip, of course. Perhaps I could drop a hint to Pendaran about mouldy bread – maybe the old Druid could do the rest. But then, that wouldn't leave anything for Alexander Fleming to discover, would it? I sighed. This time-slip business was difficult for all sorts of reasons.

'But the land, Madoc. You reached land? What was it like?' Pendaran leaned forward, eagerly.

I held my breath, waiting.

Madoc's sat up, his eyes reflecting the glow of the firelight. 'Oh, such a land, Pendaran! As beautiful as Gwynedd, green and fertile, blessed with deep, clear rivers teeming with great, silver salmon. And the hunting! Great beasts with shaggy forequarters, deer as tame as a house-cat, huge, strange birds that make a gobbling noise as they move. It is a land fit for a king, Pendaran.' His eyes flicked to me, and away again. 'And a Queen,' he added, softly.

Something deep inside me sort of lurched. I shook myself. He had been dead for centuries. That thought

149

made dread rise in my throat at the awful inevitability of it all. Madoc would go on living, here, and I would carry on there, and the other Angharad –? I felt her, suddenly, push. It was a hard push. A sort of 'get out of my way, you!' push. The other Angharad, wherever she was, was staking her claim again. I could understand that. 'Listen,' I said mentally, 'I have no designs on Madoc, OK? So stop kicking my brain around, please.'

'The people, Pendaran,' Madoc's voice was vibrant with excitement, 'oh, I wish you could see them. They are such a curious colour. Their skin gleams red as copper, and their hair is black. They wear great head-dresses made of eagle feathers, and they are noble and quite fearless. And mighty, fearsome warriors,' he added, shaking his head ruefully. 'We made peace with them, and it was a good thing that we did.'

I was about to make a flip comment about the Hollywood version of the Red Indian, and the cute little way they had of massacring white settlers – and stopped myself, just in time. The future for the North American Indian was bleak, even if it was half a dozen centuries on.

Madoc talked on and on, his voice rising and falling in the smoky darkness of the small hut, and I contented myself with listening, hearing the vibrant enthusiasm in his voice. The silvery web of the dream-catcher glistened in the flickering flames, lulling me to drowsiness. I found myself dozing, watching Madoc's face, listening to his low voice. He had turned onto his stomach, head propped on his forearms, and his left hand rested lightly on my bare foot. My eyes began to close, and I drifted, Madoc's warm hand caressing my toes . . .

Then, the other Angharad gave the sharpest push she had ever given me. It was as if my brain were being squeezed, hard. I yelped, caught unawares, and came fully awake. 'Ow!'

Madoc stopped talking, and sat up. 'What is it, Angharad?'

I stood up, quickly, pushing the other Angharad back, forcing my eyes open, taking deep breaths of the smoky, warm air. 'Nothing. Just a headache. Honestly, I'm fine.' She was strong when I was sleepy, apparently.

'You've had one of your strange turns, haven't you?' Madoc said, getting to his feet and touching my arm. 'What did you see, Angharad?'

'It wasn't a turn, honest,' I moved away from his hand. The other Angharad obviously had a jealous streak. I didn't need another prod from her to remind me I was trespassing! 'Just a bit of cramp, that's all.' I bent down and rubbed my calf muscle, to prove it. 'I'll be OK in a minute.'

'That Cei again!' Pendaran said, shaking his head. 'First Cei, then the Attila person. But it's time we got some rest.' He straightened, and stood, rubbing his aching back. 'You can tell us more of your adventures tomorrow, my boy. Now, it is late and Angharad should be in her bed.'

Oh no, I shouldn't. I frantically tried to think of a way out. I'd been there far too long already. I hadn't meant to stay so long. But then, I hadn't meant to time-slip, either. Then I remembered this was the twelfth century, and bathrooms, fortunately, hadn't been invented yet. 'I'll just pop outside,' I said, 'take a quick trip into the bushes, you know.'

151

Luckily, they did. I slipped out of the door and legged it for the woods. It was pitch dark outside: the moon was hidden by clouds, and the path through the woods to the jetty was virtually invisible. I stumbled along, tripping on tree roots, turning my ankle on unseen stones, until at last the moon broke out from behind a cloud and I saw its reflection in the calm sea. The *Gwennan Gorn*, a riding lantern glowing on deck, moved with the swell of the tide, and I felt the hard stones of the jetty under my feet. I grasped the disc, and was back, blinking in the sunlight, in my own time.

My eyes were watering in the sudden glare, and that started me sneezing. It wasn't until I stopped that I heard Marged's voice calling me.

'Angharad? Where are you? Angharad, love?'

'Coming, Marged,' I called, heading for the entrance to the bushes. Marged stood at the back door, shading her eyes against the glare.

'Oh, there you are!' she said. 'I was beginning to worry about you. I've got to go home, now, give my Einion his tea, but I didn't want to go until I was sure you were back. I don't want to leave Myfanwy on her own. Not now. I don't like the look of her.'

You and me both, I thought. 'I'm sorry, Marged. I got in among the bushes and I must have dropped off,' I said. I had, in a manner of speaking. Dropped right off into another century.

'That's all right,' Marged buttoned up her cardigan, pulling her blouse collar tidily over the V-neck. 'I wish there was something we could give her, to help. Her ankles are puffing up something terrible, look. There was something, I know there was. My Mam used to

152

swear by it, but not having had babies myself, I took no notice of what it was. Do you think I can remember? No.'

'Raspberry leaf tea,' I said, absent-mindedly undoing my trainers. 'And red nettles, hemlock and sage to bathe her ankles.'

Marged stared at me. 'Well, I don't know about that hemlock stuff, that sounds a bit iffy, but you're dead right about the other. Raspberry leaf tea for an easy labour, that's it. Well, I never. Fancy you knowing that. I expect you can get it from those healthy shops that sell the lentils and things. I'll buy some next time I'm in Colwyn. See if we can't ease her troubles a bit, poor soul.' And off she went to where her motor-scooter was parked.

Red nettles, hemlock and sage. Now where on earth had that come from? If it was any good for troublesome pregnancies, I'd never heard of it, although I remembered Mum recommending the raspberry leaf stuff to a friend once. But nettles and hemlock? Maybe the other Angharad again? I wasn't entirely sure I liked that idea, but I supposed fair was fair: I kept borrowing her body, she invaded my brain occasionally.

I went upstairs to check on Myfanwy. She was awake, and so I did the decent thing and spent an hour with her, playing Scrabble. She beat me, of course. My tiles always seem to include an X, a Y, two U's and a Z. I mean, if you aren't Ubangi or Polish, there isn't much you can do with those. The Mantis (who was getting to look less and less like a Mantis and more and more like an unhealthy suet dumpling as the days passed) got lots of useful consonants and vowels, and knew lots of seven letter words that could be added on to words already on the board, and when she added 'ZOO' to the 'LOGICAL' that was already down, and got the Z on a triple letter score, that was me done for good and proper.

'Next time, we play Monopoly,' I said, scraping the letter tiles off the board into the blue plastic bag.

'You like Monopoly?' she said, struggling up on her pillows.

'Only slightly less than I like Scrabble.' I put the lid on the box. She actually looked better. 'I don't enjoy board games too much, actually.' I saw the hurt look cross her face.

'But I quite enjoyed the Scrabble today,' I lied, quickly.

'Next time Monopoly, then,' Myfanwy said brightly.

As I closed her bedroom door, I thought I heard her whisper, 'or maybe Happy Families.' Perhaps I only imagined it.

Rhidian came back about an hour later, while I was mashing the potatoes with the electric beater. I grinned at him. He scooped up a splash of mashed spud from the worktop and sucked it off his finger.

'Have a good afternoon with whatsisname? The fruitcake?'

'Gwilym ap Emrys,' he said, and pulled a face. 'That bloke is totally twp. He's so far out he's going to fall off, soon. I asked him how he could be a reincarnation of Arthur and Guinevere's son when according to legend they didn't have any children. He just glared at me and told me that with reincarnation, anything is possible. I tried to tell him that he couldn't be a reincarnation of someone who was never carnated in the first place, but he'd lost interest in me by then and was signing copies of his book for about a hundred little old ladies who'd come in on a coach trip from Liverpool. I don't think they had a clue who he was, but they bought his books anyway, in case he was someone famous. What did you do?'

'I played Scrabble with the Mantis,' I said, omitting to mention that I'd time-slipped and spent an afternoon and evening with Madoc and Pendaran.

'The Mantis?'

I blushed. That wasn't fair. That was Mum's and my nickname for her. It wasn't kind to pass it on. 'I mean Myfanwy. My stepmother.'

'Don't you like her?'

I shrugged. 'Oh, she's all right, I suppose. I didn't like her at first, and I hated her when I found out she and Dad were having a baby, but, well . . . Oh, I don't know.'

'I feel sorry for her, stuck up there all by herself.'

'Yeah. Me too, I suppose. I'm trying to like her, OK? Only –'

'You feel loyal to your Mum, too.'

'Yes. It's not that, Rhid. Mum and Dad had split up long before Myfanwy came on the scene. It's just I suppose I'm –'

'Jealous?' Rhidian said the word I wouldn't admit.

'Mm. I s'pose. She's got my Dad, and I only see him once every couple of months.'

'And now there's going to be a new baby.'

I glared at him. He was getting a little too close for comfort. 'Yes, there is.'

'Who's going to be living permanently with *your* Dad, right?'

155

I didn't answer. To my horror, though, I felt a lump grow in my throat, and tears well up. I sniffed, hard, but one trickled down my cheek. Rhidian put his arms around me, and hugged. It was a brotherly hug, a best mate hug, a cuddle-from-a-tall person hug. It was nice and comforting. I must admit, though, it didn't feel anything like a Dad-type hug. I fumbled in my pocket for a tissue, found one, a bit tatty, and blew my nose, hard.

'I know I sound immature, and mean, and horrible,' I sniffled, 'but Dad didn't tell me about the baby. He saved it as a surprise, for when I arrived, and I was sure the surprise would be something nice, like driving lessons, and instead they presented me with the prospect of a new baby brother or sister.'

'He didn't tell you?' Rhidian, gazing out of the kitchen window over my head, shook his head in wonderment. 'I'm not the most tactful of people, everyone says that, especially my Mum. But springing that on you! That must have been a bit of a bummer.'

'That,' I said shortly, 'is exactly what it was. A major bummer.' I looked up at him, just as he stopped looking out the window and looked down. He wasn't wearing his glasses, and his eyes were inches away from mine. Our lips were closer.

That was three kisses. This was getting to be a habit.

CHAPTER SIXTEEN

It was almost a week before I could get to the library again, partly because the new group of guests turned out to be the most troublesome of the lot so far, and also because Myfanwy took a turn for the worse. She was suffering from hyper-something or other, and her ankles had swollen up again, so the doctor made her go into the local hospital's ante-natal ward for a rest. He said she was getting stressed out being at home with all the coming and going around her. He may have been right. Anyway, he promised she could come home as soon as her blood-pressure came down and her ankles deflated. Personally, I thought she'd be better off staying there until she dropped the sprog, but I didn't say that to Dad.

Some of the guests were appalling, and the tutors weren't much better. Laetitia was off with the fairies half the time, or snuggling up to Penry. She never missed an opportunity to touch him – his arm, his hand, and watching her being flirtatious was quite sick-making. Penry took to leaving the room as she came into it, and I didn't blame him.

Even Dad was fraying round the edges by Wednesday, and beginning to question the wisdom of having open house for a whole herd of maniacs. It started raining on arrival day, and didn't stop until leaving day, which made outdoor trips uncomfortable and, in the case of the painting types, impossible. It can't be a whole lot of fun trying to paint a watercolour landscape with rain washing the paint off your palette, and sloshing around your paper, even though it gave a whole new meaning to 'water-colour', I suppose. So the guests and the tutors were all stuck indoors, bickering like spoiled children.

Two of the men (and there were only three) fell in hate the minute they met, and lost no opportunity to disagree with each other, whatever the subject was. Penry took to walking out in disgust whenever they started, disappearing down to the pub in the village, so he was away more often than not. That left Dad to cover for him, as well as all his other problems, which meant more pressure and stress for Dad. Personally, I'd have given Penry the old heave-ho, but he was Dad's old school friend, so Dad, of course, didn't do anything of the sort.

Laetitia, meantime, had taken a dislike to Suzy, one of the arty ladies. Maybe her Chinese Holistic therapist thingy had warned her against normal people or something. I couldn't understand it, because Suzy seemed OK to me whenever I sat next to her at meals. She was nice, and pretty, and really interesting as well, because rumour had it that she was psychic or something, and occasionally told fortunes (although never for money). Also, she didn't chew with her mouth open, or slurp her soup, or whine, or nag, and she didn't like Laetitia, either, so we got on really well. Even better, when Penry the Smoothie grabbed her hand to slobber over it, she let him, then said sweetly, 'D'you know, the last time I had that done, it was my labrador pup this morning. I *think* I've washed it, since.' She earned lots of Brownie points for that, because just about every other female in the house turned into a simpering wuss every time he entered a room.

Despite the put-down, (or maybe because of it – perhaps he regarded her as a challenge!), Penry kept on

158

trying, but Suzy more or less ignored him, except to say stuff like 'Please pass the salt'. And yet for some reason Laetitia loathed her.

Then I popped into the studio one damp morning and understood why. Suzy was actually a much better artist than Laetitia, and the Locust must have felt decidedly threatened. Suzy was doing these gorgeous, wishy green, spooky, supernatural sort of paintings of subjects like Herne the Hunter, with his great stag horns and flared nostrils, and eerie moon goddesses, stuff like that, and a gorgeous green lady who was part tree, part human. They were good enough to stop me in my tracks when I walked past her easel. Herne, Tree-Witch and Moon-Goddess were leant against the wall, and on the easel was a painting of a tall, dark-eyed, saturnine-looking man, very handsome, wearing medieval clothes, against a background of a stormy sea. He was gorgeous, and I said as much.

'Who is it, Suzy?' I asked. 'Phwoooar! I wouldn't . . .' I stopped myself just in time from adding the rather vulgar end to the sentence. I wasn't with my mate Ceri, and a grown-up might be shocked.

'You wouldn't crawl over him to get to the lightswitch?' she finished for me, and grinned. She bent towards the canvas, adding a white highlight to the pupil of the dark eye, making it come alive. Those vivid eyes would follow a person all round the room . . .

'Oh, come on, Angharad, you can work it out!' she said, 'I thought you might have guessed. Wasn't he supposed to come from around here?'

'Who?'

'Madoc. Surely you know that legend, living here? My father told me all about Madoc ap Owain Gwynedd

159

when I was a tiny girl. As soon as I heard your Mum and Dad were opening this old place up, I knew I had to save up and come. Legend has it that he lived around here, once. Sailed from quite close, apparently, but nobody knows exactly where. He discovered America, you know, ages before Columbus. I believe it, and I don't care if nobody else does.' She tilted her head, and stood back, assessing her work.

'Oh, no!' I was caught off guard. 'Madoc doesn't look anything like that! His hair's li –' I stopped.

She froze, her brush poised over the painting. The silence almost *clanked*. Then she turned to stare at me. 'Good heavens, Angharad, you talk as if you know him!'

I went red, smiled weakly, and thought fast on my feet. 'Oh, you know how it is. You read about someone historical and you get a picture of them in your head. I suppose my idea of Madoc is just a bit different from yours, that's all.' I felt I needed to say more, throw her off the scent. 'And I never imagined Charles II looked the way he actually did, and Prince Rupert of the Rhine looked nothing like he should. They both ought to have been drop-dead gorgeous, and they weren't.' She was still looking at me strangely. I floundered on, 'Oh, and by the way, she's my stepmother, not my Mum. My Mum's in India.'

She narrowed her eyes, as if she knew something was wrong, but couldn't quite put her finger on what it was. 'Mmm.' She turned back to her painting. 'So, you think he didn't look like this?'

'Oh, what do I know?' I said dismissively, and moved away. That had been too close for comfort!

Rain saturated the garden and water dripped off the

160

trees and lay in puddles all over the lawn. If I opened my bedroom window I could hear the river rushing towards the sea, and even if I'd had time, I couldn't have walked upstream towards Pendaran's house: I'd have slid and slithered all over the place on the muddy pathway. Dad was distracted trying to do everything and rush off to the hospital for afternoon and evening visiting, and more and more responsibility descended on my shoulders, and on Rhidian's, which at least kept us busy and out of mischief, I suppose. The trouble was, we couldn't take on the teaching-writing side of it, nor help Laetitia with the painting classes, so there was a limit to what we could do. We tried to field complaints from the guests (there were many, but none we couldn't handle, thank goodness) and Rhidian went around changing blown light bulbs, fixing dripping taps, lubricating sticking window frames, and fetching and carrying, while I helped Marged with cooking and shopping, loaded and unloaded the dishwasher, peeled vegetables, made pies, laid tables and generally made myself useful.

Suzy-the-brilliant-artist, totally impressed by my efforts, decided to tell my fortune as a reward the night before she left, when we were sitting cosily together in the kitchen drinking cocoa. Everyone else had gone to bed, and I was drowsy. She took my right hand and gazed at the palm, tracing heart- and head-lines with her long forefinger.

'I can't understand this,' she said after a while, a puzzled frown on her face. 'Your lifeline is most peculiar. It's almost as if you have two . . .' She looked up at me. 'Is this a scar or something?'

I shook my head. 'Don't think so.' Then I thought about it. *Two lifelines?* 'I've got two?'

'Well, not exactly. There's this little bit of it here,' her fingernail traced my palm again, tickling, 'where it half-splits and then sort of joins and makes a chain effect for a bit. Then it turns back into a normal single line. Really odd. Never seen anything quite like that. Still, you end up with just one, and it's a nice long one.' She let go of my hand and grinned, picking up her cocoa. Then she put it down again, reached out and caught up the twin discs around my neck. 'Ban the Bomb I know, but this is lovely. It looks so old.' She separated the dragon disc from the other, and cupping it in her palm, leaned forward to look at it. Suddenly, she yelped, and dropped it.

'What?'

'That was so weird! I'd swear I got a bolt of static electricity from it!' She looked at me strangely, sucking her finger. She showed it to me: there was a small red patch at the end.

'I've never felt it,' I said, with the fingers of my right hand crossed beneath the table.

Suzy swigged back her cocoa and stood up. 'I'm going to bed.'

So. Two linked lifelines, eh? I examined my palm, looking for the chain effect Suzy had described. I found it, and traced it with my finger. And yes, it became a normal single line. I sighed with relief. Just one of us in the future, then. No long-term problems.

I was washing up the cocoa-cups when the thought hit me. Just one of us, yes. But *which one?*

When Suzy left at the end of the week, she handed me a brown-paper parcel. 'This is for you, Angharad,' she said. 'It's Madoc, to remind you of me.'

'Wow, thanks!' I said, hugging the parcel to my chest.

'I'll keep it until you're rich and famous and then sell it!' We both laughed. But as she was climbing into the minibus taking her to the station, she stopped on the step and looked me straight in the eye.

'I don't know what's going on, young lady,' she said softly, 'but I get this feeling that you know something that the rest of us mortals don't.' She raised an eyebrow at me, jumped on the bus, and swept away leaving me open-mouthed on the gravel drive. I put the parcel, unopened, in my dresser drawer. Her idea of Madoc was nothing like the real thing, after all.

Rhidian and I both worked our socks off, and when the last guest had gone, we were awarded an afternoon off, which we both agreed we thoroughly deserved. The sun came out and the ground was steaming, but it was still too wet to walk upriver. However, with the slight breeze coming off the sea, it wouldn't be long before it all dried out. I wanted to get to the library, but there was a film on that Rhidian wanted to see, so we went to the cinema instead (it had a lot of blood and violence in it, and I didn't enjoy it much) and by the time we came out, blinking at the brightness after the gloom inside, it was too late to go to the library.

Although I meant to finish my research on Madoc, the sun went right on shining, getting hotter and hotter, and the thought of sitting in a stuffy library after being cooped up indoors for over a week was too much. Tuesday afternoon, after Marged and I'd cleared up the kitchen, I folded my tea-towel and changed my flip-flops for trainers.

'Where are you off?' Rhidian appeared in the doorway of my room, making me jump.

'I'm going upriver. For a walk,' I panted, bending over tying my shoelaces. I was going to have to eat less – my waistband was so tight I couldn't breathe when I bent over. Trouble was, Marged's pies and cakes were irresistible.

'It'll be as muddy as hell, but I'll come anyway.'

And because I wasn't planning on time-slipping, I was happy to have him with me for company. We left the house, and strolled round the outside of the wall to the place where the woods began. After a while, he took my hand, and we walked along, our joined hands swinging contentedly between us, chattering about inconsequential things, joking about the last set of guests and comparing them to the current lot, who were still settling in. It felt sort of nice, holding his hand. We even kissed a bit, here and there. Not quite boy-friend and girl-friend yet, but sort of comfortable and on the way there. Then the going got muddy, and we had to walk in single file, Rhidian in the lead, me trailing behind him, slipping in the mud.

'Oh, yuk, Rhid, this is disgusting!' I muttered, clutching a branch to keep my balance, but slithering sideways anyway. He didn't answer, and I glanced up. The white light hit me, and the sea-noise rushed in my ears. Rhidian wasn't there, but Pendaran's rough, wattle and daub cottage was.

'Rhidian?' I couldn't understand it. I hadn't touched the disc, I wasn't standing on the stones – I glanced down. Yes, I was. I must have stumbled onto them without realising it, masked as they were by mud. I had two choices: keep going and find out if Pendaran was home, or step forward into my own time. But I hadn't touched the disc. How could I have slipped back in time

164

again without holding the disc? I groped at my neck, and found it, resting in the hollow or my throat, stepping off the jetty stones at the same time.

Instantly, Rhidian was back, and the cottage had gone. His face was white, and he stared at me as if he'd seen a ghost. He put out his hand, slowly, and touched me.

'You did it again, didn't you?'

I rubbed my eyes: they felt tired and gritty. I nodded.

'You went all sort of weird and transparent. It was like you were here – but you weren't here. If you see what I mean.'

'No, I don't.' I let go of the disc as if it were red hot. 'I shouldn't have time-slipped then, Rhidian. Even though I was standing on the stones, I wasn't holding the disc as well. It was just resting on my neck. And I didn't think I went – what was it? – transparent. You didn't say I did last time.'

'Last time, you didn't. You just went sort of off. Sort of vacant, not here. As if you were having some sort of funny turn.'

'Funny turn, eh?' I grinned, but I didn't think it was funny. Funny turns were what the other Angharad had – they were what made her the Wyrd Girl. She and I seemed to be getting closer. But now I was back in my own time.

'Do it again,' Rhidian commanded.

'Do what?'

'You know. Step on the wall and see what happens.'

'Why?'

'I want to watch. This time I'll take notice, I promise. Tell you exactly what happens.'

This time, I held the disc, stepped deliberately onto the stones, and was once more assaulted by light and sound. My sight cleared, and the sun poured through the branches of trees onto the small, roughly made home in the clearing. Smoke drifted idly from the roof-hole, and a chestnut horse, its halter draped across a broad brown neck, grazed contentedly in front of the door. I wondered whose it was. Half of me wanted to go forward to the cottage, find out who was visiting Pendaran; the other half wanted to go back to Rhidian and safety. I chose my own time, and stepped off the wall, clutching the disc.

Rhidian, his face screwed up in concentration, stared at me.

'That was so spooky!' he said, shaking his head. 'One minute you were there, next minute you weren't. I could hear you breathing, but I couldn't see you. It was like putting a slide in a projector, and there you were. Do it again, please.'

I shook my head. 'No. I've had enough. I want an ice-cream. Let's go down to the beach. It's too muddy here.'

'What?' He looked dumbfounded. 'You can time-travel any time you want, and you want to go to the beach and get an *ice-cream*? Oh, come on, Angharad! Where's your sense of adventure? If it was me, I'd want to go back. Find out what life was really like then.'

'Well it isn't you, Rhid, it's me. If you like it so much, you go back. Here.' I unclasped the disc from around my neck and handed it over. 'Go on. I'll wait until you get back. But you won't like it. It's smelly, it's dirty, and it's dangerous. There aren't any medicines or toilets. People ride around on horses and kill people with swords and spears. And when I was last there, some repulsive thug was trying to marry me.'

Rhidian stared at me. 'Do you mean it?' I nodded, and

166

he reached out a hand (which I was quite pleased to see was ever so slightly shaky) and took the disc. Then he closed his eyes and stepped onto the wall. He stood there, face screwed up, for a while, and then opened one eye. 'Did I go?'

'Not so's you'd notice. But how should I know? Did you hear a funny noise in your head? See a white light? See a little old cottage in a clearing in the wood?'

Rhidian shook his head. 'All I saw was the inside of my eyelids. I don't think it worked for me. Maybe it's just you can go back. Oh, damn it. There's no justice,' he said morosely. He handed the disc back to me, where I stood safely out of accidental slipping range, on the muddy path.

'I don't actually want to go back. At least, not right now. I want to find out more about what happens to Madoc. I want to read up on homeopathy, in case I get over there and catch something. What if I can't get back? Had you thought of that? I might get stuck there forever.' I felt a bit mean, laying out all these objections, even if they were entirely possible. What I actually meant was, I don't want to go back with you watching me. I want to go back by myself, to see Madoc, to tell him what the future holds for him. How could I say that to Rhidian, who was almost-special. I couldn't sort out my feelings for Madoc, either. I was falling in love with Rhidian – but the other Angharad's feelings for Madoc were all mixed up in me somehow. How could I say that? So what I said instead was, 'I'm hot. I want an ice-cream. Come on.'

With Rhidian still muttering mutinously and looking backward over his shoulder as if he were expecting

Pendaran's hut to appear the minute his back was turned, we went back the way we had come. I turned over in my mind what I'd just said. I hadn't known I was thinking that clearly about it all. And that last time-slip, when I hadn't meant to – it was as if something had reached out and dragged me, as soon as I stepped off the path and onto the jetty wall. I couldn't understand what had happened.

Then I remembered this leather jacket Mum once had. When she'd bought it, the buttonholes had been so tight she went purple whenever she tried to do them up. Then, after about a year, the buttonholes sort of relaxed, and eventually got so loose that the buttons used to fall out at the slightest tug. Maybe that was what was happening to the space I went into when I went back in time. Maybe time's buttonhole was getting baggy, and I could slip in and out without the disc getting involved? I wasn't sure I liked the idea of that happening: at least, before, I'd had some sort of control over when I went. I thought about this a bit more, and hardly noticed when Rhidian took my hand again. If I was honest with myself, even though going back scared me, it felt like a secret vice, like pigging out on jelly babies behind everyone's back: I couldn't *not* go back. Not now I'd met Madoc, and felt –

Felt the touch of his fingers on my bare, dirty foot.

CHAPTER SEVENTEEN

I didn't *decide* to go back: I really had no intention of slipping again until I'd had a chance to read up on Madoc and find out all the things I needed to know. But I couldn't hitch a lift into town to the library, and I had a free afternoon and Rhidian and Dad were driving down to Portmeirion with the guests again, and I was at a loose end. And, and, and, excuses, excuses, I know. Also, the Mantis had been fretting in the hospital, so they had slung her out and sent her home. They said if she was going to be just as stressed out and fretting in hospital as she was at Tŷ Pendaran, there wasn't much point in her taking up an NHS bed and she might as well be a pain in the butt at home. So she was back, and installed in the library with a good book since she refused to go to bed. I'd told Dad that I'd keep an eye on her, take her cups of raspberry leaf tea and stuff. We'd managed to get the tea from Nutcases' Health Shop in the village, but according to Marged they looked at her as if she was mad when she asked if they stocked an ointment of red nettles, hemlock and sage. I'd racked my brains to try and remember if I'd read it somewhere, but (rather reluctantly) came to the conclusion that the Other Angharad was wandering about in my head.

So, as I say, I didn't actually *decide* to go back: I left it up to the Mantis. If she fell on my neck and demanded to play Scrabble or Monopoly or hold her ball of wool while she knitted little booties, then I'd be a nice step-daughter and oblige. So once Marged had finished preparing dinner and had left for home, I boiled the

169

kettle, made a cup of raspberry leaf tea (which smelled all right but tasted disgusting) and took it upstairs into the library. Myfanwy was lying on the sofa, her hands supporting her back, gazing out of the window at the sea.

'Do you want another cushion?' I asked, putting the drink down beside her on a little table. 'You look a bit uncomfortable lying like that.'

She struggled to sit up, and winced. 'I would, please, Hari. I've got such a backache today. I'm going to try to get some sleep when I've drunk this.' She picked up the tea, sipped, and pulled a face. 'Ugh, this is horrible stuff. Still, if Marged thinks it will help . . .'

'If you're going to sleep, Myfanwy, d'you mind if I go for a walk? I won't be long.' OK, so I had my fingers crossed behind my back.

'No, go ahead. It's such a gorgeous day, there's no sense in you being cooped up inside as well. I'll be fine, honestly. And I know exactly how much you love Scrabble!' She smiled, and I felt a tweak of something. Affection? Sympathy? Who knows. Might have been irritation.

Anyhow, I didn't wait to be told twice. Downstairs, I changed flip flops for trainers, and crossed the lawn towards the bushes, where the wall came into the garden. Today I tried an experiment. I hunched my shoulders so the disc was barely touching me at all, and stepped onto the wall. Light-flash, white noise – and I slipped through. Those buttonholes must have been positively gaping.

When I opened my eyes, it was night. I don't know why that surprised me: I knew that time was different over here. It just seemed weird that it wasn't three in the afternoon in both places.

The *Gwennan Gorn,* a lantern glowing at her masthead, swayed on the end of her ropes, tugged this way and that by the pull of river and tide. A figure lay curled on deck, head pillowed on a coil of rope, fast asleep, but it was no one I recognised. If he was supposed to be Madoc's night-watchman, he'd sort of fallen down on the job.

By the time I reached Pendaran's hut in the clearing, my eyes had got used to the darkness, and the moon had come to my rescue so that every leaf and twig was silvered and the path ahead was almost as clear as day. The hut was a darker square against the gloom, and I paused on the edge of the wood. The chestnut horse that had been there last time had gone, and Pendaran's leather curtains allowed no glimmer of light through.

It suddenly felt so weird, knowing that I was going to cross the clearing, lift the latch, and talk to someone who had already been dead and buried for hundreds of years. I shivered. Now that some of the strangeness of 'crossing' was beginning to go, I was growing fond of Pendaran. He was kind and loving and had looked after his daughter, the other Angharad, when she was tiny and motherless, and fostered the handicapped Madoc too. I thought about him painstakingly trying to straighten Madoc's little deformed foot.

Perhaps Madoc would be there with Pendaran. I hugged myself in anticipation, and stepped out of the concealing trees towards the hut.

The sound of hooves beating on soft earth warned me, but too late. Even as I half-turned to see who was riding towards me, I was grabbed from behind, thrown across a rough wool saddle cloth, and my captor spurred the horse into a gallop away from Pendaran and the hut.

I couldn't even scream: I had no breath to do it because I was winded by the thumping of the horse's shoulders into my stomach. I tried to wriggle off, throw myself onto the ground, hoping I'd escape the pounding hooves, so that I could run back to the wall and safety, but at my first squirm backwards, a heavy hand in a leather glove descended on my back and held me down. I started to regret the second piece of Marged's corned beef pie I'd eaten for lunch. I could feel it rising in my throat with every step the horse took.

I realised where we were heading as the rider reined in the horse outside a fence of heavy wooden logs.

'*Pwy sy' 'na*?' a voice called. 'Who goes there?'

'Edwall,' my captor said.

Then I got really worried. Last I'd heard, Pendaran had said that Edwall wanted to marry me. And now he'd scooped me up and kidnapped me. I didn't particularly want to be anyone's bride just yet, but most especially I didn't want to be Edwall's. He was big, and rough, and a bully, and he could use a good deodorant, or at least an occasional wash. The gate swung open, and the horse trotted inside, Edwall bending forward over my back, ducking down to get under the lintel.

He lifted me down from the horse's back and I opened my mouth to yell, but his hand clapped hard across it, shutting me up very effectively. Then, one hand round my waist, one still clamped against my mouth, he lifted me and carried me through the door of the main hall. My mind flared with grim newspaper reports of rapes and beatings. *Not me, please, God, if you're listening!* I thought, desperately.

If Owain Gwynedd was there, perhaps I could be

172

righteously indignant, get really, really angry and demand to be taken back to Pendaran, but the hall was in darkness except for a few sputtering, smelly rush lights. Huddled shapes lay about in the straw, and since Edwall didn't remove his hand from my mouth, I couldn't do much at all to let any of them know I was there. It probably wouldn't have been any help anyway. Edwall was the Prince's son, so no one was likely to argue with him much. I struggled and squirmed, but he was far too strong for me. He went through an archway and up a flight of stairs, still holding me above ground. I didn't wriggle at this point: I didn't fancy crashing and rolling down stone stairs. At the top, however, he had to let go of my mouth to open a door, and I took the opportunity of filling my lungs ready to yell, very loudly.

I only got out a squeak: he turned me round so that my face was muffled by his jerkin, and pressed me hard against him, so that I was half suffocated. Shutting the door behind us he covered my mouth again, holding me away from him, thank goodness, because his BO was making me feel sick. The room was small, and furnished with a bed and an upright rush-seated chair. A large turf fire glowed in the corner below a square hole in the roof. Despite this, the room was smoky, and I choked, partly on the smell of sweaty Edwall, partly on peat-smoke and the oily mutton-fat rushlights.

'It is no use screaming, Wyrd Girl,' he said, his dark eyes looking straight into mine. 'Owain Gwynedd has said that you shall be my wife, and Pendaran has no say in it, since Pendaran has sworn fealty to Owain. And you have no opinion, being a woman. So shout all you will, all here know that you will be my wife. I await permission from Canterbury, and the marriage will go ahead.' He let me go, and I scrambled away from him.

'Canterbury?' I said, indignantly, straightening my dress. 'What's Canterbury got to do with anything?'

'The Archbishop must give his permission. Becket may have excommunicated my father, but he has not excommunicated me. I will not disobey Holy Mother Church. I await the Archbishop's permission.'

'Oh, *Becket*,' I said, scornfully, thinking fast for a way out, a reason why I couldn't marry him. 'Isn't he dead yet?'

Edwall took a step back. 'Dead? Why should he be?'

Ooops. Then I saw my chance to scare him a bit. I put a lot of doom-and-dire-warning into my voice. 'Archbishop Thomas à Becket of Canterbury will die.'

Edwall gulped. 'Why do you say such things, Wyrd Girl?'

I tried for sinister: I said spookily, 'Because I *knooow*! What year is it now?'

'The Year of Our Lord Eleven hundred and sixty-nine,' Edwall replied, fairly nervously, twisting his fingers together.

'Well, Thomas à Becket will be foully murdered by four of Henry's own knights before the altar of Canterbury Cathedral, in' – I racked my brains to remember the date – '1170. That's next year,' I said, in case he couldn't work it out. 'And then he'll be made a Saint, as well,' I continued, to add a bit of local colour to the story.

Edwall gulped. 'I don't believe you. Why should Henry have his Archbishop murdered? Becket is his friend. But saint he is not. In his youth he was wild.

Archbishop he may be, anyone with wealth enough may be a churchman. But saint he never will be.'

'Oh, yes, he will. Martyrdom does that for a bloke. Henry will say, "Will no one rid me of this turbulent priest?", and the deed will be done,' I prophesied. 'And whatever he did in his youth, forget it. Trust me, he gets sainted.'

It was great, this foretelling and soothsaying lark, especially with 20/20 foresight – or was it hindsight? – under my belt! It seemed to have taken Edwall's mind off immediate rape and ravishment, anyway.

I strolled nonchalantly to the bed, intending to sit on it, and then decided it would be safer to stay well away from beds. 'Becket dies, trust me. And there'll be lots of blooooood,' I hissed.

Edwall backed away a little more. 'How can you know such things?' he asked nervously. 'Are you a witch?'

I remembered, suddenly, that witches had a fairly short life-expectation back then and back-pedalled hastily. No point in making things worse than they were already. 'Not a witch,' I said, hastily. 'But my mind travels into the future. I see things that no one else can.'

His face grew crafty. 'It's easy to *say* things, Wyrd-Girl. I could say that Becket will die Thursday sennight, but only then will men know if I speak true. By 1170 we might all be dead.' He crossed himself, quickly, just to be on the safe side.

I pasted a scowl onto my face. 'I told you Brenda was going to die, didn't I? And she did, didn't she?'

Edwall scowled. 'You did. But then, you might have witched her.'

175

'I didn't!' I yelped, then calmed down, quickly. I dared not lose my nerve. 'I might have. Except that I am not a witch, Edwall. But I do know the future, believe me.'

Suddenly, the peat fire crackled and blazed, spitting sparks, startling both of us. It had the desired effect on Edwall, that's for sure – he was out of the room like a rat up a drainpipe. Unfortunately, he stopped to bolt the door behind him.

I sat on the bed and put my head in my hands. I felt like having a good howl, except that I knew it wouldn't do any good. I was stuck. If I couldn't get out of the castle, I might even end up married to smelly Edwall. And nobody knew I was there. I could rot there forever – or at least until I agreed to marry him.

And then I realised that if *I* was here, the other Angharad wasn't. That is, she was wherever she went when she wasn't in her body. So if she wasn't at Pendaran's hut, then he would know she was missing, because I was missing, and I was occupying her skin right now. And since he'd said that Edwall wanted to marry me, maybe he'd realise who had taken me and come after me.

Feeling a little bit better about my prospects, I went to the window and looked out. The night air was cold on my face, and it helped clear my brain. It was absolutely dark outside, the moon having disappeared behind a cloud, and there were no far-off city street-lights to cast an orange glow upwards. I turned from the window and looked around. I tried the big round handle of the door, but it wouldn't budge. So what did I have on my side? I didn't plan to fling myself sobbing to the bed and knuckle under. Mum wouldn't like it if I got married without telling her.

I had a long dress on, sort of one degree up from

176

sacking, tied round the middle by a twisted rope. I undid the rope, untwisted it and found it was about six feet long. I peered out of the arrow-slit window, trying to gauge how far it was to the ground. About far enough to break my neck, at a rough guess, if I jumped after I reached the end of the rope. Not only that, I wouldn't be able to squeeze myself through the window. Even if I'd been anorexic, I'd have had difficulty, and anorexic I certainly wasn't, not after a couple of weeks of Marged's puds.

So, what did I have going for me? I had my 'supernatural powers', my stickability, my bloody-mindedness and the fact that I wasn't the average sort of female that was around in the twelfth century. I didn't exactly have a chattel mentality, although I wasn't sure quite how much good that would do me, given the general brutishness of most of the male population. But they were weapons of sorts. Oh, and about two years ago I'd done a self-defence class on Saturday mornings and learned how to toss the judo instructor (who co-operated quite a bit) over my shoulder, even though it took me about six weeks to learn to stop apologising when I did it. Whether Edwall would be equally cooperative remained to be seen. I didn't intend to give in and get married to that smelly lout without at least a bit of a fight. But that was it. I thought wistfully about stun-guns and Star Trek Phasers. Even a can of hairspray would do.

I sat on the upright chair, uncomfortably, for about an hour, waiting for Edwall to come back, but my back started to ache, so I lay rigidly on the bed, stiff with nerves, afraid to sleep in case someone came to rescue me and I missed them.

But sleep I did.

When I woke it was to a murky sunshine because the arrowslits let in only small shafts of light. I sat up, completely disorientated. I didn't know where on earth I was. Then I remembered it was when, not where. I sighed. Then I realised I really, really, needed the loo.

I put up with it for a while, but then the need got serious, and even though I looked under the bed and in all the alcoves, I couldn't find a suitable receptacle. Or even an unsuitable one for that matter.

So I went to the door and hollered. No one came, so I hollered and kicked. It took a while, but eventually, there was a noise outside the door, a scraping, great-big-bolt-being-drawn-back sort of noise, and it swung open. The young woman who stood in the doorway looked vaguely familiar, and I racked my brains trying to remember where I'd seen her before.

She came in, her brown dress swishing in the dirty rushes that littered the floor, looking shyly up at me under her long eyelashes. She was pretty, but tiny. I felt like an elephant beside her. Long fair plaits swung each side of her small, pointed face.

'Angharad,' she whispered, but not because she didn't want anyone to hear, but because her voice was as tiny as the rest of her. I had to really listen to hear her. I remembered who she was, suddenly.

'You're Crisiant, aren't you?' I said. 'Owain Gwynedd's new wife?'

She nodded. 'I am his wife, yes, although I told him I would as lief wait until Brenda had been in her tomb a twelvemonth, but my Lord would have none of it. He felt it was Brenda's dying wish that we should wed immediately.'

178

'He would,' I said, sarcastically. 'Anyway, right now I need the bathroom, please. Quick.'

'Bathroom?' Delicate eyebrows puckered over the perfect nose. 'What is a bathroom?'

'Oh, hell. Little girls' room. The loo.' In the end, I resorted to rather indelicate language. She cottoned on quite quickly, and blushing, led me out of the room and down the stone corridor to a hole in the floor. It had a curtain across the front, yes, but a smelly hole in the floor was what it was. I drew the curtain across, and hung on tight to the walls. I didn't even want to think about what was below. Probably the moat, with the castle fish supply in it. Yuck.

I suddenly realised I was out of the locked room, my only guard a small, frail, shy little person who wouldn't say boo to a goose. She picked up the front of her gown daintily, and headed back along the passage towards my prison, expecting me to obediently follow her.

In a parallel universe, mate, I thought. I turned on my heel and ran in the other direction, down the spiral stairs, as fast as my legs would carry me.

Crisiant may have had a tiny voice, but apparently she could yell when it suited her, and she did. When I reached the bottom of the stairs, Edwall was waiting, and caught me as I catapulted through the doorway. I went straight into him, and didn't get a chance to hurl him over my head in a judo throw. I did manage to kick his shins quite hard, though, which made me feel a bit better, and then I was turned round and marched back up the stairs again, passing Crisiant at a window-gap on the stairways.

'Thanks a bunch, Crisiant,' I muttered. 'So much for sisterhood and female solidarity.'

She may not have understood the female solidarity bit, but she certainly knew what sisterhood meant. She followed Edwall and me up to the room, and I caught a glimpse of her stricken face as the door was slammed and locked in my own. Maybe I might have an ally after all.

CHAPTER EIGHTEEN

They fed me, at least, but the food wasn't up to much. Thick grey porridge. Still, my tummy was rumbling like an earthquake, and it filled the gap and gave me an energy boost. So then I started to worry about home. Suppose this time I really had been missing overnight? Dad would be frantic. I fretted about it for a while and then realised that I had enough to worry about in the here-and-now with a great medieval thug wanting to marry me.

After a while, a nervous serving girl escorted by a smirking man-at-arms brought me a sort of potty thing to use: obviously they didn't want to risk me making a break for it again. It was deadly boring being stuck in the tower room. There was nothing to read, nothing to do. I even started counting the stone blocks that made up the walls, but there didn't seem much point in that. At last my common sense kicked in, and I stopped wasting time and sat on the bed with my back resting against the wooden bed-head, trying to remember as much twelfth-century history as I could instead. If I was likely to get called on for the odd prediction, that sort of made sense. Trouble was, I had always been more interested in Charles II and the Tudors than anything. Of course, if I'd known I was going to end up like this, I'd have paid more attention, which was more or less the way I usually felt in exams. Only this wasn't an exam, it was for real, and since I rapidly discovered I was horribly ignorant about Henry II and all his works, I was going to have to wait for cues rather than spouting forth prophecy like the Delphic Oracle.

I wondered what was keeping Pendaran. Surely he must be worrying about me? The cottage had been in darkness when I'd crossed from my time, but even if he'd slept soundly all night and late into the morning, he should have noticed I wasn't there by now.

I was jerked out of my thoughts by the sound of the bolts being drawn. The door crashed open, and Owain Gwynedd, swaying slightly, and looking flushed and bleary, stood in the doorway looking as if he'd had gin on his cornflakes that morning. Every time I saw him he seemed to be the worse for wear, and this time he smelled like a brewery. Edwall lurked behind him, red-faced. I leapt off the bed, putting it between them and me.

Owain glared at me, rubbing his bearded chin. His hair was wild, and he looked more like a Viking than ever. His little piggy eyes crawled over me, so of course I tried to stare him down.

'What?' he said, eventually. 'This is your choice, Edwall? This untidy hoyden?' He crossed the room to stand close to me, peering into my face. 'She has a high opinion, Edwall. She will rule you unless you beat her down.'

'What?' I said, still stinging from that 'untidy' remark, 'him, rule me? Dream on, Edwall. Nobody bosses me around.' Which was hardly a tactful thing to say, given the circumstances, but I've always had this trouble with my tongue running away with me. As Mum says, 'Mouth open, brain in neutral, Angharad.'

Owain's open hand crashed across my face, knocking me onto the bed. I rolled over it, once more putting it between him and me. He'd hit me! I was flabbergasted.

182

'How dare you, you great, ugly bully!' I spluttered, longing to rub the aching place on my cheek. Owain lumbered round the bed towards me.

'Stay away from me, Owain Gwynedd,' I warned.

He laughed, and lumbered closer, his right arm stretching towards me, hand reaching to snatch at my hair. Almost as a reflex, partly because I was so mad, I suppose, I stepped inside his arm, grabbed it, reversed into him and hurled him over my back. He crashed into the corner of the chamber in a great, scruffy heap, and lay there blinking at me. And I didn't say sorry, either. Three cheers for Self-Defence for Young Ladies!

Edwall gasped, both hands covering his mouth, his eyes popping out of his head. Owain sat up slowly, shaking his head to clear it. He glowered at me for a long moment, and then a curious noise emerged from his hairy face, which I eventually identified as laughter. He rolled over onto his hands and knees, still looking at me, still chortling, and clambered awkwardly to his feet.

''Twas a fair throw, Edwall!' he wheezed. 'Watch yourself, boy. This one will best you. To hell with His Virtuousness! Marry her now, or she'll be off, mark my words. She'll give you fine sons!'

Edwall blushed, partly, I think, with pleasure, partly with relief because his father had taken his downfall quite well, considering. 'I must needs wait for permission, father. I shall not wed her otherwise. If the Archbishop consents, then her being a Wyrd Girl will not matter. Not if the Church blesses our union.'

'I don't care,' I said coldly, as Owain Gwynedd lumbered, shoulders still heaving with laughter, from the room, 'I don't care if the Archbishop of Canterbury, the

183

Queen *and* Elvis Presley all say you can, I won't do it. Read my lips, Edwall. I am not going to marry you. Ever.' I folded my arms and glared at him, still feeling ratty about that 'strong sons' bit. 'And if you try anything, I may just put a spell on you.'

He went white. 'You are no witch, Wyrd Girl. You promised me. You see the future, nothing more.'

I glowered at him. 'I may not be a witch, Edwall, but I still have the magic of herbs and potions. Take care that I don't feed you – I racked my brains, and then, suddenly another voice crept into my head – 'mouse-ear hawkweed, antimony, hemlock – and my secret ingredient!' You will never know, never taste it, but – boom-and-goodbye-Edwall!' I said.

'Boom-and-goodbye?' Edwall repeated, weakly.

'Boom. And goodbye.'

'My Lord?' A small voice came from the open doorway, and we both turned to see who it was. He wasn't very big: about four foot in his socks. His hair was carrot red, and freckles exploded like an asteroid storm all over his cheeky face.

'What?' Edwall said. Despite his fierce scowl, I got the impression from his tone of voice that he was quite pleased at the interruption. I was making him uncomfortable. Good!

'A messenger has come, Lord Edwall.' There was a tooth missing in front, which made the double-L sound doubly wet. His bright blue eyes flicked towards me, and he flashed a grin.

Edwall hurried for the door. 'Bar the door behind you, boy,' he ordered, and hustled away. I heard his feet slapping on the spiral stairs.

The boy and I stared at each other. I smiled. It was hard not to. 'Hiya,' I said. 'What's your name?'

The face split in a huge grin. 'Geraint, Lady.' He almost managed a bow, but his feet were too close together and he lost his balance and stumbled forward. Then he recovered himself and backed away. 'Is it true you're a witch?'

I pulled a face and shook my head. 'Not really. I'm just a bit weird, that's all.'

'Wyrd? How so, Lady?'

I sat on the bed and huffed out a breath. 'Well, I don't know, really, Geraint. I suppose I sort of know things before they happen. I knew Brenda was going to die the day before it happened, and that Owain was going to marry poor old Crisiant.'

The blue eyes flooded suddenly and his mouth quivered. 'Brenda was my Mam, Lady.'

I felt dreadful. Fancy me saying something like that! Impulsively, I held out my arms. He glared at me for a second, and then came for a hug. Only a short one, because he was a boy, and boys didn't apparently go in for them any more in the twelfth century than they do in the twentieth. Now me, I believe in hugs. A good hug cures loads of things, and helps lots of others.

'I'm sorry, Geraint. I didn't know.' Then an idea struck me. 'Geraint, if your mother was Brenda, then you must be Madoc's brother.'

He grinned. 'I am, Lady. One day, when I am grown, I shall go with Madoc. He has found a wonderful new land, far across the seas. I stole away to see him when I heard he had returned. He told me of the wonderful sights he saw on the voyage.' Gertaint closed his eyes

185

and hugged himself ecstatically. 'He followed a miraculous line of blue water, he said, across mighty seas, daring dreadful sea monsters, and the blue water led them to a wondrous land.'

I nodded. 'He told me. And there are people –'

He rushed on, taking over. 'There are strange people, Lady, with amazing copper-coloured skins, who wear feathers in their hair, and are brave and cruel, both at once. Oooh! I want to see them. Madoc is going back, and when I am grown, I shall go with him. He has promised.'

'He's not going back for a while, then,' I commented, smiling, 'if you aren't going until you're grown up.'

'He leaves in a month, Lady, when the *Gwennan Gorn*'s mast has been mended at Abercerrig Gwynion. And in a month I shall be twelve. My father has too many sons, and now that my mother is dead, I shall serve Madoc.'

'A month! Is that all?'

He nodded. 'Twenty ships will go with him back to the new land, Lady. And I shall sail in the *Gwennan Gorn* with my brother,' he finished, proudly.

I felt strange, uneasy. I wanted to talk him out of it. He was so young. 'It will be horribly dangerous, Geraint,' I began. 'The Atlantic has huge seas, miles bigger than the *Gwennan Gorn*. Even great passenger line-.' I stopped. Liners hadn't been invented yet. 'There are great sea creatures, terrible storms. You'll probably throw up all the way. Are you sure you want to go?'

'I'm not afraid, Lady. And I was really, really sick when I ate June mussels from the shore last year. I almost died. I'm not afraid of the sea. I'm going.'

186

I decided to change the subject. Maybe I could talk him out of it once I'd done a bit of research, found out what would happen to Madoc's new expedition. Twenty ships! I tried to picture the flotilla of little ships putting out of the tiny harbour, and couldn't. Anyway, my first task was to get out of the castle, fast. The door of the room was still open, but Geraint would get in trouble if I made a break for freedom, and I liked Geraint. Then a thought struck me.

'Geraint, do you know why I'm here?'

He nodded, solemnly, his eyes huge. 'Yes, Lady. You will marry Edwall as soon as the Archbishop says you can.'

I shook my head. 'Uh-huh. I'd rather poke myself in the eye with a sharp stick.'

He looked puzzled. 'Why would you do that, Lady? Edwall would be a good marriage for someone who is only a bard's daughter. Meaning no disrespect, Lady. Pendaran may be a bard and a druid and a fine and wise man, and know many beautiful songs, but he is not truly noble. My brother Edwall is nobly born, and strong and brave. But not as brave as Madoc,' he added, hastily.

'Edwall is a—. Oh, never mind.' I really would have to watch what I said. 'I just can't marry him, Geraint.' I racked my brains for a good reason not to marry Edwall, one that wouldn't upset Geraint. 'I've promised to marry someone else, and to marry Edwall would be wrong.'

He looked relieved. 'Oh. That's all right then. If you are betrothed already. I thought you didn't want Edwall because you didn't like him.'

Yeah, well. 'Oh, good heavens, no!' I lied. I put my arm confidentially across his shoulder. 'The problem is

187

that I'm going to be stuck here until either Becket says yes, and I have to marry Edwall, or someone finds out where I am and comes to rescue me. See? And I hate being locked up like this. It's boring for one thing.' And besides, five minutes ago I duffed over Owain Gwynedd, and sooner or later, when he sobers up, he might get round to feeling annoyed about that. 'And whatever the Archbishop says, I still won't marry Edwall.'

He nodded. 'Do you want me to help you to escape, Lady?' His eyes sparkled, but I could tell he was scared, too. 'If Edwall finds out, he will beat me black and blue,' he added.

He probably would, the big bully. 'What I want you to do, Geraint,' I whispered into his ear, 'isn't as bad as all that, honest. I just want you to tell someone where I am. Pendaran for instance. Or – Madoc, perhaps?'

He pulled away from me, and stared. A grin slowly broke over his freckly face. 'It's Madoc, Lady, isn't it? Madoc is the one you are promised to! Oh, Lady!'

Oh Lady indeed. I opened my mouth to deny it, and then the other Angharad gave a mighty push, so hard that my eyes probably bugged out. A tiny voice shouted at the back of my brain 'He's mine! He's mine!'

I couldn't say anything. I just smiled, weakly. The other Angharad was, indeed, in love with Madoc. Where before I had suspected it, now I knew. I wondered if Madoc did.

'So will you tell him? Or Pendaran. Either of them will do. Please?'

He nodded, slowly. 'Yes, I will. I must practise in the armoury this afternoon, but after that perhaps I could slip away. Just so that I am back by supper time. I must be here to serve my father at meat, or I shall get beaten.'

'Sounds like you get thumped on a fairly regular basis,' I said sympathetically.

He shrugged. 'What boy doesn't, Lady? But when I am grown, I shall not beat my sons.' He caught my eye. 'Nor my daughters, either, Lady. Even if they are wicked and lazy, and deserve it.'

'Glad to hear it. One day, Geraint, many hundreds of years from now, children won't be beaten at all. Well, not many of them, anyway,' I added, remembering newspaper horror stories.

Geraint looked uncomfortable. 'Is this true, Lady? Do you truly know?'

I nodded. 'I see the future, Geraint. I know.'

'However you see it, I am glad. Children should not be beaten.'

'And you will find Pendaran, and tell him?'

He grinned. 'Or Madoc, Lady!' And he was gone, leaving the door wide open. I went to the doorway and called after him.

'Geraint, you'd better lock me in, or Edwall will thump you for forgetting.' I heard his feet stop clattering down the stairs, and start clattering up again. Panting, he arrived at the door.

'Sorry, Lady.' He swung it shut, and I heard the heavy bolt slide across.

Now all I could do was wait.

CHAPTER NINETEEN

Waiting was still boring. I walked round the chamber clockwise, then did the same thing anti-clockwise. I tried to look out of the window when I heard a man shouting in the courtyard, but the arrow-slit was too narrow for my head. It stopped after a minute or so, anyway, so I lost interest. I looked around at my furnishings: a chair, the bed, and at its foot a beautiful carved chest.

It was in a new, light wood, as was the bed and chair. Funny, but I was surprised the wood wasn't blackened, old, and riddled with woodworm holes, but then I suppose the only medieval furnishings I had seen in my life had been in old castles and stately homes, where the furniture had centuries of dirt and grime ingrained into it. This wood was oiled, and gleamed like liquid honey in the shafts of sunlight slipping through the arrowslits. Intricate carvings of apple-boughs, with small woodland creatures peering between graceful leaves, looked as if they'd been carved yesterday. A light film of dust lay in the ridges of the carvings, though, so I used the end of my skirt to dust it, thus delaying the grime-of-centuries look by about a week, probably. Still, it helped to pass the time.

When I'd finished my spot of light housework on the chest, I got nosy and opened it. A flat, shallow tray fitted snugly just under the lid, holding a few small pieces of jewellery: cloak-clasps, brooches, pendants on chains and leather thongs. I suddenly had a wicked idea, and undoing the thong of my own necklace, I removed the metal Ban the Bomb sign and slipped it into the collection. That would be one for the archaeologists to puzzle over, if it ever turned up in a dig in my time! I lifted the tray out, to see what was underneath and discovered a gorgeous, fine blue wool cloak lined with dark yellow – saffron – linen lying on top. Lavender perfumed its folds, wafting into the air as I lifted it out, and beneath the cloak was a matching blue, fine wool gown with saffron, scarlet and white embroidery on it in a wonderful old celtic knot design. I lifted it out and held it up against me. It looked about my size. I'd hear anyone who came up the stairs – I just couldn't resist trying it on.

I slipped off my scratchy green sack-like dress and slipped the blue wool over my head. It was so fine that it felt like thick cotton, and the soft folds clung to my body. In the chest under the dress was a blue head-dress, but try as I might I couldn't work out how it was worn, so reluctantly I put it back. Whose clothes were they? They couldn't be Crisiant's, she was much too small. These had belonged to a taller girl altogether. I twirled and pirouetted, enjoying the way the soft wool flew out around me. I was so engrossed in what I was doing that I didn't hear the sound of feet on the stairs until it was too late. By the time I heard the bolts being drawn back there was nothing I could do but stand there, guiltily, wearing the dress, feeling like the worst kind of snoop.

The door hammered back, and Owain Gwynedd stood on the threshhold, grinning slyly. Then his face changed, and he took a step back, sketchily crossing himself.

'Brenda?' he said, nervously, and his florid face paled. He swung round, his feet tangling, and lurched out of the room, leaving the door wide open. I heard him crash clumsily down the stairs, bellowing for wine as he went.

Well, now I knew who the clothes belonged to! But the dead woman I had seen lying on the bed had been

191

old and fat. She would never have fitted into these in a month of Sundays unless she'd done some serious weight-watching.

But of course, she wouldn't always have been fat and old. I sat on the bed and thought about it. When Brenda had been a bride, coming, perhaps hopefully from Ireland, ready to marry the strange Welsh Prince of Gwynedd, she would have been slim enough to wear these beautiful clothes. Perhaps, once, when she had been young and beautiful, he had loved her. I hoped she'd been happy, at least for a while. Perhaps she had welcomed the mistresses that bore Owain Gwynedd his huge family. Perhaps she was glad to be relieved of his attentions. No one would ever know, now.

I slipped guiltily out of the gown and into my green sack once more, folding the lovely woollen stuff into the chest, replacing the tray and closing the lid. Then (slow, or what?) I realised that Owain's hasty exit had left the door wide open. I peered out, cautiously, ready to run back inside if anyone saw me. No one was there, and there was little noise from downstairs. The silence drew me out of the room and down the spiral stone stairway, which could have done with a good sweeping from a stiff brush. Cobwebs clung in the angles of the arched roof, many with large hairy spiders in occupation, and I guessed that Crisiant was not the housekeeper that Brenda had been, perhaps being too young to order the castle women about forcefully enough to make them de-spider ceilings. I kept a wary eye on the hairy great brutes: I am not a fan of large, black arachnids, and there were probably dozens of them queuing up to drop on my head.

At the bottom, where a stone archway opened into the great wooden-roofed hall, I paused. Three men dressed in drab brown tunics with badges on the front sat playing dice in the corner furthest away from me, and a slatternly girl with a runny nose used a ratty witch-type broomstick to sweep the soiled rushes lazily about the floor. My nose told me it wasn't before time, either. They smelled awful, and were probably full of discarded bones that the dogs hadn't finished, and much worse besides that didn't bear thinking about.

I decided my best option was to walk across the hall to the front door as if I had a perfect right to be there. Head up as if I owned the place, not sneakily. I took a deep breath and set out. I got half-way across before anyone noticed me, when one of the men looked up as I passed and smiled uncertainly. Of course, no one had actually seen me arrive: they had all been asleep when Edwall had dragged me inside. No one except the sentry on the wooden picket gate. If the shift had changed, then maybe I could get out without being stopped. If I was assertive enough. I could do assertive: we'd had classes in Personal Development in school.

The slatternly girl glanced up, gazed at me blankly with red eyes, wiped her runny nose on her filthy sleeve, and carried on sweeping. I hoped she didn't have a hand in the cooking.

And then I was at the door. The courtyard was empty except for four scruffy dogs chasing each other around a water-butt, a groom wiping mud off a horse with a handful of straw, and a smiling pig asleep in a smelly sty, her piglets attached to her like velcro sausages. At the gate, a sentry stood half-in and half-out of the wall, so that he could escape back into safety if danger threatened from outside, but was still able to poke out his head to see who was coming up the road.

Having only seen his feet on the night Edwall kidnapped me, I didn't know if it was the same one, but I had to chance it. Lifting my skirts daintily above my ankles to avoid some of the mud and slime that covered the cobblestoned courtyard, I sailed towards the gate trying to look regal, superior and as if I knew where I was going and intended to get there. The keeper stuck his head out.

'Open the gate, please.' I ordered. 'I wish to take the air.'

The sentry picked his nose, inspected what was on the end of his finger, and wiped it on the wooden gate. 'Why do I have to open this here gate for you to do that, Lady? Plenty of air inside, look.'

I decided attack was the best way. 'Mind your own business. Open the gate at once.'

'More than my life's worth, lady. You being Lord Edwall's intended, so to speak.'

Damn. He knew who I was. 'If you know who I am, then you will know that I may walk where I please.'

'Indeed you can, Lady, once His Reverence have spoke and you are safely wed to his Lordship. But they says that you ain't partic'lar about marryin' Himself. And if I let you out and you legged it, Lady, where to would I be, then? Up on the end of a rope with my heels in the air, that's where. If Edwall didn't decide to chop me in collops, first! I think you'd best go back inside, Lady, for you ain't getting out past me.'

I couldn't see anything else to do. I put my nose in the air and marched away indignantly. I was damned if I would go back into the tower, though. Well, not straight away, anyway. I walked around the outside, instead, and came upon a sunlit yard full of boys, an elderly man in battered leather clothes, and a straw archery target on a three-legged stand. The older boys had longbows, the younger ones smaller bows in rough proportion to their body size, and amongst them I recognised Geraint. He spotted me, flushed bright pink behind the freckles, and missed the target altogether when it came his turn to shoot. This earned him a savage clout round the ear from the man in charge that brought tears to my eyes, let alone his. Rubbing his crimson ear Geraint concentrated on the target this time, and hit the centre with a satisfying twang, swish and thud. I grinned at him, and made silent clapping motions. As the next boy stepped up to take a shot, Geraint slipped over to talk to me.

'What are you doing out of the keep, Lady?' he asked anxiously. 'Does Edwall know?'

I shook my head. 'Owain Gwynedd came up to see me a little while ago, and I was trying on some old clothes I found in a chest in the room. I think they were probably your mother's and I scared him. Maybe he thought I was a ghost or something, because he ran away and left the door open. I would have made a run for it, but the sentry wouldn't let me out. Have you managed to get hold of Pendaran or Madoc?'

He scuffled his toes in the dirt. 'No, Lady. I tried to slip away, but I couldn't. Cadwgan the sergeant at arms caught me and set me cleaning in the stables. I'm going to try again after archery practice. I'll do my best, Lady, but if anyone sees me slipping out, they'll sure as eggs find me a job to do. I don't get much free time.'

I sighed. 'Please do your best, Geraint. I really, really don't want to marry Edwall.'

'I understand, Lady.' His gappy grin lit his face, crinkling the freckles into one tan mass. 'If I was a girl, I'd rather Madoc, I know. Will you come with us on our voyage to the new land, Lady? Will you be Madoc's wife?'

The other Angharad shoved me so hard that my head ached. Nevertheless, I said, 'If he'll have me, Geraint.' She shoved again, and I felt sick with the pressure. 'I'm going back inside, now, before anyone spots me and drags me back. I don't like being forced to do things, I'd rather go back of my own accord with some dignity, and wait quietly in the room. Good luck, Geraint. Please, keep trying?'

He squeezed my hand and as I stood up, began to turn away, back to the butts. Then he swung round. 'It it true, Lady, that you bested my father? Threw him across the room as if he weighed no more than a feather?'

I nodded, solemnly.

His grin, this time, nearly reached his ears. 'Was it magic, Lady?'

'Sort of. But a sort of magic I could teach you, too. And then, one day, you wouldn't ever need to be beaten again.'

'If I go with Madoc, no one will beat me. You would not, I know, Lady, and Madoc has shown me kindness always. Madoc is a good man. You will be happy with him.'

This time, the other Angharad's grip on my brain hurt all the way up the spiral stairs. I had to do something about this.

'Look,' I said, firmly, when I had reached my prison and pulled the door shut behind me, 'I didn't ask to be here, did I? I came here by accident. Please believe me, I don't want Madoc. I like him, he's a nice man, and he's certainly dishy. I can see why you are in love with him, OK? The reason I keep coming back is that I intend to find out what happens to him, and tell him what the dangers are before he leaves for Ameri— for his new land. And then I shall go back to my time, and you can marry him, not marry him, marry Edwall, whatever you like, I don't care. But right now, since I'm in your body, and Edwall and Owain Gwynedd are both being complete pains, it isn't a good idea to keep giving me headaches. If you work with me to get us out of here, neither of us is going to end up married to Edwall. I'm sure you don't fancy the prospect any more than I do, right? After all, this is your body I'm in, not mine, if you think about it.'

There was a sort of silence, a blank spot in my mind while she did. Then my head stopped hurting, and I knew that she'd taken the point. Maybe now she'd work with me rather than against me.

I sat quietly in the room, and amused myself by sorting through the jewellery in the tray. Mostly it was silver, but there were a few twisted gold pieces with an Irish look about them, like the illuminations in the *Book of Kell*s. How strange that Owain Gwynedd hadn't passed the jewellery, at least, on to Crisiant. She couldn't have worn the clothes without altering them, they'd have swamped her, she was so little. But the jewellery wouldn't have been a problem, surely. I got the opportunity to find out a little later, because Crisiant brought me a wooden bowl of stew, a wooden spoon and some coarse bread at lunch-time, glancing nervously at me when she shoved open the unlocked door.

'Who left the door unbarred?' she asked.

'Owain Gwynedd paid me a visit. I was wearing his dead wife's clothes, and I suppose it spooked him a bit.' I ate a mouthful of stew: I think it was chicken, but anyway, it was hot and tasty and I was hungry. 'Look, don't run off. I'm bored stiff sitting up here on my own. Can't we be friends?'

She shook her head. 'Not until my Lord says we may. When you are safely married to Edwall, then we may be as sisters, although I shall be your stepmother. But I will stay a while and keep you company.'

'My step—,' I started to laugh. 'I suppose you would be, if I married Edwall. How weird! You can't be much older than me!'

'I am fourteen, Lady.'

Younger than me! That stopped me in my tracks. I'd thought she was about twenty, but of course girls matured and were married off at ridiculous ages in medieval times. I shivered at the thought of Crisiant at fourteen being married to Owain Gwynedd, who looked to be on the wrong side of fifty. But who could tell?

I decided to change the subject. 'I've been looking through Brenda's jewellery. How come Owain hasn't given it to you? Is he superstitious?'

Crisiant looked away. 'He says I must earn it, first.'

'Earn it? How?'

'The way a wife always earns her rewards, Angharad. By giving him children.'

My twentieth-century ideas about women's rights

were fighting to get out, but I fought them back. Whatever I said wouldn't be any help to her. I couldn't change what would happen to anyone I met over here in this time. Except perhaps Madoc, and now, Geraint.

If I could get safely back to my time and find out what was going to happen.

Crisiant stayed with me for about an hour, during which we chatted, taking care not to touch on anything difficult, skirting round awkward topics (like marriage, and children) as if they were bear-traps. And then, just before she left me, she said, suddenly, 'Oh, Lady, I cannot tell you how afraid I was when Owain Gwynedd wanted me, even before Brenda was dead. I wouldn't be his mistress, but I knew he was tired of Brenda. I was afraid he might harm Brenda so that he could have me. Oh, Lady, do you think he did? Am I married to a murderer?'

More than likely, I thought. 'Good heavens, no! What an idea!' I reassured her. 'I could tell the minute I saw her that she'd died of natural causes.' I couldn't, of course, but it made Crisiant feel better, and I'd decided I liked Crisiant. Or at least felt sorry for her.

'I am Owain's first cousin, Lady, which was why Archbishop Becket has excommunicated my husband. Our mothers were sisters. He will die cursed and unshriven, and all because of me. If only I loved him, perhaps I would not feel so badly, but Angharad, I cannot love him, no matter how hard I try.'

I took her hand and squeezed it. 'I can understand that! He's a prize-winning male chauvinist pig, is Owain Gwynedd.' I saw her blank look and changed the subject, quick. 'Look, Crisiant. You know that sometimes I know

199

what will happen in the future?' She nodded. 'Well, please believe me when I tell you that although Thomas à Becket excommunicated Owain because he married you, I know that he will eventually forgive him and let him back in the church again. OK? Honest.'

The relief on her face was incredible. That stuff really, really mattered to her. If I'd been married to Owain Gwynedd, I don't think I'd have cared one way or another about his soul. More power to the devil's pitchforks, as far as I was concerned.

'Oh, thank you, Angharad. I may never love him, but at least I am not responsible for his hell-fire and damnation.'

'You never were,' I muttered as she left the room, this time apologetically barring the door behind her.

The shadows were crawling up the inside of the wall, which was more or less what I was doing, when Edwall came for me, accompanied by a nervous woman half-hidden by a mountain of coloured fabric.

'You are to dine with us tonight,' he said. 'Esyllt will help you dress.'

CHAPTER TWENTY

Esyllt didn't actually help me much, she was shaking too hard. She seemed terrified of me. From the armful of dresses I chose a fawn wool robe belted with a thick cord, although a little devil deep inside wanted me to wear Brenda's blue and saffron, if only to wind up Owain Gwynedd, well and truly!

I washed my face and hands in the metal basin she brought before slipping the dress over my head, although I could actually have done with a nice hot shower, because I was itching. I had a sneaking suspicion that a medieval flea was using me as a walking snack bar. Esyllt handed me a bone comb, and I tried to wrestle it through the tangled mop that sat on top of my head. Fortunately the other Angharad's hair was fairly short. If it had been two feet long and hanging down my back like Crisiant's, I'd have been in trouble. The servant held up a sheet of polished metal while I combed, and in the murky reflection I didn't look too bad. Not that I wanted to impress anyone with my incredible beauty, especially not the likes of Edwall, but a girl likes to look her best, whatever the occasion.

I followed Esyllt downstairs, and she showed me to a seat at what was obviously the top table, since it was on the raised dais that Edwall had been sitting on playing 'look at me try to amputate my toes' on my last visit to try to recover the dragon disc. Below the dais, along two sides of the hall, benches stretched to the far door, leaving a space up the middle for the serving pages and girls to bustle around with ewers and dishes. A piece of coarse bread was at each place, together with a sharp knife and a wooden spoon. At least, everyone else seemed to have a knife. There wasn't one at my place. I grinned. I wasn't to be trusted with a knife, it seemed. *Owain Gwynedd's a scaredy-cat*, I thought, happily.

Edwall and Owain were already seated, and had their noses in their respective troughs. My seat was between them, and what with flying elbows and jet-propelled gravy slopped from the big lumps of coarse bread (which they were using as plates), it was a hazardous business just sitting there. The food smelled good, though, so I helped myself when the servant girl came round. Fortunately, it wasn't the runny-nosed one, who was nowhere to be seen. There was a big fish, which I thought might have been pike from the shape of what remained of its head. There were little birds, which I hoped were extremely small chickens rather than something wild, and something large, which I assumed was turkey until I remembered they hadn't arrived yet. So it had to be peacock or swan, neither of which I could bring myself to eat.

I tried some sour beer stuff, which was disgusting, and then switched to a sweet, honey-flavoured drink. I strongly suspected it was alcoholic, so I sipped rather than slurped. While I ate I ignored my companions and they ignored me. Crisiant sat on Owain's other side, her eyes downcast.

When I was full, I wiped my mouth with the back of my hand (they didn't run to napkins) and looked around for Geraint. It was a while before I spotted him, because I was looking in the wrong place, at the people seated at the long benches. Geraint, of course, was busy being a serving page. I spotted him at last, though, and managed to catch his eye. I raised an eyebrow, questioningly, and he nodded surreptitiously. I took that to mean that he'd managed to contact Madoc or Pendaran. So where were they? Why weren't they rushing to my rescue? Surely they weren't just going to knuckle under and let Edwall marry me as soon as Becket's say-so came through?

Owain tossed a large bone over his shoulder to a pair of deerhounds, which fought over it in the straw behind us, snarling and snapping. He wiped his greasy fingers on his jacket, rested his chin unsteadily on his fist and gazed at me.

'So, Wyrd Girl. Are you ready to marry Edwall yet?'

I didn't answer. Edwall pushed his trencher away and belched loudly. He leaned on his elbow, slightly unsteadily, and squinted at me.

'You couldn't be said to be beautiful, Wyrd Girl,' he said after a bit, when he'd focused, 'but you ain't ugly. I'm of a mind to have you whatever His Eminence says.'

Owain guffawed. 'Not so superstitious when you've a pitcher of mead inside you, Edwall. Are you not afraid that she will bewitch you? Turn you into a toad or some such?'

Edwall scowled. 'She isn't a witch. She sees the future, aye, and maybe she knows the plant lore, like the Physicians of Myddfai. Maybe she can cure the ague with treacle and hartshorn, or a megrim with rosemary and roasted hare brains, but she's no witch.' He glanced slyly at his father. 'She won't best me, even if she managed to flight you across the chamber like a bird on the wing.'

Owain snorted, and I was relieved to see that he could still see the funny side of his free-fall at the other end of my judo throw.

'Accident. I stumbled, that was all. She has spirit, though, Edwall. You'd best lock up your weapons,' he added, grinning.

I got fed up with being discussed as if I wasn't there at all. 'I don't care what Becket says, get this through your thick head, Edwall ap Owain Gwynedd: I will not marry you. Ever.'

I stood up, gathering my skirt up to keep it out of the smelly, stained rushes, and pushed the heavy chair away with the back of my legs, running it into a drowsy deerhound and making it yelp. I was about to turn and march indignantly upstairs when the big door at the end of the hall swung open and a familiar figure trotted in, a large cloth-wrapped object tucked under his arm. I sat down again, quick.

'Ah!' Owain said, losing interest in his son's love life. 'Pendaran. Are you come to entertain us?'

Pendaran bowed, and smiled. 'If it pleases you, my Lord.'

Geraint scuttled to fetch a high-backed wooden chair, and Pendaran sat in it and unwrapped the package, revealing a middle-sized harp which he propped against his chest. He smoothed his beard, and looked pleasantly at Owain Gwynedd.

'What is your pleasure, my Lord?' he asked politely, his hand poised over the harp-strings, one knee forward, the other tucked back.

'Your presence pleases me, Pendaran. It proves you bear no ill-will despite my son's bad behaviour. But what of the girl? My son is willing to have her to wife. How say you?'

Not that it made any difference what Pendaran thought.

He shrugged. 'If Edwall wishes to wed her, my Lord, and she will have him, who am I to object? If Edwall can make Angharad look kindly on him he will indeed be a fortunate man. My daughter is a rare woman.'

I opened my mouth to protest, but at a glance from Pendaran shut it again, quickly. What Pendaran said and what Pendaran meant were two totally different things, once I thought about it. I hid a grin behind my hand.

'So, my Lord, some music?' Pendaran rippled his harp, casually. 'What shall it be?'

'Something with a bit of go to it,' Owain muttered. 'Nothing mournful.'

Pendaran gazed at the roof for a few seconds and then swept his hands across the strings. Music tumbled into the air like butterflies, filling the room with tinkling joy, pasting smiles ranging from the gleeful to the vacuous all over the hall, depending on the amount of drink taken. When he'd finished that, he played another, and sang, his clear tenor voice ringing in the high roofed hall, bouncing off the stone walls, and the audience joined in the chorus which was extremely rude in places, a sort of medieval rugby song, which made Crisiant blush.

Pendaran played on and on, and I watched in an agony of impatience, wondering how he would get me out of there so that I could get back to my own time, back to safety and away from Edwall and Owain Gwynedd. Owain might be giving an impression of a big huggy bear at the moment, but I had a shrewd feeling that wouldn't last too long.

The men each side of me drank steadily, becoming more and more bleary, waving their pewter goblets in the air until I was soggy with sloshed liquid. I pushed my chair back, using my feet to scoot myself out of splashing range, and noticed that Crisiant had done the same.

'I think we should withdraw,' she whispered, softly so that Owain wouldn't hear. 'This is no place for women. We should retire and leave the men to their entertainment.'

'Not blooming likely,' I retorted. 'Pendaran's the only one who can get me out of here, and while he's here, I'm staying.'

Crisiant lowered her voice still further, and cupped her fingers over her mouth. 'No, he isn't, Angharad. There is another. Have you forgotten?'

I glanced at Pendaran, and saw that he was looking straight at me, a curious expression in his eyes. I raised my eyebrows, questioningly, and he jerked his head imperceptibly towards the turret stairs. He was sending me back to my room. I didn't know why, but I knew he wouldn't leave me there if he could help it.

I stood up. 'I'm going to bed,' I told Owain Gwynedd. 'Thank you for my dinner.' I could have kicked myself when I said that! But Mum always brought me up to say thank you when I ate out, and old habits die hard.

Crisiant slipped out of the hall and up the spiral staircase, me close at her heels, following the long, golden plait trailing down her back. On the upper landing, she paused. 'You cannot leave the keep without being seen, so it is no use trying,' she said clearly, and oddly loudly. 'Use the latrine before you retire. I will bolt the door of your room behind you when you have finished.' And she calmly walked to the door of my room and closed it, dropping the heavy bar across. Leaving me on the outside. Then she turned her back on me and walked away.

Bewildered, I stood in the cold stone passageway and pondered. She was giving me a chance to escape. But how? I certainly couldn't go through the great hall. Her voice drifted back to me.

'The latrine, Angharad. The latrine.'

I turned round and scuttled down the passage to the noxious, curtained hole in the wall. I reached out a hand to draw it back but a hand reached out from inside and grabbed me, pulling me inside. A tall figure, his blonde hair tied back with a leather thong, stood in the alcove. In seconds I was in his arms, and he was kissing me.

'Madoc!' I spluttered, when he let me go. The other Angharad gave me a spiteful shove. Well, I'd probably have done the same, in her position. Especially as I'd rather enjoyed it, actually. Unfortunately, she already knew that.

'Oh, Angharad! I was so afraid when you disappeared. I couldn't think where you might have gone until Geraint found me this afternoon.'

'I was kidnapped by that lout Edwall. He wants to marry me as soon as Thomas à Becket says he can. Fortunately the post is a bit on the slow side between here and Canterbury.'

'Post?' Madoc's forehead crinkled. 'I don't understand.'

'Oh, never mind that now. Can you get me out of here? Edwall's been knocking back the hard stuff all night, and I don't want him to start feeling romantic when he comes up to bed.'

'I would kill him first,' Madoc said angrily.

'That's not supposed to happen at all,' I said. 'Not as far as I've read, anyway.'

'As far as you've read? I don't –'

'I know, you don't understand. Look, can you just get me out? I'll explain later.'

Madoc produced a bundle and unwrapped it, revealing a long, dark, hooded cloak. He draped this over me, wrapping me up warmly. I had a horrible thought.

'You aren't thinking of lowering me down that latrine, are you, Madoc?' I said nervously. 'Because I think I'd possibly rather marry Edwall.'

Madoc grinned. 'No. Nothing like that. Well, something like that. But not the latrine. Even though Pendaran raised me, I know this keep well. Owain Gwynedd thought I was safely dead, if he thought of me at all, and what was one more page about the place? It was the way I kept in touch with my mother, and she with me. He never knew, until the last time, when he caught us embracing. Come on.' Grabbing my hand, he dragged me off down the corridor, past my room, to another one in the shadows of the passageway, almost opposite my own on the wooden-banistered balcony which ran round the inside of the keep walls, and tapped softly on the door.

It opened creakily, and Crisiant stood back to let us in. 'Quickly,' she said nervously. 'If Owain finds you here he will certainly beat me. Oh, hurry, please!'

Madoc towed me across the room to where a large tapestry hung on the wall, and tore it aside, revealing a large window covered by wooden shutters to keep out the cold night air. 'Thank God you chose the solar as your chamber, Cris!' he said. He unwrapped a coil of rope from his waist, and tied a double noose, slipping it over my shoulders and wrapping it round my rear end in a way I recognised. I'd abseiled down a cliff at Urdd camp, one year. It looked like I was about to do it again, down the outside of a castle keep, in the middle of the night.

Crisiant opened the shutters and I peered out of the window. 'What's down there?' I asked, dubiously.

'Geraint, holding my horse,' Madoc sounded faintly exasperated. 'Look, do you want to get out of here or not.'

'Out, please,' I said fervently. To Crisiant's obvious shock I hauled my long dress and cloak up between my legs like a nappy, and tucked it into my belt, leaving my bare legs free to abseil. This was no time to worry about modesty. When Madoc had tied the other end of the rope to the heavy iron ring on the chamber door, I clambered out of the window and down the rope, swinging into the pitch black night, my soft-soled shoes thudding almost silently on the stone walls. Madoc followed on, landing lightly beside me, although I could barely see him in the darkness. Seconds later the coils of rope snaked down from above, falling in a heap at our feet. Madoc gathered it up and coiled it, looping it over his shoulder.

'Take care!' Crisiant's voice floated down. 'God keep you.' The faint light from the solar window disappeared as Crisiant bolted the wooden shutters and replaced the tapestry across the opening.

Madoc caught my hand and peered round. 'Geraint? Where are you, boy?'

'Over here, Madoc!' The small voice sounded scared. A horse moved restlessly, and whuffled air through its nostrils. I caught a faint gleam of white and realised it was Geraint's face, reflecting the low reddish moon.

We were mounted in seconds, my arms around Madoc's waist, my face pressed into his broad back. 'Get back inside, now, Geraint,' Madoc whispered urgently. 'Give Pendaran the signal that we are away from here. Tell him we shall be hiding. We will not come back to the cottage where Edwall and Owain can find us.'

Geraint turned to go back around the keep towards the big door. In the darkness, his voice drifted back to us. 'You will take me, Madoc, won't you? When you go? I want to follow the blue water with you, Madoc.'

Madoc reined in the big horse. His teeth gleamed in the darkness.

'Aye, lad. You shall come with me. I will get word to you before we sail. You have courage enough for a grown man. I am proud to call you brother.'

I leaned down and kissed Geraint's soft child's cheek. Then Madoc kicked the horse's sides and we were away.

We rode deep into the woods behind Pendaran's cottage, uphill into the mountains, until the horse was blowing, picking its way between outcrops of stone. High up, hidden between great boulders, there was a cave, and once inside it, horse as well, Madoc lit a fire with wood from a pile stored at the back of the cave, draping our cloaks across the opening so that the glow couldn't be seen from outside.

'We'll be safe here,' he said, easing himself down beside the fire. The smoke drifted upwards, spiralling into the high roof. 'This is my place. I've known it since

I was a boy. No one else knows of it, save Pendaran, who showed it to me. No one will find us. In the morning, we'll head for Abercerrig Gwynion. I sailed the *Gwennan Gorn* there this morning for repairs to her masthead. It wasn't until I arrived back that Pendaran told me you had disappeared. He was frantic, thinking perhaps you had taken one of your turns, and were lying in the forest somewhere, half-dead. There are wolves, and even in summer they are hungry.'

I shuddered. I hadn't thought of wolves.

'And then Geraint came and told us where you were,' Madoc went on, tossing chips of dry wood onto the crackling flames. ' Did Edwall harm you? Or Owain?'

I shook my head. 'No. Although I gave Owain a bit of a shock. Threw him across the room when he wasn't expecting me to do anything other than scream and faint.'

Madoc looked disbelieving. 'You – threw Owain?'

I nodded, grinning. 'Yup. Self Defence for Ladies lesson one. It probably wouldn't work again,' I said modestly, 'not now he'd be expecting it. But it was very satisfying to do it just the once, all the same.'

Madoc eased himself across until he could put his arm round me. 'I think you should sleep, now.'

I felt very safe, warmed by the fire, comfortable with him beside me, and I wanted to sleep. But I couldn't. I lay wakeful next to him, and although he drowsed, he sensed my wakefulness.

'What is it, Angharad? Are you afraid to be alone with me?'

'Good grief, no!' I sat up, pushing my fingers through my hair. 'It's just that –'

CHAPTER TWENTY-ONE

What could I say? I was about eight hundred years too late for him? That my being there was a big mistake? That I had time-slipped from unbelievably far in the future and just wanted to pop back again to check on what would happen to him when he set sail for America? Sure he'd believe me. Not.

'I'm just restless, that's all,' I lied. 'Look, I'll try to settle. I'll just close my eyes. I'll try not to keep you awake.'

Madoc took my hand. 'I'm not tired. How could I be, when I am with you? Angharad, I know we grew up together, and that we are foster brother and sister. But there is no blood tie between us, and recently you have been so – different, somehow.'

You don't know how different, mate! I thought.

'Since I came back, you don't feel like my sister any more. You make me feel strange when I am near you. I am unhappy when I am away from you. I feel that life without you would be incomplete –'

Oh, hell. I didn't think I wanted to hear what was coming next. Being in someone else's body can be dead awkward sometimes. Also, I could feel the other Angharad prowling threateningly inside my mind. I got the feeling she was about to lose her cool. *Don't you dare!* I warned her, silently. *I can't help being here, now can I?*

I put my finger lightly across his lips. 'And Angharad,' I said, carefully, feeling her attention like a hand on my shoulder, 'Angharad feels the same.'

He looked at me curiously. The other Angharad approved. She didn't attack me this time, but I wasn't offering odds against a boot in the brain if Madoc got any more affectionate with me. That was something I had to avoid at all costs. Although... I shook myself. I was in enough trouble already without getting romantic with Madoc!

He opened his mouth as if to say something, but changed his mind. The silence was getting uncomfortable. I hate silences. I fill them the best way I can.

'Tell me about America, then Madoc,' I said. Oh, me and my big mouth. I could have kicked myself.

'A Merica? What's that?'

I sighed. I'd have to resort to the old 'seeing the future' bit.

'Madoc, I had a strange vision, and I found out that the place you found will one day be called "America". I had' (I crossed my fingers under a fold of skirt) 'one of my turns, you know, and dreamed that in hundreds of years' time, other sailors will follow your line of blue water and find it too, and they will name it "America".' It was the best I could do on short notice, OK?

Madoc sat up, excitedly. 'What? You saw my land? Then you know how beautiful it is. How brave the people are – and how fierce.'

I nodded, TV-fed visions filling my mind. Glass skyscraper canyons, wailing sirens, millions of scurrying people, New York, New York, so good they named it twice.

He beamed, and fell back, his arms behind his head. 'Oh, imagine, Angharad, a future in a great country like that – living in peace, side by side with the Mandan, for generation after generation. What an opportunity to take all that is good from Wales, and leave the bad behind.'

213

He reached across and picked up my hand, playing with the fingers, the leaping firelight gilding his face.

'We shall bring up our sons there, Angharad, if you will come with me. We shall build a house together, and not worry about whose land it stands on, because the land will be ours. Even now, the men I left behind are clearing woodland and building houses ready for their wives and children to join them.' He grinned. 'Except one or two, who have taken wives from among the new people, and will be happiest if their Welsh wives stay in Wales forever.'

Had I been the other Angharad, I might have picked up on the "our sons" bit: it was as close to a proposal as anything I've ever heard. I gulped. Keep him talking about America. That was the answer.

'Their wives are going back with you? Won't the journey be impossible for them?'

'Not impossible. Difficult. Dangerous. But not impossible. After all, I have reached Am-. What was it called, in your dream?'

'America,'

'Amerrrica,' he said, rolling the 'r' experimentally. 'America. Not as good as "New Gwynedd", which I named it. No, it shall be New Gwynedd, I have decided. Its name shall not be changed while I rule it. Where was I? Oh, yes. I have reached New Gwynedd and returned, at a cost of two men and a broken mast. No, Angharad. Not impossible.'

'What about when the weather's bad? Isn't it awful?'

He let go my hand and rolled onto his stomach, the firelight glinting on the smooth planes of his face. Propping his chin on his hands, he grinned, his teeth white in the gloom of the cave.

'Awful? No, not awful. Awesome. There was a storm early one morning, just after the sun had risen. We were so close to land we could see it like a dark, mystic shadow on the horizon – we were still following the miraculous line of blue water which flows from Wales to the new land, almost like a line of divine guidance, it is. Bedwyr was on look-out, I remember, and he had me woken in a hurry, I can tell you. The sky was a colour I've never seen before.' He shuddered. 'Nor want to see again, to be sure. The clouds were low, heavy as iron, and so dark, rimmed with purple and orange and yellow, as if the sky itself was bruised and battered. I looked where Bedwyr was pointing and there, on the horizon, was a vast spiral of cloud, dark as night, like the arm of some vengeful, warlike god, reaching down from the skies to the waves. It was like looking at the end of the world.'

He was describing a tornado, or a waterspout. I closed my eyes, trying to imagine it bearing down on the tiny boat. 'What happened?'

'We watched it. There was little else we could do. It wavered towards us, shifting its path here and there, like some terrible will-o'-the wisp. Some of the men prayed, some busied themselves battening down everything that might break loose if the thing hit us. One man lashed himself to the mainmast, his arms wrapped around it like a tree-trunk.' Madoc grinned. 'Not that it would have helped, had the thing's black finger touched us. But he had his eyes clamped shut, and his arms locked round the mast, and so much rope wrapped round him he could scarcely breathe. He was very good at praying, I remember.'

'It didn't hit you, then?' Silly question. He wouldn't be here if it had.

He laughed, and shook his head. 'It passed by with a roar like a dragon, not two ship's lengths away. We were tossed, and battered, and at one point we spun round helplessly in the whirlpool of its passing, but it missed us, praise be.'

'Weren't you terrified?' I sat up, hugging my knees, watching his face.

'Of course!' He laughed. 'There were so many times during the voyage that we believed our last hour had come. The great grey whale that almost sank us, for one. It came so close we could see its little round black eyes, and the barnacles that covered its huge back. It seemed to be watching us, assessing us, wondering if we would attack it. It was so knowing, somehow. I got the feeling it was as intelligent as any man on board.' He chuckled. 'And a lot more intelligent than some. It needn't have worried. All we wanted was to leave it in peace – and put as much distance as possible between its mighty tail and our little ship! Our very, very little ship. And there were rainstorms like nothing you have ever seen before, when the rain came down so heavily that you could not hear your own voice above the rain's roar, and it seemed that the ship might sink under the weight of water. There were waves like mountain crags, like Eryri, and the *Gwennan Gorn* climbed laboriously up them, and then fell down the other side, only to be faced with another mountainous wave, even higher than the first. There were winds that were like the pressure of a giant hand, so great that you could almost see them, and we felt them in our heads, like earache. Oh, many times we thought we had reached the end.'

'But still, you're going back.'

'Oh, yes. New Gwynedd is worth the risk. It is worth anything, any risk, Angharad. And, even amid the dangers of the sea, there are such compensations. Such beauty. The quiet of a calm sunset, the sky filled with colours that have no right to exist in nature; the magical, shimmering path of the moon on the water. And when the wind catches the sail just right, the *Gwennan Gorn* flies like a shearwater, skimming the tops of the waves. A company of dolphins escorted us one day, slipping along in the foam of the ship's passing. On days like that, it is good to be alive, and free, and at sea. On days like that, there is no life in the world better than that of a seaman.'

'How will you persuade the others to go with you? Especially those who've never been to sea before. I mean, seasickness is pretty horrible – I've been there.' I pulled a face. 'I can't imagine a journey in a boat the size of the *Gwennan Gorn*. I've been in –' I stopped. 'I mean, I'm a terrible sailor.'

He rolled onto his side, propping himself on an elbow. 'Oh, you'll get used to it.'

Wanna bet? I thought

'After the first few days, you will get your sea-legs. Your body will learn the rhythm of the swaying boat, and when you land in New Gwynedd it will take almost as long for your body to forget it. You will stagger like a drunkard when you set foot on land.'

Other Angharad? You listening? You're welcome to this particular experience, I thought.

'So, when you landed, where did you and the crew settle? Right next to the beach?'

'No. We stayed close to the sea only for a short while,

217

making small forays away from the *Gwennan Gorn*, getting our bearings, and then we took our coracles and set off upriver, although we left a small party of men with the ship for safety's sake. We travelled upriver, many, many days, until we came to a mighty waterfall, tumbling down a sheer cliff – so like home that we felt it welcomed us. We climbed up beside it, up a sheer, black cliff face, and halfway up, behind the mighty, tumbling curtain of water, we found a hidden cave where we camped for the night. We left the coracles there, rather than carry them any further, and when we return this place will be our lookout spot.'

'And the Ind— er, natives?'

He smiled, reminiscing. 'We met them almost by accident. We came face to face, suddenly, in a wood. I think they were as startled to see us as we were to see them. Coming upon each other like that, we met as equal men, face to face, and reached an agreement. They respect our ways, and we for our part respect theirs.'

'You were lucky,' I said. 'I don't think they're always so friendly.'

Madoc frowned. 'How do you know? You are so strange, Angharad. You keep talking as if you know these people. How can you? You have never been to New Gwynedd. You have lived all your life here.'

I sighed. It would be so much easier if I could explain time-slipping. But I couldn't mess up the real Angharad's life with complications like that. No, I had to stay with the visions, and I was going to have to explain. Well, try to, anyway.

'No, I've never been there. But you forget, I travel – um – sort of outside my body, sometimes. My mind goes

218

where my body can't.' A little white lie or three became necessary. 'When I have those strange turns, sometimes I glimpse a little of strange lands, like the one you have found. Sometimes I see the future. Right now,' I said, ruefully, 'I seem to be seeing more than I want. But there's nothing I can do about it, nothing I can change. Not yet, anyway. It's why Edwall calls me a Wyrd Girl.'

'Edwall!' Madoc scowled, shifting his position. 'He does not know you as I do. But these powers, Angharad. Do they allow you to see what happens to me in the future?' His voice was diffident, but he wasn't looking at me, or smiling. He was gazing down at his hands, the way people do when what they have just asked is much more important than they are pretending it is.

'No,' I said, honestly. 'It told me that you found your new land, yes. But it hasn't told me' *yet* I thought grimly, 'what will happen to you if you go back there. I am trying to find out, Madoc. But what if I see something awful happening? Would it prevent you going?'

He shook his head. 'Of course not. What sort of a man would I be to take notice of your silly visions?'

Honestly, I wanted to slap him, hard. 'But you expect me to go with you, anyway?' I asked, exasperatedly.

'Yes. And you will come, because you love me.'

Far back in my mind, a voice said *'Yes. Oh, yes, yes.'*

So that was that, wasn't it?

This is for you, Angharad, I said silently. *Not me.* 'Yes,' I said. 'I will, and I do.'

It's a strange feeling, getting hugged from inside. Rather nice, though. For once I'd done the right thing. And then I got kissed, on the outside, which was even nicer, although I had to pretend to myself that (a) I

219

wasn't enjoying it one bit, and (b) I was doing it *entirely* for the other Angharad. After all, she'd more or less just got engaged, hadn't she? I have to say, on her behalf, he was a very, very good kisser.

That didn't stop me needing to get away, though. I was exhausted, but I still had to get home. More so than ever, now, because I wanted to get back to my own time, find out what happened. My heart told me that he had returned safely to America, and settled there with his Angharad. My head told me nothing was certain. All sorts of things could have gone wrong on a second voyage. I needed another look at that reference book. And I was more than ready to say goodbye to the twelfth century for a while.

But here I was, stuck in a (nice, warm) cave, with a big (and very handsome) lug of a medieval sailor who kissed rather nicely, and there was no way he was going to let me get back to Pendaran and the wall into my time without his company. So I lay there beside him, his arm under my neck, his other arm resting across my body, snuggled up, my head on his chest, warm and comfortable – and very wideawake.

Fortunately, Madoc wasn't. Quite soon, he drifted off to sleep and was snoring gently. I waited until the light filtering in through the cloaks covering the entrance to the cave showed that it was morning, and then I slipped silently from his side, crept across the soft earth of the cave floor, collected my cloak and left him soundly sleeping. But first, I kissed him, softly, goodbye. For the other Angharad, of course.

Of course.

CHAPTER TWENTY-TWO

Outside, Snowdonia loomed all round me, the peaks like giant, brooding sentinels, and a huge bird circled lazily below me on a current of clear air. It was cold on the mountain so early in the morning, and the way down was rocky and uneven. There was no path to follow, but I at least knew that the way lay downhill, and even in the darkness of the previous night I had sensed that we were travelling more or less in a straight line, and not winding round the contours of a mountain. With luck when I reached the bottom I would find Pendaran's wood, and beyond it the jetty and safety. Always assuming I could keep out of the way of ravening wolves.

Once I was away from the mouth of the cave, out of sight and sure that Madoc couldn't hear me, I spoke aloud to the other Angharad. 'Look, mate,' I began, 'you must know the way down. You live here, I don't. So it would be in your own best interests to guide me a bit, show me the way sort of thing, OK? The quicker I get back to my time, the quicker you can snuggle up to Madoc in his cave.'

I don't know whether she helped or not, but I didn't lose my way at all. That's not to say it was an easy journey. Light, soft-soled leather slippers aren't meant for walking, and my feet were killing me by the time I finally reached the softer ground of the woods at the bottom of the mountain. Even my blisters had blisters, and my feet ached and throbbed. There was no clear path through the wood, either, but somehow I still didn't lose my way, and there was no slavering wildlife, so I think

221

maybe the other Angharad might have helped. It was a long journey, a couple of hours by the way the sun rose up above me as the morning passed, but at last, there was the cottage, and beyond it the way through the woods leading to the jetty. Clutching the dragon disc, I picked up my skirt and ran like hell, blistered feet and all, till I gratefully touched the side of Tŷ Pendaran and looked down on familiar muddy trainers.

How long had I been away? I shot into the kitchen, surprising Marged, who was just taking a fragrant fruitcake from the Aga oven.

'What's the rush, lovely?' she asked, peering over her glasses, which had steamed up.

'Oh, nothing. I just thought it was later than it actually is.'

She looked at me curiously. 'Oh, you did, did you? Well, there's nothing much you can do here. Go up and keep Myfanwy company. She's been on her own all afternoon.'

I took the stairs three at a time, so glad to be back not only in my own time, but at the right time, too, despite the fact that I'd been away for the best part of two and a half days. I softly opened the library door in case Myfanwy was asleep, but she was wideawake, gazing pensively out of the window towards the sea.

'You were in a bit of a rush, Hari,' she commented, without turning her head. 'You looked as if seven devils were after you.'

'No, only one,' I said, without thinking.

At that, she turned and looked at me. 'Is something going on? Is Penry bothering you? You can tell me, you know. If he is, then I'll speak to him myself. He isn't my best friend. I'll say what's on *my* mind. Unlike your Dad.'

I grinned at her. 'No, don't worry. Penry got the brush-off from me a while ago. He doesn't give up easily, though.'

She struggled into a sitting position, her hand resting affectionately on her bump. 'He really is a pain, isn't he, Hari! The first time I met him he chatted me up, would you believe! I had to be really rude to him before he'd stop. Honestly, some men think they're God's gift to women, don't they?'

'That one does,' I agreed. 'I suppose he's good-looking, in an older person sort of way. Laetitia seems to think so, anyway. But M –.' I just stopped myself in time.

'You prefer Rhidian?' Fortunately, she'd misunderstood.

'Mmm. Rhidian's OK. He's nice.'

'I'm glad you like him. It's good for you to have someone your own age to talk to while you're here. I'm looking forward to meeting your friend Ceri when she comes, too. When is it? Next weekend? It will be nice to have some more young faces about the place.'

I counted on my fingers. 'No, the weekend after.' And what a lot I would have to tell her when she arrived, too. *If* I told her. I mean, it would be pretty hard to accept, wouldn't it? She'd probably think I'd gone completely insane.

Marged came in then with a tray of tea, and we all had a cup and sat round making small talk. Honestly, it was so weird! Half an hour ago I'd been seven hundred years in the past, running, if not for my life, and least

223

from the traditional 'fate worse than death'. And now here I was, sitting in a twentieth-century library, drinking tea and munching Marged's buttery pikelets.

It took me a long while to shake off that sense of weirdness – a bit like the way Madoc described getting one's sea-legs and then losing them again, I suppose. Even the next morning, sitting in the warm, summery kitchen eating crisp toast from an electric toaster, and jam from a pot, and listening to the electric hum from the big fridge, and Roy Noble on Radio Wales, it still felt wrong, as if I were a visitor from a strange country, a stranger in a strange land. After my chores, Dad said that he was holding an extra session in the library during the afternoon, to help some of his students with special projects, so that he would be around for Myfanwy if I wanted to get away.

'D'you want to sit in, Rhidian?' he asked, but Rhidian shook his head.

'No thanks, I thought I'd spend the afternoon on the beach, have a swim. Would you like to come too, Angharad?' He didn't look at me when he asked, so I knew he really wanted me to go with him, but didn't like to push too hard.

I thought about it. I'd intended to hitch a lift into town, get to the library, but the appeal of an afternoon lazing on the beach in the sunshine was too much. It was so hot, the first really hot weather we'd had since I'd arrived. I'd hardly seen the beach, after all, and a swim sounded lovely. And it would be goodness knows how long before Madoc sailed. He had to get the mast fixed, and his provisions loaded, all sorts of things. There was time. I could afford just one lazy, beachy afternoon.

The sun was hot, and we found a secluded spot to sit away from the other beach-users. We could just see Tŷ Pendaran, set in its dark frame of woodland, and I lay on my stomach, sifting sand through my fingers, feeling the freckles popping up on my back in the heat of the sun. The thought of freckles made me think of Geraint. I hoped he hadn't been found out. I hoped Madoc –.

'Penny for them?' Rhidian said softly, rolling onto his back so that his head rested on the inside of my arm. I grinned down at him, squinting at the close quarters, which made my focus blur so that he had one eye in the middle of his face.

'Oh, they're worth much more than a penny, Rhid.'

'So tell me anyway?'

I shook my head. 'Nothing you'd be interested in, probably.'

He sat up, then, brushing sand from his long legs. 'Yes I would, probably,' he said crossly. 'You've been time-slipping again, haven't you? I can tell by the way you've looked since yesterday afternoon. Sort of preoccupied and far away. Go on, Hari. Admit it. You've been back.'

The urge to tell him was too strong. 'Yes, I have. And this time it was scary. I got involved in what was happening over there, and nearly ended up as Owain Gwynedd's daughter-in-law.' I told him the whole story, Crisiant helping me, Pendaran singing rude songs, Madoc rescuing me, Geraint risking a beating to help us escape his father and brother. I left out the bit about Madoc kissing me, of course. I may be daft, but I'm not stupid.

He listened, eyes wide. 'Crumbs. All that happened, really? You were away from here for two whole days?'

I nodded. 'Yup. Madoc rescued me, and I managed to get back.'

'Look, Hari, you won't keep on doing this, will you? I'm afraid something might happen to you back there. After all, from the sound of it something nearly did this time, didn't it?'

'You've changed your tune!' I said, indignantly. 'Wasn't so long ago you couldn't wait to send me back. "Do it again, Angharad," you said. Yes, things got a bit sticky, but –'

'But me no buts,' he said firmly. 'That was before I knew you were likely to end up in dangerous situations. If you keep dodging back and forth like this, something serious will go wrong. You have to stop it, Hari.'

'I know.' I tucked my hair back behind my ears. 'But I have to go back just one more time, Rhid, that's all. I need to get to the library, find out what happens to Madoc on the second voyage. Then I want to get back and tell him – maybe even warn him, depending on what the book says. And I want to make sure the other Angharad is OK, and that Madoc knows she loves him, and – oh, Rhidian, I have to know that Madoc and Geraint will be safe before I can stop. Then, I promise, I'll throw the dragon disc into the sea so that no one can use it ever again, least of all me.'

'Promise?'

'Promise. But I must go back again just once. I can't let them sail for America, all that way –' I smiled, remembering – 'following his line of blue water, without telling them how it all turns out.'

'I can understand that. But be careful, Hari, please?'

'Oh, don't worry about me, Rhid. I'll be OK.'

'But I do worry. Hari – when we finish here at the end

226

of the summer, and Myfanwy has had her baby, and we both go home, can we keep in touch? Please? I don't want to go away and forget about you.'

That made me feel funny, inside. I didn't want to forget about him, either. Gangly and clumsy he might be, and he never could keep his glasses on his nose where they ought to be, but Rhidian was special and I knew it. 'Yes. I'd like that. Maybe we can meet up, too. After all, you can drive, and I am going to learn, soon, so when we go to college . . .'

'What if we end up in the same college?' He grinned at me. 'That'd be fun.'

I thought about that. It might, indeed. I got up, brushing sand off my knees. 'Come on, lets swim.'

We swam, and splashed each other, and shrieked like kids, and kissed salty kisses, and for a while I almost forgot about the other Angharad, and Madoc, and time-slipping. We walked sandily home, our arms round each other's waist, and pecked goodbye outside the kitchen door. My shoulders were sore, my hair was wet and stringy, but I felt happy and relaxed, detached from the time-slip. My this-time life had taken over.

Penry Pritchard had obviously been spying on us, though, because he kept dropping hints about 'young love' over dinner, until Rhidian went red and gritted his teeth, and pushed away his soup without finishing it.

Penry carried on all evening, even in between the readings in front of the guests. He still hadn't stopped niggling at us even when Dad, Rhidian and I were in the kitchen making late-night cocoa for everyone, and Penry was (naturally) not helping, just standing, arms folded, dropping clever remarks.

Eventually, Rhidian had had enough. 'Look, Penry,' he said, 'no one mentions it when you go creeping around the house at night popping in and out of bedrooms.' (I noticed Laetitia turn purplish at that.) 'Just afford me the same courtesy, will you?'

Penry raised a sardonic eyebrow, and Dad spoke sharply.

'That's quite enough, Rhidian. Let's have a bit of respect for your elders.'

'Sorry,' he muttered. I squeezed his hand under the tablecloth. It didn't feel like a sorry hand.

'If we're talking about creeping around the house at night,' Penry drawled, 'it ill becomes you –'

I cut him off. 'He's referring to the night Rhidian and I were talking in my room, Dad. He's making nasty suggestions that just aren't true.'

Dad frowned. 'I'm not sure I like you having Rhidian in your room at night, Hari.'

'Why, don't you trust me?'

Dad went red. 'Of course I do, but –'

'Oh, then you don't trust Rhidian?' I said, sarcastically. 'D'you think he's some kind of mad rapist, Dad? Can't be trusted alone with your precious little girl?'

'That's enough!' he said, sharply. 'Carry this tray through, Rhidian, and let's hear no more about it.'

But my lovely day felt tarnished, somehow, thanks to Penry. The only good thing about it was that Laetitia had an expression like (as Mum says) a bulldog that's bitten a wasp.

Rhidian drove me into town to the library on the next day, using Myfanwy's car. Dad and the writing guests headed off in one minibus, while Penry and Laetitia the Locust took the other lot to do some sketching further along the coast, where they were going to have dinner and come back very late. By rights Penry should have gone with Dad, but Dad was still short-tempered, and Penry obviously thought Laetitia would be easier on him than Dad would be. From the glint in her eye as she sat beside him in the front passenger seat, I wouldn't have bet on it. She was probably still annoyed with him about the popping in and out of bedrooms revelation – or at least the fact that it wasn't her room!

Marged would stay with Myfanwy until she finished her work, and Myfanwy said she'd be fine on her own until Rhidian and I got back. We expected to be home by four o'clock at the latest, and Dad was due by five.

Rhidian had some messages to run for the guests, and he wanted to pick up the new Stereophonics CD he'd ordered from the music shop, and a couple of other things as well, so I headed for the library, arranging to meet him at the usual cafe for coke and doughnuts at three. The library was almost empty, and I found the Madoc book and settled down in the corner with it.

CHAPTER TWENTY-THREE

Madoc, I read,

'. . . *leaving his brother Rhirid behind in America to establish a Welsh colony, returned from his discovery of the new world beyond the sea full of stories of its wonders. He then persuaded a good number of his countrymen to return to the New World with him, and when his vessel the "Gwennan Gorn", damaged by the hazardous journey it had undertaken, had been repaired (it is believed at Abercerrig Gwynion, once a thriving seaport) he set off for his second voyage accompanied, according to various sources, by between twelve and twenty other vessels. Questions have been raised regarding the likelihood of such small vessels successfully crossing the Atlantic, and some academics have dismissed the idea as impossible. However, if Madoc had been caught up in the Gulf Stream Drift, which skirts the Northern coast of Wales, he could have followed this current all the way to America, most likely making landfall on the shores of Mobile Bay, Alabama, in the Gulf of Mexico.'*

The Gulf Stream! Of course! Madoc's 'line of blue water'. I closed my eyes, picturing the tiny *Gwennan Gorn,* tossing in the terrible seas Madoc had described. I still couldn't imagine it: I'd crossed to Northern Spain in a force nine gale, in a huge great passenger ferryboat, and I'd been sick as a dog. I'd taken to my bunk and stayed there, surrounded by a mountain of sick-bags, for the twenty-four hours it took us to reach solid land, and Mum had had a hell of a job getting me back on board when the holiday was over. It had been horrible. And yet Madoc had managed a far longer and more dangerous crossing in that tiny, insignificant little boat.

'The vessel "Gwennan Gorn" was possibly a captured Viking longboat, since the Mandan Indian tribe, with which Madoc and his countrymen are believed to have made contact, recorded in their earliest legends and pictograms that a "Lone Pale Man" came in a great "war canoe" bearing the head of a great beast on its prow. Viking raids on Anglesey and North Wales were common in the eleventh and twelfth centuries and it is likely that one may have been taken by the Welsh. The "Gwennan Gorn" would probably have been clinker built (of overlapping planks), made entirely of wood fastened together with wood or horn pegs. Iron implements were not used on board, partly because their weight added to the risk of capsizing, and also for fear that they might confuse the rudimentary compass, or lodestone, which, together with the positions of the stars, would have been their only navigational aids. The boat would have been widely curved, with either one or two proportionate square sails, and might have been sufficiently buoyant to survive all but the most swamping seas. It is possible, therefore, that this legendary voyage may in fact have taken place, especially when one adds the evidence of the 1897 voyage in a rowing boat between New York and the Scilly Isles. That voyage took 55 days.'

I closed the book on my finger while I thought about that, remembering Madoc, filled with enthusiasm, telling me about his vessel. What had he said? Oh, yes – 'built from the finest Gwynedd oak, and her planks are *fastened with nails made from the horns of stags that roamed the Gwynedd hills'.* Not a stolen Viking longship, then, but built by Welshmen. It felt strange, knowing something the historians weren't sure about. I went back to the book.

'When Madoc first made landfall on Mobile Bay, Alabama, it is believed that he made his way up the Alabama River, establishing a lookout at the confluence of the Alabama and Coosa Rivers, behind the majestic De Soto Falls. It is recorded that Post-Columbian explorers discovered rotting leather armour and coracles behind these falls, and it was discovered that the Mandan Indians used "bull-boats", coracle-type boats remarkably similar to those found even today on the rivers of Wales.'

So Madoc's 'great waterfall' was identified for me – as well as his look-out cave. One day, I might even visit it. A shiver of excitement went up my spine. I would get there, somehow. I couldn't wait to tell Rhidian. Maybe we could go together. I buried my nose in the text once more.

'Further evidence for the establishment of a Welsh colony there in the early twelfth century is found in the existence of the Old Stone Fort on the Duck River, Tennessee. This triangular fortification covers an area of about fifty acres. It is a twenty feet high by twenty feet thick wall of stone, shale and flint, in almost all respects identical to ancient ruins in Wales.

It is surrounded by a moat, and this fort, together with those at De Soto Falls and Fort Mountain, are unlike anything hitherto discovered attributed to Native Americans.

Additionally, during excavations to construct cellars near Old Stone Fort, Roman coins were unearthed, and it is a well-established fact that Roman coins were minted in Wales during the Roman occupation of Britain. It is possible that these particular coins may have travelled to the New World aboard the "Gwennan Gorn".'

Goose pimples rose on my arm. All this proof – as if I needed any. I knew that Madoc had reached America. So why was Christopher Columbus getting all the credit? Good grief, a few years back – when was, it, 1992 – they'd celebrated the five hundredth anniversary of Christopher Columbus making landfall in America, and made a real fuss over it. And yet Madoc got there first! Didn't seem right, somehow. I flicked to the back of the book, riffling the pages. Not much more, then I'd know it all.

'Further evidence of a Welsh colony established in America is given by the evidence of early settlers who wrote extensively of a tribe of "white Indians", many with fair or blonde hair, who used coracle-like bull boats and whose language included many words bearing a great resemblance to the Welsh language. Sadly, it is known that the Mandan tribe, through intermarriage and outbreaks of disease (possibly smallpox introduced deliberately by white settlers), is virtually extinct, and only the very diluted remnants of their tribal characteristics remain for comparison. In the absence of scientific proof, therefore, the tale of Madoc ap Owain Gwynedd must remain merely a legend.'

What? What was he on about? All that evidence was good enough for me – the coracles, the white Indians, the Roman coins, the old stone forts – what did the guy want, letters of fire or something? Of course Madoc discovered America. But he hadn't finished.

'*What became of Madoc and his expedition of tiny vessels must remain pure speculation. After sailing from (it is believed) Abercerrig Gwynion (although some sources suggest he may have sailed from the now vanished small settlement of Pendaran, near Rhos on Sea, nothing further was ever heard of him or his valiant companions. It is likely, therefore, that while his brother Rhirid, who had remained behind in America, settled and colonised the area, inter-marrying with the Mandan tribe, Madoc, braving the fury of the Atlantic for a second time, perished at sea, together with all who accompanied him.*'

Coldness crept up my spine. What? Madoc what? Perished? He couldn't have! Madoc was fine, I'd seen him just the day before yesterday. *Yes, you fool,* my inner voice said *but that was before he set sail for New Gwynedd on his second journey.*

No! It couldn't happen. I wouldn't let it. I had to get back to Tŷ Pendaran and the wall, go back, warn him, tell him not to go. I slammed the book shut and sprinted past the startled librarians, down the steps of the library and along the street to the cafe, ready to drag Rhidian out, make him drive me back. He wasn't there. I looked at my watch. He wasn't due for another hour, and I hadn't a clue where he was.

Raking my hair despairingly back from my face, I looked around, hoping against hope that I'd see his gangling, clumsy figure wandering towards me, early for once. No such luck. What I did see, though, was a bus. The one bus that went from Rhos to Pendaran, once a day, every Tuesday if there was an R in the month and it wasn't raining. Talk about luck! I was miles from the stop, but that didn't matter. I flung myself into the road in front of it, waving my arms. It screeched to a halt, inches away from me, and with a muttered apology to the driver/conductor, I climbed on board.

'You could have got killed, you could, doing that,' he muttered as I paid him the last one pound fifty I had in my purse. 'I could have run you down flat.'

'I know, I'm sorry. But I have to get back home, quick, it's urgent. I knew if I let you go past I'd never get to the stop in time. I'm really sorry, honest.'

He sniffed, and put the bus into gear. I'd be willing to swear in a court of law that he drove that bus deliberately slowly. He didn't go over fifteen miles an hour the entire way home, and we crawled past fields, trees, houses, shops, until I was ready to scream.

At long last he pulled into the stop in the village, half a mile from Tŷ Pendaran, and took about ten minutes, I swear, to open the bus door. I almost fell down the steps, and put my head down, my back-pack bumping my spine, and ran for it. I intended to go straight to the jetty, timeslip, find Madoc and warn him not to risk it. I groped at my neck while I ran, feeling for the security of the dragon disc.

It wasn't there. I skidded to a halt, panting and panicking, then remembered that I'd taken it off when I'd showered that morning, and popped it in the china tray on my dressing table. I had to go back to the house first, then. I knew I could timeslip without it, sometimes, but I didn't want to risk it now. Not now, when there was so much at stake. Lives, even.

I reached the bottom of the dusty beach road leading to Tŷ Pendaran and had to stop, doubled over with a stitch. When I got my breath back and the agony eased, I set off again, wheezing faintly, specks of over-exertion floating before my eyes. When this was over, I'd need to stop eating Marged's apple teabread . . .

I reached the house puffing like an ancient walrus, flung my backpack onto the hall floor, and sprinted up the stairs. I raced into my bedroom, grabbed the dragon disc and headed back downstairs again.

That was when I heard the panicky voice calling from the library.

'Hari, is that you? Oh, Hari, please, I need you!'

I thought about pretending I hadn't heard. But there was something in her voice: I couldn't ignore her. Gritting my teeth with fury and impatience I opened the library door. 'What, Myfanwy?'

'Oh, Hari. I think the baby's coming!'

'What?'

'The baby's coming. I'm scared, Hari.'

'I'll get Marged. Stay there, Myfanwy.' As if she was going anywhere!

'Marged's gone. And about an hour ago your Dad rang to say the minibus has broken down and he's going to be late. I didn't tell him, didn't want to worry him. I thought I could get downstairs, ring the hospital, get an ambulance, but I couldn't.' She grabbed her bump, suddenly, and fastened her teeth in her lower lip.

'What, what? What's happening, Myfanwy?' I yelped, panicking. She went very quiet, breathing slowly and calmly, in-in-in, out-out-out. When she relaxed and let go her bump, she said, 'Just a contraction, that's all.

236

Only they're coming quite quickly now, and they're lasting a long time. I think the baby's nearly here.'

'I'll phone an ambulance.'

'No, there isn't time. Don't leave me, please!'

'I've got to, Myfanwy. Don't be daft. I can't do anything! You need a doctor or a midwife or something.'

'There isn't time, I tell you. Trust me, Hari, I know. You'll have to do it. I can feel the baby. It's coming now. Help me on to the floor, hold my hand.'

'Look, I'll get some towels from the linen cupboard, and phone an ambulance.' I helped her onto the floor so that she was sitting, knees bent, her back resting against the sofa, then I sprinted across the hall and into the linen cupboard, scooping armsful of sheets and towels and some spare pillows. I propped Myfanwy up, hurling the towels at her.

'Now I'll go and phone.'

Myfanwy's face was purple with effort. 'Noooo – tiiiiime!' she grunted. 'Dammit, will you listen, Hari! Can't you see I'MMM HAVING THE BABY!'

I pushed Madoc firmly to the back of my mind. This was now. This was urgent. This was important. There would still be time to warn him, wouldn't there? Time was so flexible, so different. I was probably panicking over nothing. I took a deep breath. And hoped.

'All right, all right,' I said, soothingly, 'no need to lose your temper.' I knelt down next to her, feeling utterly useless. What did I know about helping babies get born? I'd never had one, had I?

Then I remembered the film I'd watched in Year Nine at school. The one when three boys fainted, and one of the girls had hysterics, silly cow. Childbirth was

237

straightforward so long as no one panicked. I could do calm. I was good at calm. And suddenly, amazingly, I was. I took a deep breath and felt my heartrate slow. I was In Charge. Capable. Ice-cold and Coping.

I don't know where it came from. It was as if the wisdom and patience of ages was suddenly inside my mind. And then I knew. The Wyrd Girl. *She* knew. She must have seen lots of births, helped, probably. She'd known about the raspberry leaf tea, hadn't she?

I got Myfanwy to lie down, her shoulders and lower back propped on the pillows, and got her to lift her hips so that I could slide towels underneath her. At frighteningly fast intervals, the mighty contractions took her again. She didn't scream or cry, though, the way they do in the movies. It was as if she was battling against a high wind, or climbing an invisible mountain. She got this look of deep concentration on her face, turned faintly purple, then darker purple, and grunted deep in her throat with the effort of it. It looked like *bloody* hard work. In between, she got her breath and rested. I felt like we were part of a team. We even made jokes – in between the scary bits, that is.

I thought it would be over quickly once I could see the wet, dark circle that was the top of the baby's head. I thought the baby would pop out like a cork from a bottle. But it didn't. It took long, long, hard time, forever, it seemed, and yet it somehow passed in a flash. I was so calm! I held her hand, breathed with her, laughed with her in the short (and getting steadily shorter) intervals between contractions. Despite everything, it was exciting, exhilarating, and somewhere along the line, I discovered that I liked her. For herself.

Despite her being my Dad's new wife that I used to be jealous of. Not because I was in charge and she needed me. She was kind, and brave, and tough, and hey, this was MY new baby sib!

And then, at last, she gave one last, mighty push and the head was born. I made her pant in and out like a dog while I checked that the cord wasn't around the tiny red neck and then, just as the rest of the baby – it was a boy – slithered out, red and squirming and bellowing his head off, I remembered to tie the cord in two places (I used bits torn off sheets – not sterilised, but clean enough, I hoped) and cut between the ties with the embroidery scissors Myfanwy had been using. Then I wrapped the baby in a towel and gave him to her. She cried a lot, then, and so did I, but it was happy, silly, giggly crying, and we hugged a lot. He was a gorgeous baby. He had a mop of curly hair and a nose like a button mushroom, although his eyes were tight shut. His mouth was about the prettiest thing I'd ever seen, especially when he stopped bawling, and I felt this great, impossible, incredible, amazing *swell* of love for him. And if I felt like that, what must Myfanwy be feeling?

'I'll go and phone the ambulance,' I said at last, when we'd both had a good admiring session. 'I think you need to get to hospital. Bit late, I suppose, but that's the way it goes.' I grinned at her. 'But hey, Myfanwy! We coped!'

She grinned back, but there ere tears in her eyes. 'We did indeed, Hari. We coped.'

I tripped downstairs, feeling on top of the world, and phoned the ambulance, then filled the time it took to arrive with collecting the hospital bag she'd packed and leaving a note for Dad when he finally got back. It was there within twenty minutes, and half an hour later Myfanwy and the baby were admitted to the maternity ward at Rhos-on-Sea. I went up to the ward with her, settled her in, was thoroughly praised and made much of by ambulancemen, nurses, midwives and a rather dishy young doctor, and was then dismissed while they gave Myfanwy and the baby a thorough check over. I grinned, sitting in the waiting room. I had a new baby brother, and I had helped deliver him. Wow. I also had a new friend in my stepmother. A bit of a drastic way to go about it, I suppose, but it felt good inside. I was still, for some reason, slightly out of breath. Vaguely, I remembered running, rushing somewhere, before all this happened, before I'd been taken over, caught up in the excitement of the birth. But then Dad arrived, hot and panicky and I had to calm him down and reassure him. He went off to find a nurse to take him to Myfanwy and the baby, and –.

Madoc.

CHAPTER TWENTY-FOUR

Memory rushed over me like a waterfall. How could I have forgotten so completely? I borrowed money from Dad and phoned for a taxi to take me back to Tŷ Pendaran. Waiting in the hospital foyer for it to arrive, I tried to calm myself. To forgive myself for forgetting Madoc in the need to take care of Myfanwy and her baby. The panic and emergency of the baby arriving had driven him from my mind as surely as if I'd been hypnotised.

Surely Madoc *couldn't* sail before I got there? There had to be some purpose in all this, some meaning behind my time-slipping. Why, otherwise, had I been the one to discover the disc and its amazing abilities? Why not Dad, or Marged, or Rhidian? Why me? I tried being reasonable, talking sternly to myself, telling myself not to panic. Of course I would get back early enough to warn Madoc, to prevent him from sailing the second time. I had to. He might not listen to me, but at least I could warn him. Then he wouldn't take risks, he'd take care. As if he could 'take care' in a tiny boat in the middle of a ferocious sea.

The taxi arrived, and I sat in the battered back seat, clinging tensely to the ratty strap, swaying from side to side as the Jack-the-lad driver tried to chat me up, failed miserably, and then tried to impress me by driving like a lunatic instead. At least he got me back to Tŷ Pendaran in one piece. Scared stiff, but in one piece. I paid him, and the car rocketed off down the beach road, sending up clouds of dust in its wake.

I slipped into the cluster of bushes, into the dim greenness, clutching the disc ready to step on the wall. Crossing here, close to the house, I would be closest to the *Gwennan Gorn*: if he was still there, I could stop him sailing straight away. I rounded the thick patch of bushes, full leafed now with high summer, and ran straight into Rhidian. Rats. Now I would have to explain, which would mean more time lost.

'Oh, Angharad!' His face was relieved. 'I thought you'd time-slipped again without telling me. I couldn't work out what had happened to you when you didn't turn up at the cafe. I hung around for ages, went to the library, asked just about everywhere before coming home. I was afraid I was going to have to tell your father I'd lost you.'

'Lost me? You make me sound like a parcel or something.'

'Well, you do have this habit of disappearing, don't you?'

'Look, Rhid. Have you been inside the house since you got back?'

He shook his head.

'Then you don't know. Myfanwy's had the baby.' I grinned, filling up with pride despite my panic. 'It's a boy, and I delivered him. Me and Myfanwy. We did it together, all by ourselves, and then I called an ambulance. She's in hospital.' It was gratifying, seeing his jaw drop open. 'But right now, I don't have time to talk, Rhid. I have to get back to Madoc.'

He wasn't listening. 'What? You delivered it?'

'Him.'

'It, him. You did it?'

242

I nodded. 'Yes. But Rhid, I really have to –'

'Wow. Were you scared?

'Too busy to be scared. Look, Rhid. Not now, OK? I'd love to stay here and tell you all about it, but there's something I have to do. Trust me, it's a matter of life or death.'

He looked suspicious. 'What is? You're going to time-slip?'

'Yes. But I must do it *now*.' I tried to push past him, but he barred my way.

'Well, it's fairly obvious you found something in the Madoc book. What was it? According to the librarian, you took off from there like a bat out of hell, *and* without putting the book back on the shelf. So, what?'

'I don't think Madoc makes it, Rhid.'

He looked blank. 'What do you mean, he doesn't make it? You met him, didn't you? So therefore he makes it, right?'

'Wrong. I met him, yes. I met him before his first voyage, then again when he came back. And then just before he left for his second voyage. According to the book, he left Wales the second time and was never heard of again.'

'How do they know?'

I glared at him, exasperated. 'What do you mean, how do they know? He sort of drops out of history, Rhid, that's how. He disappeared at sea, somewhere between Wales and America. Or else he got there safely and was never heard of again. But according to the book, the *Gwennan Gorn* most likely sank in rough seas on the second journey.'

He shoved his glasses up his nose and peered at me

through them. 'So what do you think you can do about it?'

I stared at him, disbelievingly. 'If I go back, I can warn Madoc, stop him going, can't I?'

Rhidian shook his head. 'Doubt it. That would change history, wouldn't it? It's the old faithful time-machine problem.'

'What do you mean?'

'You know that old sci-fi brainteaser. If you could go back in time to before Adolf Hitler was born, would you kill his mother so Adolf would never arrive? Thus preventing World War II and the concentration camps.'

I stared at him. 'But no one has ever been back before.'

'How do you know?

'Well, because . . .' I frowned. 'I don't, do I?'

'No. You aren't going to tell anyone that you've done it. You'd get carted off to the funny-farm if you did. Who'd believe you, after all?'

I made up my mind. 'I don't care, Rhid, I've got to try, at least. I can't just sit back and let him go. He's going to take Geraint. He's only a kid. I can't let him risk it. All those people – maybe twenty ships, each with about twenty people on board, I expect. All drowned. No, I don't care what happens. But I've got to try.'

'I wish I could come with you. I could at least keep an eye on you. Help you persuade Madoc not to go. Talk the neanderthal man out of trying to marry you. What was his name?'

'Edwall.' I'd almost forgotten about Edwall. That would make it doubly hazardous, going back. Trying to warn Madoc and avoid Edwall. Still, I had to try.

'Edwall. Look, if you are serious about trying to stop Madoc, maybe I can come with you then – if I hold your hand.'

'We tried hand-holding, remember? It didn't work.'

'Try hugging then. Please?'

'All right. But come on. I can't bear the thought of him sailing and not knowing.'

We went deeper into the bushes, and Rhidian put both his arms round me while I grabbed tight hold of the disc. With a sort of sideways hobble, we stepped simultaneously onto the wall. Maybe this time . . .

But when the whiteness of sound and vision had cleared, I was once more alone on the jetty. The evening sun was a ball of red fire on the horizon, streaking the sea with colour, the weather set fair except for a few small purple clouds partially veiling the sun. The great iron rings which had tethered the ship to the quay hung empty. There was no sign of the *Gwennan Gorn*.

Nausea hit me, and I swayed. Was I too late? Stunned, I stood for long minutes gazing hopelessly at the empty sea. A seal's head rose from the water a few yards away, and inquisitive eyes in the sleek black head surveyed me. I felt very alone.

And exposed. I suddenly remembered Edwall and his habit of scooping me up from behind. The safest place for me was probably out of sight at Pendaran's cottage. Picking up my skirts I sprinted to the end of the jetty, and keeping in the darkening shadows of the trees I hurried through the woods as quietly as I could until I reached the familiar small cottage. I crept round behind it, and listened at the hide-hung window opening. If Edwall was inside, waiting for me, I didn't want to walk

245

in and let him get me. I might not be able to escape next time. Especially without Madoc to help me.

But the cottage was silent, save for a soft snoring noise. I slipped round to the door, and eased it open on the latch. Pendaran lay huddled by the embers of the fire, nestled in sheepskin, curled in a ball, the red glow painting the thin, sharp bones of his face. He looked like a small white mouse. I tiptoed towards him, and almost jumped out of my skin when, without opening his eyes, he spoke.

'You are back, Angharad. When Madoc said he had taken you from Edwall, I was glad, for though you are foster brother and sister, there is no tie of blood to complicate matters, and Madoc loves you. But your turns are happening more and more. I worry that one day you will find it impossible to come back.'

'Come back?' I hedged.

The old man sat up, passing both hands across his face, the heels of his hands rubbing the sleep from his eyes. 'Come back. When the moods are upon you, Angharad, you leave us. Oh, not in body. But you are strange, afterwards, and you know things that no mortal could possibly know without the magic of the Old Ones. Whatever, I ask no questions. But you agreed to go with Madoc to his new land. Why have you come back? Our parting was painful enough the first time. Must I suffer it again?'

I had no time to explain. 'Where is the *Gwennan Gorn*, Pendaran?'

'And that is another thing. I have always been "Father". But lately, it is "Pendaran". You have changed so much, Angharad. Sometimes you are like a stranger.'

'OK, Father,' I said, not caring what I called him so long as I found out where Madoc was.

Pendaran sighed. 'Oh, Cei again. Is this person the reason you reject Madoc, Angharad?'

'Reject M—. Oh, for Pete's sake,' I exploded. 'I haven't rejected anybody! Will you tell me where Madoc is? Please, Pendaran. Father. It's more important than you'll ever understand.'

He climbed laboriously to his feet, easing his aching back. 'Madoc? But you have left him. Do you care what becomes of him?'

'Pendaran,' I said, putting menace into my voice, 'I care more than you'll ever know. If you don't tell me where he is, I'll, I'll –'

He regarded me with a mild and infuriatingly calm expression. 'Madoc – and the *Gwennan Gorn* are at Abercerrig Gwynion, of course. You knew that his mast was broken in storms off the Scilly Isles. The whirlpool caught him, as it usually does. Which is why the islanders call it Madoc's Downfall. He cannot sail until the repair is done.'

My knees gave way with relief. 'Then he hasn't left for America?'

'America?' Pendaran looked puzzled. 'Where's that?'

'I'm sorry. It's just that – well, one day, that's what Madoc's new land will be called.'

'Am-er-ic-a,' Pendaran rolled the word around. 'And your visions have told you this?'

I nodded. 'Sort of. But I really have to talk to Madoc now. I've got to warn him.'

'Warn him? Of what?'

'If he leaves Wales again, he won't come back. Ever.'

Pendaran shrugged. 'I don't think he cares. What is there for him here? When Owain Gwynedd dies, Madoc's wretched brothers will fight over every coin in his coffers. His mother is dead, he has no lands save that he has found. Rhirid awaits his return: of course he must go.'

'But you don't understand,' I pleaded. 'Pendaran, if Madoc sails away again, he and all his companions – all the ships, all the people on board them all – they might all die.'

'Nonsense. By the laws of nature, some will reach the new land. Of twenty ships, some will succeed. Who is to say otherwise?' He glared at me, and then his expression softened. 'Your visions are sometimes wrong, Angharad. You prophesied that Wales would one day fall to England, and Wales would be ruled by English princes. That has not happened.'

'But it will, Pendaran,' I said urgently. I didn't know what the other Angharad had learned during her turns, but with the hindsight of my history lessons, I could guess. 'Pendaran, the last true Prince of Wales will be a Prince of Gwynedd. His name will be Llywelyn, and he will be ambushed and killed beside a stream in mid-Wales. I know this will happen. I know exactly when, in a little over a hundred years. I can't remember the exact date, 1282 I think. But I know it, just as I know that man will one day walk on the moon, as surely as I am standing here, and you are here opposite me. Just as I know that if Madoc leaves Wales he will be lost. I don't know how, maybe a storm, maybe a whale, maybe aliens will whisk the whole damn lot of them into outer space. I don't know. But Pendaran. You must believe me. They might all die if I don't warn them.'

Pendaran, frozen, stared into my eyes. At last, he believed me.

'Then we must ride,' he said. 'With fortune's help, we shall be in time.'

CHAPTER TWENTY-FIVE

Madoc's horse grazed the woodlands, his legs loosely hobbled to prevent him straying. He was, of course, only one horse, and there were two of us, and once again I found myself pillion on his back, being bumped along cross-country, the bones of my bottom apparently fracturing each time it and the horse's back collided. It wasn't nearly as comfortable cuddled up to Pendaran as it had been to Madoc. The unprotected insides of my legs rubbed raw on the animal's rough hide, and I began to feel that we were riding to John O'Groats rather than a few miles down the coast of North Wales to Abercerrig Gwynion. But I gritted my teeth and bore it. I was Madoc's only chance.

We reached the fishing port just before dawn, when only the birds were awake, and they were sleepy. The first rays of sunshine slipped between the cluster of small shacks that edged the harbour walls as we clattered onto the cobblestoned jetty. There were other boats tied up, small fishing boats, but the graceful curved shape of the *Gwennan Gorn* wasn't there.

Pendaran slid off the horse in front of the nearest shack, and hammered on the door until a toothless old man appeared, bare-chested, wearing only a wrap-round sort of nappy thing which would have tickled my funny-bone at any other time.

'Who hammers my door at this godless hour?' the old man complained, gummily. 'You'll likely wake the dead, you will.'

'Pendaran, Bard to Owain Gwynedd,' Pendaran answered, shortly. 'The *Gwennan Gorn*, where is she?'

'The *Gwennan Gorn*?' The ancient nappy-wearer peered round Pendaran dopily, as if expecting to see the ship lurking behind him. 'Oh, the *Gwennan Gorn*. She've gone out on the tide, likely. Her were finished last night, and his Lordship was anxious to get under way on this morning's tide. Oh, you'll have missed her –' he squinted at the water, then at the rising sun, 'oh, a while, now. Tide'll be full about mid-arternoon. Give or take a bit. Her'll be well on 'er way be now, her will.' He scratched his hairy armpit and yawned.

'On her way where?' I asked, urgently.

The man gazed at me, as if surprised that I could speak. 'Forrard miss, en't she? Young girls was learned to speak when they was spoke to, in my day. Young folks nowadays. Don't get beat enough,' he grumbled.

'True,' Pendaran agreed. 'But answer her, man. Where is the *Gwennan Gorn*?'

The man frowned, thinking hard. 'I can't just remember. O' course, my memory might get better if you was to –'

Pendaran produced a coin, which disappeared into the nappy at the speed of light.

'Ah. Now I remembers. His Lordship said he was stopping off along the coast. Say goodbye to his foster-father, he said – then he was meeting up with the rest of his ships off Lundy Island. If you was wantin' to talk to his Lordship, mind, you'd have to move fast – he misses the tide a-goin' out from any port along here, he be stuck 'til tomorrow. He were waitin' for his woman last I 'eard, but she weren't nowhere about. I said, looks like she don't fancy a sea voyage, but he din't laugh. Said he'd wait until the tide turned, then 'e couldn't wait no more. So 'e went,' he added unnecessarily.

251

His woman! That was me – or at least, the other Angharad. By being here, had I forced her away? Had I saved her life, or deprived her of being with Madoc whatever happened? Now I felt guilty, as well as miserable.

Pendaran groaned. 'We have missed him. Pray that we reach home in time, Angharad. We must ride now, quickly.'

The pain of that ride will stay with me until I'm ancient and in a wheelchair. Actually, it's something of a miracle I didn't end up in one. I had blisters on my legs, raw places on my behind, and my spine felt as if it had been fractured at just about every one of its vertebrae.

But we made it back at least in one piece. We skidded to a halt, the poor horse puffing like a grampus (whatever that is) outside the cottage. But it was as empty as it had been when we'd left, the fire out, the inside smelling of dust, herbs and rushlights.

'Quick, Pendaran. The jetty,' I gasped, and began to run. 'We must be in time. We *must*!' Every joint aching, every step agony, I plodded at a sort of hobbling gallop towards the jetty. When the sea came in sight, to my joy the unmistakable shape of the *Gwennan Gorn* was in the bay. I gazed at it, willing it closer. Relief made my wobbly legs give way. I clutched Pendaran for support. We'd made it. Just a few hundred more yards now, to the end of the jetty The dragon figurehead, poised majestically over the creaming bow-wave, cut through the still air, gulls wheeling and screaming about it, and the great square sail bellied in the wind. Thin black lines of oars linked boat to sea, dipping in and out of the glassy waves, drawing the boat strongly out into the pull of the tide, inexorably picking up speed.

Following blue water. The *Gwennan Gorn* was heading out to sea. Fear gave me the energy to run the last yards.

On deck, on the small, square platforms at bow and stern, figures moved in a graceful ballet, bending, climbing, coiling ropes, stowing barrels, lashing down. I filled my lungs and yelled.

'Madoc!'

I sensed how tiny my voice was, even across that calm, sunlit sea. Tears blurring my eyes, knowing that every yard further out to sea was closer to failure, I ran along the jetty, keeping pace with the movement of the boat, until I reached the end. I shaded my eyes. I could just make out the tall figure of Madoc standing on deck. Pendaran, puffing, arrived beside me, and lent his voice to mine.

'Madoc!' we shrieked into the wind, trying vainly to make our voices carry. '*Madoc!*'

The tiny boat suddenly heeled, the sail collapsing and then bellying in a new direction as the sailors swung the mast-boom round. At first I thought he'd heard us, was coming back, that against all the odds we'd cheated both history and destiny.

I dropped my waving arm, suddenly. They hadn't heard our voices. They'd caught the tide, and now the boat was picking up speed, skimming the waves faster and faster. They would never hear us now.

I stared miserably after the *Gwennan Gorn,* my eyes straining to make out the figures on deck. Bright hair caught the sun, glinting red, Geraint's slight figure unmistakable beside the tall shape of his adored older brother.

253

But there was someone else, too. Someone young. Someone slim, with short, straight brownish hair, and a familiar green dress. Madoc didn't see me. But she did. She was watching me, even over the distance between ship and shore, her eyes pinning me like a butterfly to a board. I knew her. And she knew me. Behind Madoc's half-turned broad back, she raised her arm, silently, and waved.

And I waved back, myself waving to myself, standing both on the jetty and on board the doomed ship, my eyes blurring with tears so that the *Gwennan Gorn* shimmered like a mirage as it disappeared into the pearly mist that lay on the morning sea.

Pendaran saw her too, and his face went white as he looked from the other Angharad to me and back again. His mouth opened, his face creased with pain, and he took a step away from me.

In that instant, driven almost by some power outside and beyond me, I stepped off the jetty, back to my own time, landing with a jolt in my world, tears pouring down my face, my hand clutching the tiny dragon disc.

Rhidian caught me as I stumbled and fell, his arms went round me, and he held me while I sobbed out my tale of failure.

Then he dried my eyes, and hand in hand we walked out of the garden of Tŷ Pendaran, onto the seashore, and to the edge of the tumbling waves. Night had come, and the moon was low, splashing the dark sea with silver streaks. Slowly I undid the thong holding the dragon disc, and freed it. I held it against my face for an instant, then hurled it as far as I could, glinting in the moonlight, to splash into the whispering sea beneath which the treacherous sands waited. I hope the mermaids took it to the other Angharad, wherever she was. Then Rhidian and I, arms round each other, turned from the past and set off for our future.

The night my brother was born, Laetitia the Locust arrived home, very, very late, driving a busload of weary guests. When everyone had climbed off the minibus, stretching and groaning (and some of them staggering slightly) Penry wasn't among them.

Dad and I exchanged glances, and Dad's right eyebrow shot up. 'Laetitia?' he said, uncertainly. 'Where's Penry?'

Laetitia tossed her head, scooping her handbag off the floor of the bus. 'I really don't know, Jack,' she said coldly. 'And to be honest I care even less. My Ka is UTTERLY depressed.' And she stalked into the house, straight up the stairs, and shut herself away in her room.

Dad and I looked at each other, mystified. 'Is that the sort of car to take to a garage?' he asked. 'Or some other sort?'

I grabbed one of the steadier guests on his way past, and swung him round, hanging on until all the others had gone inside.

'Where's Penry?' Dad asked.

The guest scratched his bristly chin. 'Well. He could be lots of places. Like, he's either walking back from a little pub just outside Caernarfon, or sleeping in a ditch, or if he's really lucky, he found a bed and breakfast place to take him in at gone midnight. Which I doubt. He was at least seven-eighths ratted and I wouldn't have let him in. Laetitia left him behind.'

255

Dad gaped. 'She *left him behind?*'

I felt a smile of pure joy creeping up on me. I tried to fight it, honest.

The guest nodded. He was having a hard time keeping a straight face himself. 'Penry spent the entire evening chatting up the barmaid, and when Laetitia decided she'd had enought and it was time we all came home, Penry wanted one for the road. And then another for the dual carriageway, and then another for the M1. He'd got to about the M25, I think, when Laetitia told him he either came right then, or he didn't come at all. He didn't. Last we saw of him he was staggering down the road behind us, waving his arms and shouting something rude. I don't think Laetitia saw him in her rear-view mirror.'

'I'll bet she did,' I muttered.

That night, I stared out to sea from my bedroom window, physically and mentally exhausted by the exertions of the day, so weary that tears were barely a breath away. Far out, the moon slipped down the night sky, making a glinting pathway on the mirror-calm sea. Perhaps I imagined the small ship sailing along the moon-path. Perhaps I didn't. It didn't matter. Whatever had happened to Madoc, Angharad and Geraint, they had been dead for centuries, and nothing I could have done would have changed that. But still I mourned their passing.

I drew the curtains across the window for the first time ever, shutting out the sight of the sea. Turning, I opened the dressing table drawer to find a clean night-dress, and Suzy's brown-paper parcel caught my eye: the picture of Madoc she had painted. I smiled, wearily. She had got him *so wrong*. But then, nobody had seen Madoc, except me, so how could she have known? Listlessly, I unwrapped it, revealing the ridged brown back of a piece of hardboard. I turned it over. And sat down, suddenly, on my bed.

In my hand I held a picture of Madoc. My Madoc. Not the tall, dark, saturnine character Suzy had originally painted, but my Madoc. She'd changed it. Clear blue eyes crinkled at the corners, white teeth showing in a familiar smile, his sun-bleached hair tied in feathered-decorated Indian plaits. He wore the same tunic and leggings I'd last seen him wear, and about his neck was the unmistakable, spider-web Dreamcatcher. He stood, his weight resting on his right leg, the left bent and eased, favouring the foot that had been twisted at his birth, the deformity that had condemned him in Owain Gwynedd's eyes.

I let out my breath in a long, shaky sigh, finally believing in Suzy's psychic powers. Unbelievably, she had painted the real Madoc. I gazed at the picture, a lump the size of an elephant in my throat. Madoc stood on the deck of a ship – not quite the *Gwennan Gorn*, because the figurehead was a carved coronet, not the fierce dragonhead that had swayed so proudly over the tumbling waves, but the curved longboat shape was almost right.

Then I noticed, seated on a coil of rope, another figure. It was me: except that I knew it wasn't. She wore the familiar rough green dress, her chin cupped in her hands, her eyes staring straight out of the picture at me. She was smiling, and I knew that whatever had happened to them, they had been together in their time and their lives, however long those lives had been, and were together still.

Dad sent a fax to Mum in India to tell her about the baby, and she rang Tŷ Pendaran next morning.

'I'm so sorry I didn't warn you about the baby,' she said, her voice surprisingly clear despite the distance. 'I wanted to, but your Dad begged me not to. He wanted to surprise you.'

'Well, he certainly did that,' I agreed, laughing. 'But hey, Mum. Water under the bridge. He's here now and he's gorgeous. I love him to bits already. I can't wait for Ceri to get here so she can see him.'

The relief in her voice was obvious. 'Oh, Angharad love. I'm so happy everything is all right. I've been worried stiff ever since I left. I thought it was a lousy idea, not telling. Look, this is costing me a fortune. Send me a fax when you get your A-level results, OK? I love you, I'm incredibly proud of you for the way you coped with the birth, and I'll see you in a couple of weeks. Give the new baby a kiss for me.'

'I will. Love you too, Mum. Take care.'

Later still, we all went into the hospital to see Myfanwy and my new brother. Dad was still full of praise for me, amazed that I had coped so well, introducing me to doctors, nurses, other patients, ecstatic at his new son – but so amazingly proud of me, too. I felt a rush of affection when I saw Myfanwy, and gave her perhaps the first genuine not-just-to-be-polite hug I ever had.

'Hari,' she said softly when we let each other go. 'Here. Hold your brother.' She scooped him out of the perspex cot and put him gently in my arms. I looked down at the tiny face, the head no bigger than a grapefruit, the dark hair lying straight as my own on the tiny skull. He yawned, miniscule hands starfished, and opened the bluest eyes I'd ever seen.

'Hello, little brother,' I whispered. He screwed up his face, ominously. 'Hey, don't cry!' He pouted, whimpered, then settled into sleep again. He was warm and light as a kitten in my arms.

'What are you going to call him?'

Dad cleared his throat. He sounded as if he was about to do pompous. Dad does pompous extremely well, if he's allowed.

'We thought you might like to suggest a name, Hari. I'm not saying we'll agree, mind,' he warned quickly, 'just in case you want to call him Moon Unit or Dweezil, something like that.'

'Moon Unit and Dweezil are your generation, Dad, not mine. However, I suppose there's always Keanu. Or Brad. Or Axl . . .'

Dad shuddered. 'Ha. Very funny. Be serious, Hari. Any ideas?'

I didn't have to think for long. 'Madoc,' I said, and waited.

'Madoc?' Dad said.

'Madoc,' Myfanwy repeated.

'Madoc,' they said together, tasting the name.

Madoc, my beautiful little brother, yawned.

AUTHOR'S END-NOTE

For someone with a passionate interest in the people whose lives make history, but who is by no means an historian, tackling a semi-historical novel was an intriguing and daunting task. It was rather like having a jigsaw with several important pieces missing: I had the four corner pieces and most of the outside edge, but some of the frame and the bit in the middle were left to my imagination.

I have taken liberties with what is known of Madoc's life and times: I have given Owain Gwynedd an imaginary north Wales castle because Dolwyddelan (where probably Madoc was born to Brenda and Owain Gwynedd) is too far away from my imaginary village of Pendaran to allow Pendaran and Angharad to visit it easily.

The Druid and Bard Pendaran existed, according to one source, and fostered the infant Madoc, who may have been physically flawed in the way described. The meeting between Brenda and Madoc is said to have taken place, and also that they were discovered embracing by Owain Gwynedd, who accused his wife of taking a lover.

Abercerrig-Gwynion is not found on modern maps of Wales, but the name is believed by some sources to have been corrupted to Abergele, which is.

The jetty, according to Showell Styles, can be found at a private house named Odstone, on a walk beginning at Rhos-on-Sea. It now forms part of that house's entrance drive, and bears an inscription to the effect that Prince Madoc sailed from there in 1170 AD.

The warlike Owain Gwynedd died (to most historians' surprise, in his bed) in November 1169. Thomas à Becket was murdered in 1170, but not before issuing a posthumous pardon to the deceased Owain Gwynedd for the sin of marrying his first cousin, Crisiant.

Madoc had brothers called Rhirid (who lived in Ireland, and where Madoc took refuge) and Edwall (who was, apparently one of those who accompanied Madoc on his second journey to America). Edwall may, therefore, have been a 'goodie': however for the purposes of my book, he has been turned into a bit of a 'baddie'. Madoc may have had a brother named Geraint, (there were, after all, according to some sources, as many as 27 legitimate and illegitimate offspring credited to Owain Gwynedd) but as far as I am concerned, he is purely imaginary.

I have tried to tell Madoc's story as best I can, but this is a work of fiction filtered through fact: I hope that historians will forgive me. Madoc's discovery of America was too wonderful a story for a romantic to ignore.

Sources

Brave His Soul: The Story of Prince Madoc of Wales and his Discovery of America in 1170 Brenda Pugh (Dodd, Mead & Co, USA)

Welsh Walks & Legends Showell Styles (John Jones, Cardiff)

Pamphlet: Madoc ap Owain Gwynedd Kathleen O'Loughlin (Printed 1.11.47, St Catherine's, Ontario)

Welsh Tribal Law & Custom in the Middle Ages T P Ellis (Oxford 1926)

Americans from Wales Edward George (Octagon Books NY 1978)

Madoc & the Discovery of America Richard Deacon (Fredk Muller 1967)

Madoc: The Making of a Myth Prof. Gwyn A Williams (OUP 1987)

Princes and People of Wales John Miles (Starling Press 1977)

The Herbal Remedies of the Physicians of Myddfai Tr. John Pughe (Llanerch Enterprises)

From almost all of which I have 'cherry-picked' to suit my tale . . .

THE BACK END OF NOWHERE
Jenny Sullivan
sb   £4.95   1 85902 497 1

For Catrin Morgan of Pennsylvania, U.S.A., the new factory that her father has to open up in Wales means *tragedy*. It means leaving her normal life in America, leaving her best friend, leaving her place as cheerleader for someone else to fill and, worst of all, leaving her almost-boyfriend, Kurt. To go where? The Back End of Nowhere, that's where. Wales, where she'll have to live in a house full of antiques and go to school in *uniform!* Her father thinks it's all so wonderful—the land of his ancestors, history and all that. What on earth is Catrin supposed to make of those old Welsh legends—of the sea-harp, the sky-egg and the earthstone?